Masked Flaws
and Other Stories

by Carrie Dalby

Table of Contents

Introduction

The following is a collection of historical short stories I wrote over the past half dozen years. All were written to be included in various themed anthologies by both Mobile Writers Guild and Bienvenue Press. Several were plotted to fit into romance collections—which means the stories are sweeter than my typical novels—but they all fit into the turn-of-the-century Mobile Bay world I have painstakingly created during the course of writing sixteen books (as of right now) set between the 1890s and 1920s.

For those unfamiliar with my books, I hope you enjoy this sampling of Southern Gothic stories with historical drama and details. For those who have read *Fortitude* or any of my series novels, enjoy this return trip to old Mobile with memorable main characters, those who haunted the background of the scenes, and one story that's filled with all new people. There's a little something for everyone, from charming holiday scenarios to scandalous Mystics of Dardenne masquerades.

Enjoy!

Carrie Dalby

Autumn 2023

"Masked Flaws"

A prequel short to The Possession Chronicles

Edmund Easton spent the minutes before his lunch hour scowling at his brother's office. Maxwell flaunted his full partnership with Easton and Sons by leaving his door ajar—thereby providing a clear view for his only living brother to witness him indulging in cigarettes and cigars whenever he felt like it. Cramped in his corner desk in the main room with the secretaries, Edmund wasn't allowed to smoke. Though it was 1903 and women were ready for voting rights, his father, James Easton, deemed it ungentlemanly for him to light up in the same room as the ladies.

I'm nothing but a secretary in pants to those two. Easton and Sons be damned! The sign might as well read Easton and Eldest Son.

Stomping out of the building as soon as the clock struck noon, Edmund paused long enough to light a cigarette before making his way through the lunchtime crowd.

"Eddie!" Maxwell called from behind. "Wait up!"

He exhaled a cloud of smoke and turned, hazel eyes glaring. "What do you want?"

Maxwell clapped his shoulder, giving it a squeeze. "You're wasting away, little brother. I ran across Freddy the other day and had to take a swing at him to test his burgeoning strength. You two used to box together as often as you could. Why'd you stop?"

"He got married." Edmund smirked to hide the bitterness over his childhood best friend inheriting an accounting firm. Sure, Frederick Davenport had lost his father and new bride within half a year, but he didn't have to answer to anyone for his choices.

"Father always said he'll make you a partner when you settle down."

"I'm not in the least ready to settle in with a wife. And it didn't do Freddy a lick of good either as he's stuck in mourning bands for carnival season." Edmund elbowed around Maxwell. "I'll see you after lunch."

He finished his cigarette as he neared Bienville Square. A group of lawyers were congregated before the bandstand, men he'd gone to grade school with who were settling into roles as important fixtures in the legal scene about town. Alexander Melling turned his icy blue eyes on Edmund and smiled with a dark glint amid his fair complexion.

"Easton!" Alexander, the third generation and only son at Melling and Associates Law Firm, waved him over. "Where have you been hiding yourself? I only see you at mass these days."

Rupert Lyons, long face as serious as ever, gave a sardonic laugh. "He's hiding in that dusty warehouse by the river, counting cargo."

Some of the others smirked and turned away from the newcomer, but Alexander shook his hand. "I'm glad to see you. How are things looking for your carnival season?"

Edmund shoved his hands in his pockets. "Order of Mayhem with my family on New Year's Eve. No other invitations yet, but they'll come along. I attended five balls last year."

"Poor sop," Rupert muttered.

"What do you expect for a guy who grew up amid so many sisters?" Sean joked.

"The sisters are his only saving grace," Rupert replied.

"Is sweet little Lucy coming out this season?" Sean asked with a leer.

"Get your facts right," Rupert said. "Lucille Easton was presented last New Year's Eve, though she failed to make another appearance all season." He moved his hands in an hourglass shape. "Believe me, I've kept my eyes out for that filly, but she keeps eluding me."

Edmund fisted Rupert's suit jacket, his other arm moving back to strike. "You better keep your hands off my sister!"

Alexander took Edmund's elbow. "I'd be careful if I were you, Rupert. Eddie was a champion boxer in school, and I've heard he's taken out a few guys who looked not even two seconds at his sister's assets. I think his legendary strength is what we need. How would you like to join a society for yourself rather than rely on your family's meager social connections, Easton?"

Bristling with indignation—his family was as well-off as any of theirs, but his father would rather spend his downtime playing golf than hobnobbing around at parties—Edmund controlled his anger enough to force a smile.

"What, you think you have a monopoly on Mardi Gras?"

Alexander threw an arm around him and whispered from his several-inch disadvantage. "As a matter of fact, we do. Mystics of Dardenne members tend to rule the revelry." He mussed Edmund's brown hair. "We'll save a spot for you, Easton. Let me know by midnight mass."

***

Edmund held the sleeve of Lucy's pale green dress as they climbed the steps to the portico of the cathedral for Christmas Mass. Her nineteen-year-old figure—two years his junior—was displayed to its best advantage in the flared ensemble. Her blonde hair was skillfully wrapped high on her head, adorned with holly sprigs and her white mantilla. Edmund followed the path his parents and youngest sister took until he spied Rupert and Sean nearby. Hoping to steer Lucy from their hungry eyes, he angled her toward the far door.

"Easton!" Sean called.

Lucy elbowed him. "I think your friends are trying to get your attention. I don't mind if you say hello."

Giving an inward groan, Edmund brought them to the column the men leaned against.

"Eddie," Sean said as his grin flashed his chipped tooth, "how about an introduction to your lovely sister?"

"Lucy, this is Sean Spunner and Rupert Lyons. I'm sure you've seen both of them around. *Gentlemen*"—he stressed the word, as if willing them to behave—"my closest sister, Lucille Easton."

Her smile was tight, her offered hand stiff as they each took it. Edmund wanted to knock the smirk off Rupert's face as he visually took Lucy's measurements.

Rupert brazenly kissed the back of her hand. "The pleasure is mine, Miss Easton."

Alexander made a show of brushing against Lucy as he maneuvered into the group. "After making the acquaintance of a charming young woman, you can't say it was a wasted evening at mass."

Rather than shying away, Lucy's green eyes appeared to brighten as she took in the sight of the Alexander as he shamelessly pressed against her before settling beside Rupert. She smiled and managed a hello before Edmund had her by the elbow.

"We must join our family," he said. "Please excuse us."

"A moment of your time, Eddie." Alexander leaned across Lucy. "What's your response to my question from the other week?"

He narrowed his eyes, inclining his head toward Alexander's hand hovering near Lucy's backside. "Yes, though it must be understood that some things are forever off limits."

Alexander grinned. "You'll hear from me this week, Easton."

"Melling, you dog." Sean's voice snaked through the boisterous chatter of the parishioners as Edmund took his sister inside. "You nearly pinched her seat under Eddie's nose!"

Edmund carried the taint of the encounter with him over Christmas. He'd heard the stories—both from the guys themselves and others—of the conquests made by Alexander and Rupert, but to think of anything happening to his naïve sister was too much to fathom. Lucy spent the better part of her life with her nose in a book, though in their youth she was just as eager as the neighborhood boys to join in games of knights and castles. She and Frederick had been the best players, but Edmund no longer wished for his friends to play with her. Not at their present games.

***

On Thursday, two days before New Year's Eve, the doorbell rang after supper. Edmund heard Alexander's smooth voice coupled with Lucy's tinkling laughter and nearly spilt his brandy in his rush to the foyer.

"Alex," Edmund said as he came around the corner, "what brings you here?"

"I require your advice. Would you step out with me a moment?"

"Of course." He turned to his sister. "Thanks for getting the door, Lucy."

She glanced at Alexander and bowed her head as though embarrassed before returning to the parlor where she'd been reading. Alexander eyed her departing figure with open appreciation.

"Stop looking." Edmund collected a coat, still holding his drink in the other hand.

Alexander relieved him of his brandy. "To chase away the unrighteous thoughts. You owe me that much for parading her around." He swallowed the rest in one gulp and set the empty glass on the credenza.

Edmund yanked him to the porch. "Like hell I parade her! I've been shielding her for years from cads like you."

"And for good reason." Alexander jumped off the steps and removed his cigarette case from his pocket, holding it out for Edmund. They both lit up and after the first few puffs, Alexander gazed at the parlor window where Lucy sat in profile under the lamp, head bent over a book. "I never noticed how perfectly formed she is."

Edmund swung but Alexander dodged the punch. "If you ever touch her, I'll—"

Alexander laughed. "I'm not in the habit of deflowering debutantes. I prefer my women experienced—something you'll learn in the days ahead if you complete your initiation. There's a wide world of pleasures to be had, and Mystics of Dardenne members are the ones that gather them with gusto. Don't you want in?"

Edmund nodded. "But like I said Christmas Eve, Lucy's off limits to all of you."

"We tease. Well, maybe not Rupert." Alexander removed an envelope from his breast pocket. "Your instructions. Look for me at the Mayhem ball when you're ready to embark."

***

Edmund adjusted his black tuxedo jacket and scanned the ballroom at the Battle House Hotel. With his blond hair, Alexander stood out amid the masked crowd at Order of Mayhem's ball. Combined with his metallic Columbina mask and bowtie, he proved to be the golden boy of the night, from his practiced moves on the dancefloor with a variety of women, to his infectious laughter among the men. Edmund would be lying if he said he didn't envy the notoriety of the young lawyer, not to mention his confidence. He did whatever he wanted and others followed.

Unable to cut in while he danced, an hour passed before Edmund had the opportunity to join Alexander. Without speaking, Alexander nodded toward the punch bowls and slipped Edmund a flask when he came alongside him. With the first of his three-part initiation complete, Edmund helped himself to a glass of the spiked punch.

Alexander laughed. "Easy there, Easton. You'll need all your faculties for your next exhibition. Meet me in the alley in twenty minutes."

Throat burning from the whiskey-laced drink, Edmund watched Rupert carry a glass toward Lucy. She stood with Maxwell and his wife on the edge of the dancefloor. After rushing to her side, Edmund took Lucy's arm by the silk of her long gloves.

"How about a dance, sister?"

Without waiting for a response, he began a waltz. Rupert stopped a few feet away, shaking his head before drinking the punch himself. When the song ended, Edmund escorted Lucy to their parents' table.

"Be careful tonight, Lucy," he whispered as he kissed her cheek.

Maxwell followed Edmund into the lobby. Taking him by the shoulder, he shoved Edmund into a corner behind a potted palm. "What's got you on edge tonight?"

"Nothing." Edmund pushed him out of the way, but Maxwell blocked his escape.

"Tell big brother Max all about your troubles, Eddie."

"There's no trouble. I've been invited to join a society, and I need to be somewhere."

Maxwell crossed his arms, his broad-shoulders intimidating. "Does it have anything to do with your yanking Lucy about?"

"Some of the guys keep insinuating that they'd like a go with her. Please watch her while I'm gone."

Maxwell laughed. "You have *one* sister to defend. I had to keep tabs on Susan, Cora, *and* Emma when they were all out at the same time. But don't worry. Lucy's too reserved to get swept away by any revelry makers."

"Even debonair Dardennes?"

He scoffed. "Those types aren't interested in deep thinkers. They want ones who don't wish to philosophize."

"They're interested when she's built the way Lucy is. I've heard more than enough from several of them."

"Mystics of Dardenne members?" Maxwell looked skeptical. "I find it hard to believe those guys would ever announce themselves to you. You're not their type."

"Shows how much you know!" Edmund charged past in his anger, heading for the exit.

Maxwell caught him on the sidewalk and nudged him against the stone wall. "I know more than you think, Eddie. It can't have changed that much since I was a bachelor. I was a member before I married, and as recent as last decade they only invited the highest on the social ladder from influential families."

Shame burned his clean-shaven face. "I'll prove I'm just as worthy of membership as the next guy! Especially you, since you're only the son of an import salesman, same as me."

"The *eldest* son who was given full partnership upon graduation." His mask shadowed his hazel eyes, but Edmund knew they were as challenging as ever—just as his own. "Go ahead, Eddie. You won't last a night with those animals."

Minutes later, Alexander stood lookout while Edmund crawled under all the carriages and automobiles belonging to the city council members to disconnect the axles and then leave Mystics of Dardenne calling cards on their seats. Afterward, Edmund followed his friend back into the ballroom.

"Which young woman will be blessed with your attentions tonight, Easton? Kate Stuart?"

Edmund gave a nervous laugh at the mention of the sharp-eyed ruler of the debutantes. "Hardly."

Alexander's pale eyes flashed with mischief within his gold mask. "I get the feeling she'd skin you alive and run you up the flagpole in front of the courthouse. You need a meek soul who won't spread gossip. Too bad you can't use your sister."

Edmund scowled. "No one touches Lucy!"

"I swear to you we haven't. A sweet conquest like her wouldn't pass without bragging." Alexander's gaze roamed the ballroom. "What about Grace Anne Marley? I hear she gives and takes a bit with each of her escorts without playing pious."

His stomach soured at the mention of Lucy's best friend. *She'd better not teach my sister her tricks!* "No, she'd be sure to tell Lucy if something happened between us."

Alexander slung an arm about his shoulders. "Judith McGowan?"

"But she's friends with Kate," Edmund protested. *Who would have thought feeling up a woman would be the most difficult initiation to pass?*

"Yes, but unlike frigid Kate, she'd welcome the attention. I'll ask her to dance and you cut in. And remember, it doesn't count unless you've got her whole buttocks or breast in your hand. I'll be watching. Do this and I've got a special celebration planned for you."

Edmund slunk to a nearby chair, keeping his gaze on Alexander's arrogant stride. Judith smiled at his invitation, and he set them around the dancefloor in a lavish display of fluidity and charm, to the strains of the string quartet. Where most men would shy away from taller women, Alexander didn't allow his average build to be a disadvantage. He'd danced with women of all shapes and sizes, and Judith was no exception.

After a minute, Edmund took his chance. "May I cut in?" he asked Alexander.

"Miss McGowan, you know Edmund Easton, don't you? His family owns the largest import company in the city."

Her smile widened. "Why, yes, Mr. Easton. I'd be happy to dance with you."

Edmund's right hand set comfortably on her jutting hip beside her abnormally tiny waist. Her brunette hair, piled in a pompadour, almost reached his own height, but he kept his eyes on her face—plain but pleasant. Judith's hand traced the definition of his shoulder as she angled closer, giving him a clear view of her cleavage that proved to be as shapely as her lower half.

"You're a fine dancer, Mr. Easton. Why have we never shared one before?"

Taking the opportunity, his gaze lingered at her chest several seconds as he tugged her closer. "It appears I'm finally outgrowing my shyness around beautiful women."

"I admire a man who knows what he likes."

"Your warmth puts me at ease, Miss McGowan." He gave her his best smile and chanced another look at her front.

"It's Carnival, Mr. Easton. You needn't be bashful if there's something you'd like to try."

Wondering if Alexander had set him up, Edmund raised his brows.

"Don't go telling your friends I offered," she whispered. "I'd only do so for someone as respectable as you. I've never heard gossip about your exploits, unlike Alexander Melling. Unless he changes his ways, he'll have to find a wife out of state because no respectable young lady in Mobile would accept a cad like him, with or without his father's fortune."

"Is that so?"

She nodded. "Keep us moving briskly and bring your hand up from my waist. No one will notice."

Edmund did as requested, feeling her corset seams through the blue gown until he reached the softness of her left breast. Judith gasped with pleasure and clutched his shoulder. Fingers spreading to palm her generous mound, he squeezed as they reached above her décolletage, gently nudging the ruffle lower.

"So soft and feminine," he whispered.

"Mr. Easton." She was near breathless.

"Call me Edmund." He smiled as his hand snaked back to her waist and then around her hip to grasp her buttocks.

The song came to a close and she stood before him with dewy eyes. "Will you ask me for another dance?"

"Sometime this season, if not tonight, Miss McGowan." He kissed the back of her gloved hand. "It's been a pleasure."

***

"Rupert didn't think you had it in you, but I knew you did!" Alexander slapped Edmund's back as soon as they were outside the ballroom. "You had her all worked up and then scored a bonus point! Does she feel as good as she looks?"

"She does, though I don't see how she can breathe all bound up in that corset."

"All the more fun to undress when things come spilling out." Alexander laughed and led him to a waiting carriage. He glanced at the driver. "You know where to."

"Yes, Master Melling."

"How did Judith compare to others you've handled?" Alexander asked once they were underway, hands cupping his own non-existent breasts.

Edmund fiddled with the coat in his lap. "She was soft…"

"Easton, have you no experience? For the love of all that's holy, don't let the others guys know!" He patted his knee. "It's a good thing I've whisked you away. By the time the others arrive, you'll know plenty."

Arrive? Edmund looked out the carriage window and saw they were entering the red light district. *Maxwell was right. I'm in over my head, but I can't back out now.*

Swallowing his fear, he managed a smile. "I appreciate this, Alex."

"Here." Alexander pulled a bottle of medicinal tooth ache drops from his jacket. "Take a swig or two. It makes for an amazing experience where we're going."

The liquid cocaine was meant to be taken in tiny doses not mouthfuls, but Edmund needed the courage, so he took a swig as directed. By the time they climbed the steps of the brothel, Edmund's head was buzzing with energy that couldn't escape.

"Happy New Year's, ladies!" Alexander called as he let himself in the front door.

Several women lounging in the front room looked to him with smiles. A petite brunette tucked herself under his arm, and he immediately cupped a breast possessively as he claimed her mouth with a kiss.

Edmund stood awkwardly before the display while the women watched with perceived jealousy. *He has it all, even the envy of the other harlots.*

When they came up for air, the woman had a hand tucked in the waistband of Alexander's tuxedo. "Consuela, I need your help."

"Anything, Alexander the Great."

His impish smile doubled as he pulled an envelope from his jacket. "I need you and as many of your friends to attend the Mystics of Dardenne masquerade in a few weeks. Arrive together and this will provide entrance for you all."

She clutched the invitation. "A real masquerade rather than waiting for you to stumble here in the middle of the night?"

"Yes, Consuela. I want you to come to us this time. There's no reason our revelry can't handle more indulgences, especially with new blood in our group." He nodded to Edmund. "Meet our finest newbie. He had a deb gasping under his touch in the middle of the ballroom."

She giggled and looked to an older woman who'd followed the conversation. "You hear that, Hazel? We're going to a masquerade, and there's a fresh crop of men to delight!"

The willowy woman nodded and sucked on her cigarette. "The Dardennes never disappoint."

"Come on, Eddie." Alexander steered Consuela toward the stairs as Edmund followed. "I'm going to need Prudie's assistance tonight. Is she busy?"

Consuela crossed her arms.

"For my friend." Alexander groped her backside. "You know I need your ministrations more than anything. Go ready yourself for me."

He knocked at the first door on the landing. A voluptuous blonde with a surprisingly innocent face opened the door. The smile she gave Alexander was wanting, and she did nothing to cover her scanty nightgown beneath the open robe.

"Good evening, Alexander."

"Prudie, my dear." He claimed her mouth much like he'd done with Consuela, hands splayed over her broad hips. "May we come in?"

Her eyes widened as she seemed to notice Edmund for the first time. "Both of you?"

"Yes," Alexander said with a wink, "but nothing too naughty this time."

Prudie flushed and looked up at Edmund when he followed Alexander into the room. Closing the door behind them, she crossed to the bed where Alexander motioned to her. She settled on the tidy bedspread where he sat beside her, a hand going to her bare knee.

"I've got an important job for you," Alexander said with a seductive tone, pointing to Edmund where he stood before the dressing table. "My friend, Eddie Easton, is the newest Mystics of Dardenne member this season. He has a little secret I need you to confidentially address."

Face heating, Edmund studied the gold carpet.

"I've brought him to you, dear Prudie, because I know how sweet you are and that you won't talk about this to anyone. Can you believe this handsome fellow is inexperienced? We need to remedy that, don't you think?"

"Yes, Alexander. I can help."

He kissed her and ran a finger down her neck. "He needs a gentle hand to guide him, but look at that shoulder span! He was a championship boxer a few years back. In his exuberance, he'll likely require a sturdy partner. I'm sure you'll work him into a frenzy at some point tonight, but I know you can take whatever he delivers. What do you say?"

"Anything for you, Alexander the Great. But he won't be a hardship." She looked to Edmund and smiled. "You're very attractive, Mr. Easton, and I'm honored to be your first."

Alexander pulled her to the mattress with a dominant stance. "Don't get too comfortable with him, darling Prudie. You know I relish our monthly exchanges. I won't let him take that from us."

Hands roaming, they necked and touched, exchanging whispers. Edmund tried not to follow every movement and moan.

A minute later, Alexander stood and grinned at Edmund. "Do you need me to demonstrate any positions or techniques?"

Wanting Alexander to leave so the woman's appreciative gaze would focus on him, Edmund shook his head. "I'm sure Prudie's a capable teacher."

Alexander laughed and took him in a brotherly embrace. "Do whatever you want within this house, but Consuela is mine."

Prudie watched him leave from her perch on the now rumpled bed, but smiled warmly at Edmund once they were alone. "Would you care for a glass of brandy?"

Head still buzzing from the shot in the carriage, Edmund declined. "Maybe later."

She nodded and patted the spot beside here, blonde hair shifting across her shoulder with the movement. "Then join me, Mr. Easton."

"Call me Eddie."

***

Edmund woke with a splitting headache. Groaning, he rolled facedown to hide from the ambient light through the curtains.

Prudie's soft hands massaged his back. "Eddie, may I get you some coffee?"

"Mmm, please."

The mattress shifted when she left him and he tried to remember the details of the night. He recalled Prudie's guidance the first time. Though he knew Alexander would take credit for arranging things, it was Prudie who deserved the praise. At some point, Rupert's loud voice sounded in the hall. Doors slammed but no one disturbed them, so Edmund had indulged again and again—both with Prudie and alcohol.

By the time Prudie returned with a tray, he sat on the bed in his underdrawers. Bumping the door closed with a magnificent hip, her smile brightened the room.

"Please don't tell anyone about this. We aren't supposed to serve men in our rooms, except a shot of whiskey or brandy during their paid time."

He blanched as he took his first sip. "I'm sorry, Prudie. I wasn't expecting to come here. I don't know if I have enough in my billfold to cover—"

She laughed and settled beside him. "Don't worry about it. Alex told me he would see to the payment when he's around later today."

Trying to understand how much of the night was pre-planned, he questioned her. "When did he decide that?"

Her cheeks turned pink and she tucked her hair behind her ear. "While he had me on the bed before he left. But I'd have stayed with you without payment, Eddie. It was an honor to share that with you."

Edmund grinned and straightened his posture. "Would I be as sought after as Alex if I make a habit of coming here?"

"The young handsome clients are always fussed over, but Alex most of all. He's good to us girls, those of us lucky enough to be chosen. But he doesn't disrespect the others. He's a gentleman to all while most of the men leer at us like we're ham hocks in a butcher's window."

"I'd never treat you that way, Prudie." His finger caressed her lip as he leaned in, plundering her mouth to seal himself as worthy a lover as Alexander Melling.

"We're advised not to kiss," she whispered.

"But Alex does, and I aim to indulge you even better than him."

"I'll look forward to your return."

True to her obliging nature, she helped him dress. He tucked his bowtie into the pocket of his tuxedo before leaving. It was nine in the morning, but the streets were near empty after a night of partying. Edmund walked to the safety of Dauphin Street before encountering anyone he knew.

"Eddie!" Frederick Davenport called to him from across the road. He jogged over, hair slightly damp as though he'd just showered. He shook Edmund's hand with a firm grip. "I haven't seen you in months."

Edmund grinned and thumped him on the back. "How do you look so alert this morning?"

He nodded over his broad shoulder. "I just finished at the gym. I didn't have a partner for the ring, so I had to take extra time on the rowing machine and punching bag." He did a few arm rotations then took a sparring stance. "Join me sometime, Eddie. I'd like another go at you."

Edmund ran a hand through his tousled hair and laughed. "After the night I just had, you'd knock me flat. And I haven't been in the ring for over a year."

"It's never too late to get back to it, and it'd be good to see you on a regular basis again." Frederick motioned to his tuxedo. "You've been out since the ball?"

Edmund nodded with a grin. "I now understand what a man like you enjoys."

"What do you mean by *like me*?" Frederick crossed his arms.

"You know. Having been married."

Frederick cleared his throat.

"Have the months been rough?" Edmund asked. "We haven't talked since the funeral."

"I'm getting along."

"It's a shame you have to miss the balls this year. Lucy was there last night. I always fancied you two together, but instead I'm stuck chasing the cads away because you had to go to Pennsylvania and marry a stranger last winter. Why didn't you bring Harriet over to meet us?"

Frederick's fists tightened. "It never seemed like the right time, and she was sick much of her time here. How are your parents?"

"Well as anything. Opal's with a private tutor now but is still giving Mother trouble with her moods. Father's hinting to me about settling down so he can retire."

"And Lucy? Is she still writing?"

Edmund noted the emotion in his friend's voice. "She's forever scribbling and watching the mail for word from publishing companies when she doesn't have her nose in a book. Come over and see her sometime. I'm sure she'd appreciate the visit. The only caller she ever has is Grace Anne."

"It wouldn't be proper." Frederick pointed to the black band around his upper arm that set him apart as being in mourning. The Davenports were all about honor and tradition.

Edmund guffawed. "You're family to us, Freddy. No one would mind, and I'm sure Lucy would be a sympathetic listener to your woes. You two always got along splendidly."

A bittersweet smile found his clean-shaven face. "I've always had a soft spot for Goosy. We three had fun together with our battles when we were kids. It'd be nice to escape reality and return to those carefree years."

Rubbing the stubble on his jaw, Edmund nodded. "Those were the days."

"We can relive our games in the boxing ring at least. Find me in the gym any day after work or Saturday mornings."

"I'll let you know. It's good talking to you, but I need to get home and sleep this off."

"You shouldn't need to sleep off a pleasant night. Take care of yourself, Easton."

He looked to his scuffed dress shoes. "You too, Freddy."

***

Ever since meeting Frederick New Year's morning, Edmund's soul grew heavy with guilt. Seeing his oldest friend morally and physically fit despite life's upsets cast a shadow on the choices he'd made since Alexander had offered him camaraderie. To hide from himself and to help him feel more distinction amid his peers, Edmund decided to grow a beard like the European royalty wore.

In the weeks leading up to the masquerade, he attended four planning meetings with Alexander where he met the full Mystics of Dardenne society and felt the rush of being among the wealthy bachelors he used to run about with as a boy. A chasm had grown between them as they had gone away to universities and oversea adventures after graduation, while Edmund was stuck in the family business. But now they were equals. The meetings were followed by visits to the brothel, where Edmund furthered his liaisons with Prudie on his own dime.

The Friday afternoon of the event, he met Alexander after work. They were one of the first to arrive at Temperance Hall, and Alexander showed Edmund the layout of their party. The main room was decorated as a cemetery, complete with false headstones and monuments. A mausoleum erected in one corner added to the atmosphere, and potted trees throughout the space gave the appearance of the outdoors. The second floor offered a full bar and facilities for guests, the third story a private oasis for members to indulge in whatever they saw fit.

On the top floor, Alexander and Edmund relaxed with a few drinks as the others arrived. An hour before the doors opened to their guests, they all dressed in matching costumes—full-body skeleton suits on black material. The hooded skull masks were the last things to be pulled on. Then the Mystics of Dardenne members lined the red carpet in the foyer like a gauntlet of death for guests to pass between as they entered the ballroom.

The thrill of being in a position of dominance over the captive arrivals brought Edmund to a new high. Following the other members' leads, he began touching women as they passed before him. A caressing hand down an arm. A pinching touch on a backside. When Consuela and her friends arrived, the skeletons increased their boldness. Many broke rank and absconded into the ballroom with the women.

For the members-only first dance, Edmund chose a striking brunette dressed in all black whose escort gave him a frown as he led her onto the floor. Her feathered Venetian mask offset her porcelain skin, and the cut of her gown showed much of what she had to offer.

His hand migrated from her waist to her hip. "Do you mind?"

Her painted lips parted into a smile, and she shook her head. "But my cousin might."

"Why would a man bring a cherished family member to a ball like this?"

She giggled. "He's visiting from Birmingham and didn't know better."

Edmund took her merriment as invitation for more and did what he'd done to Judith at the New Year's Eve masquerade. By the end of the waltz, he wished to take the woman to the third floor den and explore her further, but it wasn't his break time.

"May I find you later?" he asked as his gloved hands lowered.

"Please do."

Knowing there were willing women that didn't need to be paid delighted Edmund. He settled near a punch bowl with a glass and drinking tube that allowed him to partake of the laced punch through his mask. Head woozy, he almost fell when someone knocked his shoulder. A skeleton leaned next to his ear.

"I know that's you, Easton," Alexander whispered. "Don't disappoint me by loafing around on our night. Go up to the den and see Lyons. He's got something that will get you going. And take a guest with you."

Under the lights of the ballroom, Prudie didn't shine as she did in her bedroom, her fleshy form not as comely as the others and her blonde hair too reminiscent of his sister's. Scanning the crowd for someone new, Edmund noticed Hazel coming out of the mausoleum with a guest, the man's tuxedo in disarray. Understanding it was a place for the non-members to indulge as they weren't allowed on the third floor, he felt himself heat beneath the mask.

Complete debauchery! But I can't blame them.

He went for the stairs and found Consuela pushing away a man who couldn't keep his hands off the black corset she wore on the outside of her red gown.

Edmund shoved the guest to the ground and took Consuela's hand. "Come with me."

"Thank you." She clutched his arm and climbed to the third floor with him.

With a nod to Edmund's skeleton costume, the man dressed as The Grim Reaper standing guard allowed them into the Mystics of Dardenne den. Consuela squealed in delight over the ice buckets full of bottles and the couples in various positions on the settees about the sitting area.

"Welcome, brother!" Rupert, unmasked, waved him over to a table in the corner. "Bring that sweet little woman over here so both of you can get a hit."

Consuela tugged Edmund's hand until he followed her to the offering of white powder displayed on a flat tray. As he stood beside her, Rupert studied him.

When she'd snorted her fill, Rupert took her by the neck. "That's not Alex."

"I don't know who he is, but he was nice enough to defend my honor."

"Like you have any." He sneered and shoved her before turning on Edmund. "Who do you think you are, bringing Alex's whore up here?"

Edmund pulled his mask off and slapped Rupert across the face with it. "I'm a Dardenne! Who do you think *you* are handling Alex's girl like that?"

Rupert's face went from shock to humor as he laughed. "Easton, you've proved me wrong. I thought Melling had lost all sense when he invited you because I believed you were like saintly Davenport since you were such friends with him. How wrong I was!" He emptied another metal case of cocaine onto the tray. "Load up, Eddie. Then you can unload in Consuela. I'll get Alex high to keep him from interfering. He doesn't like to share and sometimes needs to be reminded that Dardenne brothers need to sacrifice for each other."

Edmund did as Rupert suggested and brought Consuela to one of the chaises in the partitioned-off space in the rear of the room. By the time they emerged, Edmund felt the effects of his binging and Alexander was face down in the middle of the room. Consuela laughed and went to Rupert for another fix.

The guard burst through the door. "There's a raid! Get out the back!"

Edmund immediately sobered. Rupert grabbed his supplies and led the way to the fire escape out a back window. Consuela went with the throng.

Feeling guilty for being the reason Alexander was plastered, Edmund hauled him by his armpits. "Come on, Alex!"

He moaned and started twitching.

"Police are coming, Melling. We've got to scat."

As he pulled him through the window, Alexander went limp as though he'd passed out. Edmund slung him over his shoulder, wishing he'd spent time at the gym the past few weeks so that carrying him wouldn't be as taxing. When they got to the alley, he realized their only means of escape was on foot. Edmund toted Alexander through the night to the closest safe place he could think of—Frederick Davenport's house.

***

The first Friday in February, Edmund forced himself to The Cathedral of the Immaculate Conception for confession. Thanks to the look on Frederick's face when he'd opened the door to Edmund and Alexander on the night of the masquerade, Edmund had managed to stay sober and away from the red light district the previous week. Disappointment and disgust were what his old friend had conveyed without words, and the feeling still loomed over him.

Edmund went so far as to go to the gym once—he was sore for two days afterward—and had spent one evening at Frederick's house playing chess as a means to pacify the upset in their friendship. At Easton and Sons, he worked harder and volunteered to go every time something was needed from the warehouse. But it was all for naught, because after the fast times with Alexander and his crowd, nothing was fulfilling.

Then the invitation came that morning.

Edmund Albert Easton

Of Mobile, Alabama,

Is hereby invited to join Aethelwulf Club

Please arrive on the evening of…

The premier men's club of the city! Within those smoking rooms, political deals were made, business partnerships were forged, and the downfall of lesser men was plotted. The Melling and Lyons men had all been members for generations. Edmund's father and Maxwell were members but obviously had given no thought to mentoring him into their folds, because Alexander

Melling was listed as his benefactor—probably because he'd saved him from being arrested at the masquerade.

But no matter the reason, Edmund wasn't going to let the opportunity slip away. He promised himself he'd start fresh after confessing his indulgences since New Year's Eve and would be free to mature into a position of respectability among his peers without the aid of Mystics of Dardenne mischief.

He paced the marble floor as he waited in the rear of the nave for an opening in the confessional booth. When the curtain finally parted, a contrite Alexander stepped out. Catching Edmund's gaze, his typical puckish grin returned. Nodding to greet him, Edmund stepped into the enclosure as Alexander held the curtain for him.

Falling to his knees, Edmund's heart raced as he crossed himself and waited for the window to open. Going through a watered-down version of his sins, Edmund promised to carry out his penance when prompted with how to make amends.

Breathing a sigh of relief when he exited the cathedral, Edmund faltered at Alexander's mirthful expression as he leaned against one of the portico columns.

"Feel better, Easton?"

He shrugged. "Better than I felt last Friday."

Alexander laughed. "Thanks for helping me out of that mess. I assume you've received your invitation."

"It was most unexpected. Thank you."

"You deserve it. It'll be another place we can drink and cavort. For now, let's go celebrate our lightened souls. There's never a wait in the district on confession day." Alexander started down the steps.

Edmund hovered at the edge of the portico two whole seconds before following Alexander back to the indulgent revelry of carnival season.

~~~
~~~

"Dashing Through the Snow"

A Washington Square Secrets/Malevolent Trilogy/Possession Chronicles Short

Sean Spunner sneaked through the kitchen while the cooks prepped dinner for his uncle's household. It wasn't a completely successful exit. Althea, the assistant cook, caught his eye and winked at him before he closed the back door.

Outside, he raised his face to the falling snow and opened his mouth to catch the snowflakes he hadn't seen for several years. Mobile rarely got snow, and today's weather with multiple inches accumulated had halted all normal activity in the city. Sean watched his breath puff out as the freezing temperature made his face ache.

In an attempt to stay warm, he ran down Palmetto Street, his feet making satisfying crunching sounds through the inches of snow. He didn't stop until he got to Washington Square Park. The gaslights around the square flickered against the ice and snow, giving a magical luster to the neighborhood park at twilight.

"Spunner!" John Woodslow shouted as he sprang out from behind a bench and ambushed his best friend with snowballs.

Laughing, Sean scooped up a handful of snow and hastily packed a ball to throw back at his friend. After several rounds—all with John victorious—they silently signaled a truce and came together.

"Did you do it?" Sean asked when they were a foot apart.

John grinned and tugged down his blue knit cap over his blond hair. "I sure did."

John was fourteen—ten months Sean's junior—but he was more experienced in the scheme of life. He'd told Sean that morning that he was going to deliver a Saint Valentine's Day card to the Easton twins and promised to meet Sean in the park to report about it before supper, no matter the weather.

"Did you give one to both of them or make them share?"

"Neither. I only left one for Cora. That way she'll know I'm serious about her and don't want her sister."

"So you signed your name?"

"You bet I did."

"But your signature is atrocious. She probably can't read it."

"Her loss." John shrugged.

"You did that on purpose because you know if a sixteen-year-old girl knew a boy your age gave her a Saint Valentine's Day card, she'd laugh in your face."

His fair complexion showed a hint of a blush in the dim light. "At least I was brave enough to leave a card, unlike you, Scholarly Spunner."

Sean had known John since he first came to his uncle's house as a twelve-year-old orphan. In an attempt to catch his nephew up to his new peers of the highest social class, Patrick Finnigan had pushed Sean academically, setting him up to become the top student within two years after transferring to the private school. Sean knew his uncle didn't want the other boys looking down on him as the poor orphan from the wrong side of town, so he supplemented his education during the school breaks and made sure he was in top physical shape to defend himself through a place on the school's boxing team.

"I couldn't have gotten away today even if I wanted to deliver a sappy card to some girl," Sean said. "Uncle Patrick had a list of reading for me to do as soon as he heard the school was closing due to the weather."

"We'll start out early tomorrow, before he can disrupt our plans," John said. "Meet me here at eight in the morning. There'll be snowball fights and maybe sledding if we can find something to use."

"I'll be here." Sean brushed the snowflakes off his hair and hurried home.

* * *

Sean threw his quilt to the floor, eager to greet another day off. The gift of no school on a Friday during Mardi Gras season was too wonderful not to take full advantage of it.

The fire in his bedroom hearth was almost out, but he wouldn't need it. Why spend a moment inside when there was at least half a foot of snow outside to enjoy? He snatched a pair of long underwear from his bureau and took yesterday's pants off his bed's footboard, not caring if they were rumpled. White shirt buttoned and tucked, he grabbed his socks before scurrying for the stairs.

"You better slow down," his cousin Megan called from her bedroom.

He skidded to a stop outside her room at the top of the stairs and leaned against the door frame as he pulled on his woolen socks, balancing first on one foot then the other. Megan sat at her dressing table, brushing her brunette locks. At fifteen, she wore her maturity like a badge of honor, draped in a bustled red dress befitting a morning at the cathedral rather than a stroll in the snow.

"Are you going outside in *that?*" Sean said.

She gave him an exasperated sigh. "It's better than dirty trousers and a smelly shirt. My mother wouldn't let you step a foot outside dressed like that. Be glad she's in bed with a head cold."

"I refuse to be joyful over Aunt Cecilia's poor health." Sean eyed Megan's ensemble when she stood. "I suppose you want to look like a cardinal, complete with a big tail rump."

"You're a buffoon, Sean Francis Spunner!"

"And you used to be fun."

He ran down the stairs, fleeing the memories of his childhood visits to this house and the capers he and Megan used to go on together—neighborhood frolics and household catastrophes. But all that had been before his parents died and Megan grew breasts. She had been kind to him that first year he'd moved in, and her friends had doted on him. But as the years passed they'd grown apart, boys against girls.

When Sean reached for the boots he'd left by the front door the evening before, Patrick Finnigan spoke from the dining room door. "No so fast, young man. There's something I need you to do today. Join me."

"But I told—"

"Now, Sean."

Still holding his boots, Sean gazed from where his uncle had disappeared into the dining room to the freedom beyond the frosted glass of the front doors. He sighed.

On her way to the kitchen, Althea paused on the pretense of checking the potted palm in the entry hall. Her dark face leaned close as she rubbed a frond between her thumb and finger.

"Breakfast, Sean Francis," she whispered. "It won't take long. Besides, you won't get far on an empty stomach. Cajun sausage and grits—a hearty meal to keep you warm all morning."

Sean dropped his boots and they both straightened. Nodding, he grinned at the woman in possession of the one voice that always gave him sound logic.

His uncle lifted his freckled face upon Sean's entrance into the dining room. Uncle Patrick's fine auburn hair was similar to his deceased sister's, making Sean—with his thick brown mop—appear to take after his father's family at first glance. But their tall, sturdy frames were similar.

With a nod, Uncle Patrick crossed himself. Sean followed his lead and sat reverently for his uncle's uttered prayer over the food. Althea stepped in from the kitchen as soon as the blessing was said and poured coffee for the man of the house.

"Sean, just because you aren't going to Spring Hill for school today," Uncle Patrick said, "doesn't mean you have a free pass."

Sean glanced up from ladling a big helping of grits into his bowl.

"I have an important delivery I need you to bring to Melling and Associates," Uncle Patrick said. "Then I expect you home at noon in time to wash up for midday dinner."

"Yes, sir. I can do that." Sean stabbed two large sausage links from the platter Althea held.

Uncle Patrick did the same when Althea came to his chair. "I know you can. And I expect you at your studies this afternoon."

"With all that snow outside, Uncle Patrick? This doesn't happen every day, or even every year."

"You're nearly fifteen, Sean. It's time to hang up some of your boyish games and focus more on your studies."

"Boyish games?" Sean laughed. "No man is ever too old to throw a snowball."

Uncle Patrick tried to keep a straight face, but the corner of his mouth quirked. "Perhaps not, but there's much to keep up with if you're going to graduate early."

"Yes, sir."

Sean sliced the spicy sausage and stirred the pieces into his grits so he could eat quicker. When he stood to leave the table, Uncle Patrick met his eye.

"The envelope addressed to Mr. Melling is on my desk. Remember, you're acting as a law clerk on my behalf. He expects it by ten o'clock."

"Yes, sir." Sean practically collided with Megan on her way into the dining room.

"You might ask your junior law clerk to put on clean clothes, Daddy," she said.

"He'll have a coat on and be covered in snow by the time he crosses Government Street," Uncle Patrick replied. "No one can stay fresh for long in these arctic temperatures, Megan. Not even you."

After fetching the letter then tying on his boots and buttoning up his wool coat, Sean poked his head back into the dining room to bid them farewell.

"A hat, Sean," Megan chided. "Just like a child, you have to be reminded of everything."

Uncle Patrick looked up from the newspaper. "And a scarf, young man."

With a frown and glance at the mantel clock that showed his morning wasting away, Sean reached for the banister to haul himself back to his room. He met one of the maids hurrying down, his cap and scarf in her hands.

"Althea said you'd need these, Sean Francis," she said.

"Dear Althea saves me again." He set the green hat on his head, pulling it low about his ears, then he wrapped the matching scarf twice around his neck and smiled at the maid. "Thank you."

A minute later, he was at the corner, reveling in the freezing temperatures and sparkle of the snow-covered houses and trees as he pulled his leather gloves from his pocket. It had snowed enough after nightfall to cover the prints from the previous day's pedestrians. The blanket of white crunched under his feet as he traveled another block toward the park.

John Woodslow, wrapped in a black coat and topped with his blue hat, was building a snowman at one corner of Washington Square and sent a snowball straight at Sean. It struck him in the middle of his gray coat. Laughing, Sean hastily gathered a handful of snow and hit John in the back.

"I can't believe you came unarmed again, Spunner!" John reached for two more snowballs hidden behind his snowman and let them fly, striking first Sean's arm and then his thigh.

The battle continued several minutes, with John heavily armed and sporting a good aim against Sean's quickly formed weapons and haphazard throws while he laughed. Children and adults from the houses circling the park joined in the fun and games.

When Sean spotted priggish Kate Stuart mincing her way through the snow in a bright purple cape, he motioned John to his side and nodded toward the newcomer. She was only thirteen but already thought she ruled the world, or at least all the young ladies at the cathedral. John immediately understood exactly what his friend had in mind. They both set to work packing the tightest snowballs yet, unbothered that they were bombarded by a dozen strikes in the process.

As graceful as a choreographed cotillion dance, they moved across the park to get behind Kate. Another girl saw what they were about to do and gasped. Using the girl's exclamation as a signal, the boys let their snowballs fly. John struck Kate squarely between the shoulder blades, jolting her forward. Sean's snowball struck just below her buttocks, marring the cape with a splattering of ice from its softer hit.

She turned with venomous eyes. "You rascals! I'll tell Father Quinn on you both!"

They laughed and escaped the neighborhood, not stopping until they reached Government Street. Clouds of air steamed before their faces as they caught their breath from the flight. The busy road typically teemed with streetcars, wagons, and carriages, not to mention pedestrians and horses, but now it was as clean and quiet as an empty field. Eerie, deserted, and calm.

Sean patted his coat where Mr. Melling's envelope was tucked into the interior breast pocket. Hearing the crinkle of paper, he relaxed to know he hadn't lost his special delivery. He checked his watch and was surprised that it was already heading for nine.

"I've got to go to Melling and Associates for my uncle this hour. Want to come with me?"

"Only if we can go through the district on the way. You can always see the finest horses in the stables behind the red-light houses."

Sean bit his lip and nodded. They had both grown up hearing about the tenderloin district, the area of town where some men went to be satisfied by women bolder than their sweethearts or wives—especially during Mardi Gras. The district had a mythical quality to boys their age, just a couple years shy of being old enough to enter one of the houses of ill repute located a handful of blocks northwest of the business section of town. Sean couldn't help wondering which of his friends would be the first to walk in as a boy and emerge a man?

He wasn't sure if he would, especially if he had fallen in love by then. After his parents died, Sean had promised God he'd be a faithful spouse like his father had been. He didn't want to be like his uncle and his society friends, who paraded their wives to masquerades and fundraisers only to indulge in sin at their own gatherings, especially during the weeks leading up to Lent.

Sean's father might have been a humble bricklayer, but he'd made sure his son was taught to be true to his religious and marriage vows, because he'd seen how—even as a young boy—Sean had been dazzled by the splendor of Patrick Finnigan's lifestyle, from the rich foods to the impressive personal libraries.

John led the way to Broad Street, instinctively staying on the unseen sidewalk like the other adventurers. At the intersection, Sean marveled at the vast expanse of snow covering all the streetcar tracks and horse dung typically seen in the road. Only a few marks marred the smooth snow, most likely left by the milkmen and newspaper boys.

With a whoop and a holler, Sean ran diagonally across the street. In the middle of the road, he dropped to his back and began moving his legs and arms to make a snow angel, laughing at the thought that it was probably the closest he'd ever get to Heaven. Especially with girls like Megan and Kate tattling on him all the time.

John was beside him a moment later, following Sean's lead. After leaving their divine mark, they ran north, snow and ice dropping off them like droplets from fog. Bells clanged and two racing buggies whizzed down Government Street, the young men at the reins oblivious to the pedestrians. The tracks made by the single horses and wooden boards instead of wheels sliced right through their snow angels.

"That's a bit of luck that we weren't still laid out on the road," John remarked, looking back.

"A blessing, not luck." Sean frowned at his marred angel a moment before heading north again.

Following the excited sounds of children and adults at play, Sean and John tromped through the fringes of the Creole neighborhood on their way to the red-light district. They paused to help a few girls build a wall for a snow fort and assisted a boy lifting a huge snowball on top of an even larger one to make a snowman.

"Stay and play with us!" the boy said.

"We can't," Sean replied, patting his coat. "I've got a delivery to make."

Another wagon-sleigh passed, spraying icy snow behind the rickety runners. The riders sang about jingle bells as they rode. Sean's nose was beginning to ache from the cold.

"This way." John motioned down an alley between Cedar and Lawrence Streets.

He led Sean toward a stable that serviced several of the brothels. The young man on duty was huddled in a pile of straw just inside the open doorway.

"Is it okay if we look at the horses?" John asked.

The fellow grunted. "Ain't many here today. Guess the gents are keeping their wives warm in this weather."

Sean knew John recognized most of the thoroughbreds in the city and knew who owned them. His father took him to the riding club a couple times each week, and he was on a polo team with several other young men from the parish. Sean enjoyed riding every once in a while, but he preferred boxing. For now, the break from the chilly north wind was appreciated, though it pained his nose more as the feeling returned to his face. There were three horses in residence but only one captured John's attention, a chestnut stallion in the furthest stall.

"It's Janus!" John reached out a hand to stroke its muzzle.

"Don't go touching 'em," the stable hand called out.

"But I know this one."

"No touching unless you want to pay to keep me quiet. And you'd have to tip me better than the fancy man who rode him in. I doubt you can afford that." The stable hand tucked his dark hands under his armpits. "What, is it your daddy's or something? You out spying for the old lady?"

"Nothing like that," John said. "This horse belongs to my friend Al—"

"No names given here!" the stable hand remarked. "But I doubt the gentleman would appreciate being called a friend by a mere boy like you."

"He must have taken his son's horse because Janus is younger and more spry than his own." John defiantly stroked the horse and then rushed out through the rear door.

Sean stumbled after him as the shouts from the worker chased them from the stable. In their hurry to escape, they went further north, out of their way. At Lawrence Street, they doubled back south and encountered a mixed group of bawdy women playing in the snow. They didn't look like much, all bundled in ill-fitting coats with their hair in disarray from the wind.

"You boys lost?" a brunette called out.

"No, ma'am," Sean replied, trying not to gawk at her chest that peeked from beneath her fastened cape.

"Y'all best move on then," she said. "You're not old enough to be paying visits here."

"Maybe they're wanting work," a blonde said. "You boys want to shovel snow from a few walks for a nickel?"

John laughed. "How about for a kiss instead?"

The brunette shook her head. "Don't sell yourself short, young man. You'll have girls lined up to kiss you, if they're not already. You don't need her used lips."

Sean checked his watch and elbowed his friend. "I have to deliver that envelope. Are you staying here or coming with me?"

"You'll be a charmer too," the brunette said to Sean. "But if you want to pay me a visit in another year or two, ask for Hazel. I've turned many boys into men in this city."

"Thank you, ma'am." Sean gave her an uncomfortable smile.

"Do I know your father?"

"He's dead." Sean refrained from insulting her by saying that his father never would have come to this neighborhood. "I've got to make a delivery now. Enjoy the snow, Miss Hazel."

Sean walked away without waiting for John, but he heard his footsteps crunching after him.

"Goodbye, ladies!" John called before reaching Sean, then he said, "That's Alexander Melling's horse in there. He got Janus for his birthday last autumn. Mr. Melling must have ridden him this morning and might be in one of these houses with a woman. You should have asked those ladies if they knew him."

Sean shook his head. "Like the stable hand said, these people don't deal in names. At least not without a price." He increased his pace. "Besides, I doubt my uncle would appreciate me delivering one of his correspondences to a red-light house. I was instructed to bring it to Melling and Associates by ten o'clock, and I will."

They hurried on without conversation, turning left on St. Francis Street toward town. Sean ignored the snowballs hurled at them, though John did pause to lob one back if they were struck.

"Should we stop in the cathedral to confess to Father Quinn before Kate gets to him?" John asked when they approached Claiborne Street.

"Maybe on the way home." Sean looked at his watch and stepped up the pace more until he slid on a patch of ice.

"You better slow down," John said. "I'm not going to carry you if you twist an ankle."

Sean started a shoving match that ended when they were both on their backs in the snowy road. Laughing at each other, they stood and Sean threw an arm around his friend.

"Hold it together a couple more blocks, Woodslow."

When they reached the north side of Bienville Square, Sean gazed across the road to the trees frosted with snow, like the fancy cakes his aunt served at tea parties. Icicles hung from the three tiers of the fountain, winking in the morning sun like sequins on a Mardi Gras mask.

Sean gripped the slick brass of the doorknob at Melling and Associates, difficult to do with his gloves on. It finally turned and he stepped into the space he had visited many times before, both with his uncle and as a runner between offices. No secretary sat at the front desk, nor did he hear any clerks in the file room. John followed him inside, closing the door behind them.

"Hello?" Sean called from the bottom of the stairs. "I have an important delivery for Mr. Melling!"

The man himself came down the stairs, smoothing his cravat. He paused a few feet in front of Sean, his blue eyes staring coolly as he took a drag on a cigarette.

After whipping the cap off his head, Sean ran a hand over his unruly hair. "Good morning, Mr. Melling. I'm here with a delivery from Solicitor Finnigan. Six inches of snow can't stop the legal profession from rolling forth."

Mr. Melling laughed. "You're Patrick's nephew, aren't you?"

"Yes, sir." Sean shoved his cap under his arm and opened his coat to retrieve the envelope.

"I remember you from last summer. Bright mind, good worker, quick on your feet, and a sense of humor." He exhaled a cloud of smoke. "How old are you?"

"Fifteen in less than two weeks, Mr. Melling." Sean handed over the envelope.

Melling tapped it against the wall. "Do you have your eye on law school?"

"Yes, sir. My uncle already has me studying for it alongside my classes at Spring Hill."

"Excellent. There's nothing like a young man who applies himself." He paused to puff on his cigarette, his eyes flickering to John standing near the door. "Is that you, Woodslow?"

"Yes, sir." John took a few steps closer, taking the cap off his blond head.

"Did your father get you a new stallion for Christmas?"

"Yes, sir. He said it wasn't right for a boy as young as Alex to have a better horse than me on the polo field."

Mr. Melling laughed, eyes brightening. "Nothing like envy to spur a man along. Janus is an exceptional horse. I rode him into the city today since my carriage couldn't make it. I refuse to allow the coachman to remove the wheels for a rare day or two of snow."

"Are there proper facilities nearby for a horse?" John asked with a lift of his fair brows. "The community stables don't offer enough protection in this weather."

Mr. Melling cleared his throat. "I'm using a private stable, not too far from here. Janus will be well seen to."

"That's good to hear, sir. Alex loves that horse."

"Now, young man," Mr. Melling said as he turned to Sean. "How would you like to be a junior clerk at Mobile's most prestigious law firm this summer?"

"Thank you, Mr. Melling, but Uncle Patrick has my schedule planned out for the next five years."

"He's putting you to work for his gain, no doubt. Do you need to stay for a reply?"

"Not that he mentioned, sir, but we'll be in the square for a few minutes if you need to call me over."

"Very well. Regards to your uncle, and to your father, Woodslow."

The boys hurried out the front door, pausing on the sidewalk to don their caps before dashing across the street, where they crafted a few snowballs. John elbowed Sean and motioned to an approaching sled-buggy.

"It's the Eastons. Well, almost half of them."

"The good half," Sean said with a smirk when he saw the three oldest sisters riding with their older brother, Maxwell.

Cora and Emma were close friends with Megan, and Sean could never keep his eyes off the Easton twins when they visited at the house. Halos of blonde hair, blue-grey eyes, and perfect curves on their still-budding bodies were enough to make any boy ogle them. And with their oldest sister Susan looking like a full woman at seventeen, the odds of the fifteen-year-old twins being perfection in another few years were good.

"Let's ambush them," John said.

"That's not the way to get the attention of girls like those."

The sled whooshed past them, the twins in the back waving.

"I'm not waiting around to quote poetry to them." Expecting Maxwell to circle the park, John took off across the square to cut them off on the other side.

Not wanting to be left behind, Sean ran after him. The Eastons slowed for the turns, and Maxwell flicked the reins to increase their speed once they were on Dauphin Street. Staying several feet away from John so he wouldn't be mistaken as the ambusher, Sean watched with open mouth as his friend's true aim clocked Maxwell on the shoulder. The snowball burst, showering Susan with the powdery ice.

Maxwell immediately pulled the horse to a stop, and by the time he'd thrown the reins to his sister and jumped out of the sled, John was running. But Maxwell was bigger and faster. He tackled John in a snowdrift at the base of a lamppost.

"You might have hit one of my sisters, Woodslow!" Maxwell yanked him around, but instead of pummeling John's face, he punched him in the stomach several times then ground handfuls of snow into his mouth.

"Aren't you going to help your friend?" Cora asked Sean as he stood beside their buggy.

Sean shook his head and stepped onto the runner, peering at the twins, warm within their lap blanket and furs. "I told him not to do it. He deserves the beating."

Emma giggled. "You could have stopped him if you wanted."

"I was too overcome by the beauty within this sleigh to intercept him." Sean grinned and started reciting a Keats poem. "'O thou whose face hath felt the Winter's wind, Whose eye has seen the snow-clouds hung in mist—'"

"Enough of that, Sean," Susan snapped. "You're too young for any of us here. Try your poetry on Lucy in a few years. She'd appreciate it, at the very least."

"She's the bookworm, not us," Emma said.

"Susan is too." Cora straightened her shawl. "But as she said, you're too young for us."

"But you're sweet and adorable," Emma said. "Never change, no matter what Megan says." She leaned over and kissed him on the cheek.

To Sean's despair, his face was too numb to tell how soft her lips were.

"Emma, you minx!" Maxwell left John lying in the snow and stomped over. "Don't make me beat up two boys today."

Emma lifted a shoulder in a coquettish way. "Sean meant no harm. He was only reciting some Victorian drivel about winter snow."

"Spunner, go!" Maxwell pointed toward John. "Make sure Woodslow gets home without trouble. I tried not to rough him up too much."

"How about giving us a ride?"

"It's the least you can do, Max," Susan said. "He's just a boy having fun. You didn't have to jump on him like that. He's still holding his middle."

A cloud of breath escaped Maxwell when he sighed. "Get in, the both of you, before I change my mind."

Sean went to where John was sitting in the snow and hauled him to his feet. He pushed him toward the front bench, next to Susan who had shifted closer to her brother.

"I'm sorry I struck you with the snowball," John told Maxwell as he took a seat beside Susan.

"Sorry you did it, or sorry I caught you?" Maxwell asked.

"Both," John admitted with a grin.

Sean climbed in the back row, snuggling between the twins when Emma pulled the lap blanket aside with a naughty smile. He knew he'd enjoy every minute of this ride.

"Maxwell, would you be able to go around the square once more?" Sean asked. "I see Mr. Melling leaving his office, and I need to make sure he doesn't have a message for my uncle."

"So now I take directions from my younger sisters and from random boys as well?" Maxwell muttered.

Susan poked her brother in the ribs, and Maxwell steered the horse around the corner. Mr. Melling, turning to the sound of someone calling his name from next door, slipped and fell on his side. Several men and ladies rushed over, including a newspaper reporter.

"Could we be of assistance?" Maxwell asked when they reached the scene.

"Do you need to get to the hospital, Mr. Melling?" One man pointed to Maxwell. "These folks have a sleigh."

"It's just my elbow—nothing to fret about." Mr. Melling was clearly trying to downplay his embarrassment. "I'm not as old and decrepit as that, gentlemen and ladies."

Sean stood, knocking the blanket to the floorboard. "Any message for Mr. Finnigan, Mr. Melling?"

"No, thank you. I'll be in touch with him next week." Mr. Melling held his arm and tried to disperse the audience.

With nothing to be done on their part, Cora tugged Sean back to the bench and Maxwell set the horse back to a trot. The twins lowered the lap blanket simultaneously, trapping Sean's arms beneath. As they flew over the snow-covered streets of downtown, Emma's hand found his, their gloved fingers intertwining. She brought his hand to her knee and pressed it against her leg. Sean bit his lower lip.

Maxwell half-turned to check on his sisters. "Spunner, you get your hands above that blanket right now or I'll beat your—"

"Max!" Susan shoved him as Sean brought his hands straight up, over his head. "You're barbaric today. You can put your arms down, Sean."

John shot his friend a sneer of pure jealousy as Sean settled his arms around each of the twins' shoulders. Emma and Cora giggled, causing John to turn back with an annoyed huff.

Emma's hand—still beneath the blanket—went to Sean's knee. As though not wanting to be outdone, Cora set her gloved hand on his opposite thigh. Sean nearly melted into the upholstery at the stimulating weight of their hands on him. He could sit forever between such heavenly beauties, but he wished he could return the attention.

Before he realized it, they were turning down Broad Street and onto Palmetto, stopping before his uncle's house. Megan, still in her ridiculous dress, was building a snowman in the front yard. Seeing Sean tucked between her friends, her pleasant face fell into shadow.

Sean quickly kissed Emma's cheek and then Cora's. He nimbly hopped over Emma's leg and landed on his boots in the dirty snow on the well-traveled sidewalk.

"What do you think you're doing, Sean?" Megan asked with annoyance.

"Telling my seat-mates farewell." He spun back to face the buggy and pulled off his cap to bow. "My thanks, Easton family. It was most enjoyable."

"You don't have to be nice to him," Megan said as she approached her friends.

Emma giggled when Sean winked at her. "He's charming."

"He's wearing yesterday's dirty clothes!"

"Who looks at clothing when a fellow has a smile like Sean's?"

Sean bit his lip at Emma's flattery. Megan frowned at the twins.

"Max clobbered John," Cora said.

"I did not!" Maxwell's knuckles strained against his black gloves.

"He isn't handling the cold well," Susan said. "And we wanted to make sure the boys made it back in one piece."

"The only thing I'm not handling well is being outnumbered by sisters!"

"There were three females and three males in this sleigh for the last few minutes," Emma pointed out.

"Lucky me," Maxwell grumbled. "Next time I'll bring along Edmund, Peter, and Aaron so we don't need to pick up stragglers."

"No," Emma whined. "Big brothers are the only type of brothers to keep around."

"They're the only useful ones," Cora agreed.

"Let's go home, ladies," Maxwell said and then smiled at Megan. "The snow agrees with you, Miss Finnigan. I'll turn the care of these ruffians over to you. Hopefully, you can keep your cousin and his friend out of trouble."

John crossed his arms. "We don't need watching."

"I would disagree," Maxwell said as he signaled the horse to move.

Emma waved at Sean as they pulled away. Relishing the attention, he was oblivious to all else, so Megan's shove sent him to the ground.

"Hey!" He jumped to his feet, not bothering to knock the snow from his backside.

John inched away, laughing over Sean's predicament. "I'll see you later!"

Ignoring John's retreat, Sean turned to his cousin. "What did you do that for?"

"Keep away from my friends, Sean Francis!"

"I can't help it if they wanted to share their lap blanket with me." He gave her an arrogant smirk.

"You filthy jackanapes!"

Megan lunged at him, but he was ready. Rather than shove her and possibly ruin her red dress or crush her bustle, he clasped her arms to her side and loomed over her with his superior attitude.

"I won today, Megan. Accept the fact that even in wrinkled trousers, your younger cousin attracts more females than you attract men in your fine gown. Although Maxwell Easton did pay you a compliment."

"I'll have you know I've had dozens of kind words from people as they walked by this hour." Her chin lifted and she looked away, unable to move as Sean still held her.

"Is that why you're building a snowman in that dress—to attract men? That's pathetic."

"You don't know anything!"

"But I do. I may still be young, but I can tell you that men don't want a woman they're afraid to touch. If you want interaction more than fleeting comments, go change into something a boy wouldn't be afraid to strike with a snowball."

"Don't be ridiculous! And I don't want the attention of boys anyway."

"Sure you do. Boys come in all ages." Sean released her arms, flipped her velvet cape, and nodded toward the house. "Go change into a regular dress and coat. I bet you a nickel you'll have a flirtation within ten minutes of returning."

"From a boy my age or older?"

"Sure enough, but plenty of younger ones too, I'll wager. You're pretty, Megan. Don't let high fashion stand in the way of possible beaus."

She pursed her lips and marched into the house. Sean set to work building an arsenal, piling the balls behind Megan's snowman so they wouldn't readily be seen from the road.

"Sean Francis!" Althea called from the porch. "I've got a cup of hot cocoa if you want it."

He left his work and wiped his gloved hands on his trousers as he climbed the steps. "Thank you, Miss Althea."

"If your nose gets any redder, it's going to fall off. Wrap that scarf around your face after you're done drinking."

He took a sip of the hot sweetness. "It's not bothering me."

"Because you can't feel it. That's not good, child." Her hands were on her slim hips, mouth set in a straight line.

"Thank you for caring about me, Miss Althea, but I think I'll survive until dinner."

"You better. I've got your favorite bread baking, and a hearty stew for y'all."

"That sounds wonderful, but what about you standing out here with no coat?"

"It'll help me work faster to warm up when I go inside."

Sean knew she was waiting for his cup, so he drank the rest as quickly as he could without burning his mouth.

"Thank you, Miss Althea. It was delicious. I feel warmer already."

Megan joined them on the porch. "You need to quit coddling him, Miss Althea. He's got a high enough opinion of himself as it is."

"And for good reason, Miss Megan. Sean Francis is the best boy that ever roamed these halls."

Megan rolled her eyes as Althea went back into the house. Sean took in the length of Megan's black skirt, made full from functional petticoats that would keep her warm, and the gray wool cape that hung over her plain blouse.

"Don't you feel better?"

"I suppose I do." Megan straightened the cuffs of her lined gloves.

"I've set you up with a supply of snowballs here," Sean told her as they stepped into the yard. "Don't be afraid to use them."

"What do I do? Stand around and wait?"

"Play, build, frolic." Sean motioned to the snowman. "Make that bigger for a start. Do you want me to help?"

Megan nodded and set to work making another tier while Sean padded the base with more bulk.

Freddy Davenport, a lively twelve-year-old who was best friends with Edmund Easton, came whistling by.

"Nice snowman, Sean," he said.

"It's Megan's. I'm just helping finish it."

"You did well, Miss Megan," he said with a blush, too well-mannered to say more.

"Thank you, Freddy." She'd seen him enough times at the twins' house to know him by name, though he didn't attend the parish.

"There's going to be a battle at Eddie's house at two o'clock," Freddy added.

"I'll be studying, but thanks," Sean said. "Be sure to tell John. He might be at the park."

Freddy nodded and stuck his hands in his coat pockets, continuing on his way.

"Little Freddy doesn't count," Megan said before Sean could breathe an *I told you so.*

He was still laughing when a group of boys a year or two older than him strolled by. They stopped, elbowed each other in a way that meant *look at her.* One boy let a snowball loose, striking Sean on the side of the head, and another got Megan on the chest.

"Sorry about that!" another boy said as he crossed into the yard. "My friends are a bit rowdy today. Are you all right?"

She nodded.

"I'm Mason," he said as his friends on the sidewalk threw snowballs at him.

Megan laughed as she brushed the ice off her cape. "I'm Megan, but please don't stand too close if your friends are going to keep throwing those."

Sean discreetly pointed Megan and her visitor to the pile of snowballs tucked away. They glanced at the cache and then at each other with a nod. In one swoop, they gathered armfuls and started tossing them at the boys on the sidewalk. Grinning, Sean took a seat on the front steps and watched his cousin behave as she hadn't in years.

Megan and Mason rallied their efforts as they fought two against four. When they ran out of pre-made snowballs, she ripped apart her snowman to toss chunks of it at the boys, laughing the whole time. The battle ended with her sitting on the frozen ground and Mason shielding her.

"That brother of yours ain't worth much!" one of the boys shouted. "He sat it out and watched you get walloped!"

"He's my cousin, and he had a rough morning!" Megan called back.

Surprised at Megan's defense of him, Sean watched as Mason helped her up and invited her to visit the soda fountain he worked at for a complimentary drink.

"Could I bring Sean with me?" She motioned to him still on the steps. "He's the one who stocked the snowballs."

"Of course, but come sometime after the snow clears. I don't want you risking yourself on account of a measly soda."

"Thank you, Mason." She gave him her best smile—the genuine one. "I'll see you soon."

When he got back to his friends, they jostled him and looked back at Megan several times before making it to the corner. She waved the first time and then pretended not to notice. But as soon as they were out of view, she plopped down beside Sean, resting her head on his shoulder.

"Thank you."

"For what? According to them, I sat around like a lump."

"I'm glad you did. The battle wouldn't have been as magical if you'd participated."

"It wouldn't have been much of a fight if I hadn't stocked the ammo for you either. Not to mention, it never would have happened if you were still wearing that cardinal showpiece."

She sat up straight and scooched away a few inches. "That's doubly true. You helped in every way and made this the best day of the year so far. What can I do to repay your thoughtfulness?"

"The only thing I'd like is to be on good terms with you once more."

"Then don't be annoying. Cease chasing my friends, and—"

"I'm never going to be perfect, and we're bound to see the worst in each other from time to time, but if you could show me some respect like you—"

"You're no longer a mournful boy."

"I'm still an orphan." He let his lower lip pout and gazed at her dolefully.

"That doesn't work on me, Sean Francis." She shoved his shoulder. "But I'll try to be nice, so long as you keep away from my friends."

"Then I'll admire them from afar."

"Not if you know what's good for you."

"Empty threats, dear cousin."

Megan grabbed a handful of snow and shoved it in his face. "That wasn't empty, was it?"

She jumped up and ran, and Sean chased her down Palmetto Street.

"Don't forget you owe me a nickel!"

She laughed and slowed until he caught up with her.

Sean raised his brow. "Do you want to join the neighborhood fun like you used to?"

Megan nodded and they united for the snowball battle in Washington Square.

John got clobbered.

~~~
~~~

"Courtship and Courage"

A *Fortitude/*Possession Chronicles short

Claire O'Farrell tucked the broom and dustpan in the cupboard of the one-room schoolhouse. She picked up her carpetbag and settled on the front stoop to await her father's arrival to bring her home for the mid-December weekend.

A minute later, Joe Walker came up the path. Several times since she began teaching on the Creole island that fall Joe rode along with her father, but it had been weeks since she'd sailed home with him though they spent most Saturday afternoons together.

Standing, she met the young captain at the foot of the steps as she straightened her brown shawl. "What are you doing here? Mrs. Mathieu made it clear she won't release me to anyone except my father."

He took the bag from her and flashed his crooked smile. "Mrs. Mathieu ain't here."

Claire crossed her arms and glared.

Joe took her elbow. "Your pa's old knees are bothering him in this damp weather so I offered to fetch ya. You'll see him on my new boat in a minute."

He'd purchased a decent fishing boat that summer while she volunteered as a nurse for the soldiers in Tampa as they prepared to fight the Spaniards in Cuba. "What do you need with another boat? There's only one of you."

"This one isn't for fishing." His blue eyes danced with merriment. "I aim to set up ferrying and cargo services."

Claire made a humming sound to prove she'd heard him without commenting. They cleared the trees and approached the public dock.

Stopping mid-stride, she turned to him with blazing temper. "What do you mean by saying you bought a new boat? That's Pa's!" She could have slugged the smirk off him.

"It's mine now, Claire. Been mine since before Thanksgiving. Look again. See that smokestack between the masts? I've done converted it to a steamer. I'm setting it up as a bay runner. It's smaller than most, but once I get steady customers, I'll be able to trade up for something bigger."

She stared at the Island Lassie. It had been her father's boat since the year she was born and realized he had only used the skiff to bring her to and from Mon Louis the past month. Her father stood from where he'd been mending a net and waved. Rushing onboard, Claire embraced him and kissed his cheek above his bushy beard. In his arms she always felt like a child though she was a few months shy of turning eighteen.

"Claire, my lassie, you're more a woman every week. You sure you're still my baby girl?"

"Yes, Pa." She looked around at the improvements. "Why didn't you tell me about this?"

He settled back with a sigh and rubbed his knees. "Didn't think it'd matter to you one way or the other seeing as how you're working away from home. It's Kevin it'll affect, but Joseph already said he'd hire him on after he's done with school next spring."

Claire flopped onto the bench across from her father and shot another glare at Joe as he untied the boat. Usually she helped, but if he was going to lord it over her family by taking over her father's fleet one boat and worker at a time he could do it himself. Without the larger boat, Emmett O'Farrell would never get back into business for himself. He'd been forced to slave away for Joe since Claire destroyed his prospects that summer by serving the Buffalo Soldiers in Florida alongside her best friend. Not only was Claire shunned by Mobile and Dauphin Island society, her family had been too, forcing Emmett to take work with his former first mate because no one would buy fish directly from him.

Anger curdled in her veins quicker than milk in the summer, and Claire frowned as Joe steered them into the bay.

"It's as smooth as anything," Emmett said. "Joseph did a fine job with the conversion. Studied up and did it all himself with the help of books from the mainland."

Claire raised her brow at the information, trying not to smile over the memory of Joe declaring he was "literate and all" in one of his first letters to her when she started teaching.

"Go on and see the expanded wheelhouse. He's gifted with a hammer."

She trudged across the deck without wobbling amid the sway of the boat. Joe's cocky grin met her when she paused in the doorway.

"Come for the grand tour? Look, I built a little bench on the side here." He patted the narrow seat. "It's just the place for a feisty girl to perch and keep me company."

"I'd rather sit with Pa."

"Ain't it something both my boats are named after you?"

Claire ran a hand along the bench's smooth wood. "You can rechristen her, especially since you made so many changes."

His shaggy, dark blond hair struck his jaw when he shook his head. "I like *Island Lassie*. And my *Fare Marie*. Having a boat named after the one who keeps your heart is a seafaring tradition I proudly continue. And me having two proves my feelings doubly, wouldn't you say?"

Claire rolled her eyes at the mention of the ridiculous name for his fishing boat. As she stayed mute, his strong hands on the helm gripped tighter.

"Haven't you got a kind word to spare for me, Claire Marie O'Farrell?"

Raising her eyes to meet his once more, she managed to keep her heart from beating out of her chest. "You did a fine job on the boat, Joe. And thank you for keeping my father employed and looking out for my brother. I appreciate your kindness. I'm sure my whole family does."

He smiled at her before looking back to where he steered. "I hold you and all your kin in high regard. Let me know if there's anything I can do for you."

Thinking of her students and the approaching holiday, she knew what she wanted more than anything. "Are you going to Mobile tomorrow?"

"I've got a market run to make at eight with a load of fresh pickings from the first boats."

"May I come along? I've saved up a little and would like to shop for Christmas presents."

"I'd be honored to bring you with me."

Feeling nervous under his intense stare, she took a step back. "Pa's coming, isn't he?"

"He'll have charge of the fishing boat." His calloused hand touched the back of hers. "But Mrs. Collier and her daughter are riding into town for shopping, so we'll be chaperoned."

Laughing nervously, she tucked her hair behind her ear. "I'm not scared of you, Joe Walker, though you've filched one too many kisses this past year."

Instead of joking, he met her with the most straightforward expression she'd witnessed on his typically smug face. "You can be sure the next time our lips meet you'll want it as much as me."

***

Coming in from the chicken house, Claire set the clutch of eggs from her apron into the catch-all bowl on the kitchen table.

"Seventeen, Ma," she told her mother who was elbow deep in bread dough.

"They don't lay like that when you're gone. Now you best get to the dock before Captain Walker leaves you behind."

Claire removed her apron and took the reticule holding her spending money. "Did you think of anything you need me to get?"

"No, you have fun. I reckon the captain will be more than happy to carry parcels for you."

Knowing it was true, Claire couldn't stop a grin before she kissed her mother's cheek. "See you this afternoon."

She found herself hurrying through the golden morning as though she couldn't wait to see Joe. Forcing herself to slow, she called forth the fading images of her time in Florida. It was in the memory of the noble Buffalo Soldiers she'd taken the post in the Creole school. Her feelings for Joe needed to be suppressed because the ache from her time in the war camps was still too fresh.

But Claire couldn't stop the flutter in her middle upon seeing Joe standing proudly on the dock beside his steamer.

"And my final, most precious cargo has arrived." He held her elbow as she stepped onto the boat. With a nod from him, the deckhand immediately started uncoiling the moorings. "Would you care to sit in the wheelhouse with me?"

She looked to the Colliers and their unfriendly expressions, then to the crates of seafood along the stern. "Yes, please. Thank you."

He saw her to the bench and shouted a few orders to his deckhand who dropped into the hull after the last line was pulled in.

"He's seeing to the engine," Joe remarked as he set about adjusting numerous dials and valves beside the wheel. "So long as the fire doesn't go out, I can control everything from up here. It's a bit like magic not having to rely on the wind for everything. I'll be fixing *Fare Marie* up for steam after Christmas. I don't know why more on the island haven't adapted. I think once people see the comfort I enjoy with this power they'll pay me to convert their boats. I'll be able to fetch a pretty penny doing that and it should keep me in business a good long while."

"I never knew you were so driven to succeed." Claire fingered the wrist strap on her bag as the boat pulled into the bay.

"You haven't given me much of a chance." There was a slight tone of disappointment in Joe's voice, but he grinned at her before refocusing on the water before him. "I admit I was a wild cuss as recent as this spring, but I've done a bit of growing this year, Claire—same as you. When you left here in May you were idealistic and carefree. You returned just as wounded as any of the soldiers, full of sorrows and matured beyond your years."

A lump rose in her throat and she tried to swallow the tears before they could reach her eyes. "Joe, I…. why are you trying to make a name for yourself in cargo services rather than sticking to fishing? Pa said you're as good as him with scouting the best locations for a good haul."

"Your pa once told me he didn't want you tied to a man that came home reeking of fish everyday—that you were too fine a young lady for the likes of that and I agree." He spoke while watching the horizon, but there was a quirk on the corner of his lips. "You're the smartest, prettiest gal on the island and I aim to be the type of man that you'd be proud to call your own. I've secured property that I've been clearing in the afternoons and building furniture for my future house each evening."

Heart swollen with compassion, Claire laid her hand on the sleeve of his navy jacket. "I'm not worth the trouble, Joe."

"Like hell you ain't, Claire O'Farrell." He swept her hand up to his lips, quickly kissing her knuckles. "I've never been surer of anything in my life than I am of knowing I'd give everything to have you as my girl."

His declaration left her emotionally charged and mute. She folded her hands in her lap and studied her fingernails.

Once they were north of Mon Louis Island, Claire finally met his blue eyes made more intense with his dark coat. "I should have planned ahead about Christmas shopping and asked about seeing Loretta and Aunt Norah on a trip to town."

"You could always stop in."

"I don't know. It'd be a bit out of the way and if they aren't home—"

"I'd see you there on the streetcar. If they're home, you stay and visit while I see to my cargo. Then I'll come back to assist you on your errands."

"Don't you have other things to do?"

"There's nothing more important to me than your comfort and safety, Claire."

She stared in disbelief. "Who are you?"

"The same cantankerous cuss who hid a letter mailed to you last spring in order to have an excuse to bring it to your house and steal a kiss."

His smile returned and she couldn't help laughing.

"That's the best sound in the world." Joe looked from her eyes to her lips and back. "You forgive me, don't ya?"

"Yes, though it might have been ruder of me to spit afterward than it was for you to plant your lips on mine."

"That fiery temper of yours gets you into trouble sometimes, doesn't it?"

She nodded, and with the admission the urge to spill her troubles poured out. "I fancied I was in love with one of the soldiers. He took a beating for being helpful to me, in part because the head nurse didn't like my attitude."

"The lady who wrote the newspaper?" Joe asked in reference to the Letter to the Editor that told of Claire's supposed shameful behavior that led to her family's shunning.

"Yes, and the soldier was nothing but good. He did many chivalrous things in the short time I knew him." Her eyes blurred with tears. "I held his hand and watched him die, Joe. With all my training, I was helpless when it mattered most. I failed him."

"You did nothing of the sort." Joe touched her shoulder. "You gave him your radiant spirit to look upon during his final minutes on this earth. The sight of you alone is enough to bring courage to a man."

Claire brought her embroidered handkerchief from her pocket to dab her eyes. "I tried, I truly did."

"I'm sure you succeeded." He squeezed her shoulder before turning back to the wheel.

***

Joseph Walker held his heart in his fist as he strove to prepare the young woman he loved to receive his forthcoming declaration. He saw to his deliveries and securing a rocking chair he'd purchased with the hope of seeing Claire and their baby in it one day. Returning to the Davis home on St. Francis Street an hour and a half after dropping Claire there, he thought back on the times he'd sailed with her father to bring her for monthly visits in town. Her aunt, Norah, the Davis family's cook, was only half the reason for Claire spending regular time there in recent years—and also part of the reason she was always looked at sideways on the island. Their neighbors couldn't understand why Claire chose to spend her time in a mixed-blood household.

"Joe Walker, you're the most excellent of young men." Norah pulled him into a hug after answering the door, squashing him against her plump figure. "Brigit's gone on about your kindness in her letters the past few months. I dare say she's ready to welcome you into the family with open arms."

He grinned. "That'd be up to Miss Claire."

"And have you asked her?" Norah's typically stern mouth twitched like it wanted to smile with the impending good news.

"Not yet, but I'm working toward it."

Taking his elbow, she leaned closer. "I'll pray for you Joseph. Lord knows Claire's as stubborn as my sister, and that's saying something. Brigit strung poor Emmett along for months."

Joe followed Norah into the fancy parlor. Claire and Loretta were on the velvet settee with a pile of books. Anyone seeing them together would understand they were the best of friends, bonded over the stories they both loved.

"Greetings, Princess Loretta," he said with an exaggerated bow.

She laughed over him referring to how she used to call herself a Creole princess, but like Claire, Loretta had changed from her time as a nurse to the Buffalo Soldiers. Gone were her flirtatious ways and flashy clothes. She currently wore a sensible blue dress and not a plumed hat to be seen.

Loretta met him in the middle of the room, hand outstretched. "Welcome, Joe. Would you care for something to drink?"

He shook her hand. "No, thank you. But is there anything I could be of service with before I help Claire on her errands?"

"Such manners!" Her giddiness peeked through. "I hear you own a couple boats now."

"Yes, Miss Loretta, I sure do."

"I suppose I should call you Captain Walker now. Soon you'll be able to call me Mrs. Lieutenant Washington because my Samson is finally back in the states from Cuba. I told Claire he sent word asking for Mother to see me to San Francisco as he's to report to the Presidio there. I'll have to be married in a strange city, but it won't matter because we'll finally be together for 1899 and beyond."

"I'm pleased for you, Miss Loretta."

She smiled in her sly way. "There *is* something you could do for me. Make sure Claire wears the green dress I gave her for her birthday this Christmas. She was saving it for my wedding, but since she can't attend I want to make sure she wears it soon."

Claire blushed under her freckles. "It's too fine to wear on the island."

"Nonsense," Loretta said as she waved her hand with a superior air. "I'm sure your parents would love to see you dressed up. And Joe would appreciate it as well."

"That I would, though Claire's pretty just as she is." Joe looked to the redhead in her best calico dress. "Are you ready?"

She nodded, but Loretta motioned to the pile of books. "I'll see what else I can find, Claire, and post the books to you next week."

"If you need to get something to Claire, I'm happy to help as I'm making regular trips to Mobile now."

"Thank you, Captain Walker," Loretta said with a smile. "I'll have a crate of books to send her at the school."

"It'd be my pleasure to deliver them."

"Will you be in town Monday?"

He smiled. "I will."

"Then I'll see you when you stop by." Loretta turned to Claire and embraced her. "And you enjoy shopping. I'll send word before I head to California. Maybe you can visit one more time before then."

After the farewells were said, Joe led Claire to Dauphin Street and she opted to walk to the bookstore. He figured it was because she didn't like him paying her streetcar fare, but walking proved more opportunity for discreet conversations than riding on public transportation. They reached the bustling section of town and she made no objection to him taking her gently by the arm to ensure the crowd didn't part them. True, their island clothes weren't as fine as the city shoppers', but he felt like he owned the world with Claire beside him.

After browsing the bookstore for quarter of an hour, she found Joe in the reference section.

"Why the frown, Claire?"

"I was hoping to purchase a book for each student, but they're all too expensive. I thought there would be some little Christmas books with Bible verses or poems, but there's nothing to fit my budget when needing to purchase seventeen copies."

The urge to fix things for her sparked his brain to a dozen options as he stared into her green eyes. "There's a stationery store on the next block. Could you purchase some nice paper and fasteners and do up your own booklets?"

She pressed her lips together. "I don't know if I could manage making them all by Friday."

"I'd help ya. I ain't one for writing nice, but I could cut and do other things when we get home and tomorrow before you leave."

A smile brightened her face as she looked up at him. "Then let's see what they have."

Several minutes later, Claire ruffled through stacks of decorative paper with glee. "This one would be perfect for a cover! And this for some verses from St. Luke…"

Her fingers counted the right amount of sheets as she figured dividing them to use in multiple booklets and tallied her expenditures. Joe couldn't help but grin at her joy.

Claire shuffled her stack of papers to his arms so she could browse for coordinating ribbons. Quick as a lightning bug winks, she balanced on her tiptoes and left a kiss on his cheek. "Thank you, Joe. For everything."

He could have crowed like a rooster, but settled on a smile instead. "I'd gladly do anything for ya."

***

Claire kept stealing glances at Joe as they worked across from each other at the kitchen table. His moves were precise and concentration high, endearing him more to her each minute. He made quick work of cutting the papers she laid out. Stacking them the way she wanted, she then folded them and passed them back for Joe to nick fastening holes. Once they were returned to her, she threaded the festive red ribbon and tied a bow to join the six page booklet into one piece.

"You'll stay for supper, won't you?" Mrs. O'Farrell asked when she came in to stir the pot of stew.

"Yes, ma'am. Thank you."

Claire's mother caught her eye and winked on her way out.

Joe saw the exchange and chuckled. "I'm glad you stopped scowling and are giving me a chance."

Blushing, she focused on tying the ribbon. "You've been more than generous with my family this year."

"I don't aim to buy affection, Claire O'Farrell." His voice held a touch of anger and a dash of disappointment.

"I didn't mean—"

"You think so poorly of me that I have to win over any female because I'm too rough and uncultured otherwise." He stabbed his knife through the last folded pages and handed it to her, pain fully on display on his tanned face. "I might not have it in me to quote poetry and my hands are too rough to ever finger a piece of silk without catching on it, but I promise you any woman I choose will lack for nothing in life. Not food, shelter, or a loving bed."

She stood from the table so fast she flipped the bench. "Joe—"

"Claire." He met her head on with a challenging inflection in his voice as he stood before her, blue eyes lit with passion like she'd never seen. "I said 'any woman' but there's only one I want. Is there any part of you that thinks you might ever give me a proper chance to sweep you off your feet?"

Raising a hand to his cheek, she felt the prickles of a beard beginning and trailed her fingers along his jaw. "Part of me has always liked you, but it scared me because you weren't what I imagined after reading all those romance novels I borrowed from Loretta. I kept you at bay with sharp comments and my temper. Then what I went through in Tampa… sometimes it feels like I don't deserve to be cherished or happy."

Joe wiped the lone tear from her face with his thumb before cupping her cheeks with his hands. "Everyone deserves joy, and you of all people deserve to be cherished."

With her guard down, she felt it all. Every ounce of love streaming from his body like water sluicing off a jumping dolphin. And it scared her. She trembled before him as the complementary rush of her own denied feelings burbled to the surface.

His softening eyes mirrored her dissolving fences as she opened her heart to him.

"You best not be playing me, Claire," he whispered. "And you better not look at another man like this with your emerald eyes."

"Never, Joseph Walker." Her arms went about his neck.

He angled down to her as he raised her chin. Their lips met on mutual ground for the first time in the years they'd known each other.

After the tender moment, Joe lowered his arms around her waist. "I love you, Claire."

"I think I love you too, Joe." She snuggled against his broad chest and breathed in the scent of the bay she knew he'd always have—grateful the fish odor was almost non-existent.

***

On Sunday afternoon, Claire returned to Mon Louis Island with eight completed booklets. After eating supper with the

Mathieu family, she retreated to her room. There she copied the verses and poems into two more Christmas booklets before turning down her oil lamp. She snuggled into her warm bed, images of Joe playing through her mind like a million stars reflecting on the Gulf of Mexico. He'd sat beside her during mass for the first time that morning and held her hand as they walked home afterward. When they managed a window of privacy on the porch after dinner, he'd kissed her thoroughly.

She woke Monday with the memory of his strong, warm body against her as they'd embraced.

At breakfast, Mrs. Mathieu studied her. "Did something happen when you were home? Your father looked to be slowing down when he brought you back yesterday."

"That he is, but Captain Walker is watching out for him. He has my father running his fishing boat with two helpers so he doesn't have to do much more than steer and tell the others what to do."

Mrs. Mathieu frowned. "I got word last night that Captain Walker collected you from the schoolhouse Friday. I set the rules down when you arrived and you're not to be unchaperoned with a man."

"Yes, ma'am, but it was just the quick walk to the dock. It was damp that day and Pa's knees were—"

"It doesn't matter. While you're staying under my roof you have to abide by my rules. I'll not shelter a young woman who is discussed because she spends time alone with a man."

"Yes, Mrs. Mathieu. I'm sorry. It won't happen again."

Samuel, the oldest Mathieu boy at twelve with a head of curly yellow hair, accompanied Claire to her schoolhouse before he continued on to the school for the more affluent Creoles. A handful of her students were already playing marbles in the yard.

"Mornin', Miss Claire!" Nanette, the youngest student, ran to her side. "I heard you got a beau."

She felt her cheeks heat and looked at the beaming smile amid the brown face. "Word travels this island faster than wildfire."

"What's got Miss Claire as red as her hair?" Raymond lumbered into the yard.

"Our Miss Claire's done got herself a man!" Ines hooted.

Annoyance prickled Claire's insides and she stomped into the building. "Y'all have five minutes before I ring the bell."

Not long after she'd arranged the day's lessons and wrote the date on the board, the students filed in. They spent the morning on Bible verses and geography with the help of the globe Loretta's mother donated when she'd come to spend Thanksgiving with her cousins, the Mathieus.

After dinner the children straggled inside, meager jackets pulled around their necks from the chill wind. They settled in for arithmetic. It was Claire's least favorite subject but she knew the children needed to add and subtract to get by in life, the older ones were also mastering multiplication to be sure they weren't shorted wages when they began work. With her back to the room, she wrote five distinct problems for each of the grade levels to figure on their slates. As soon as she wrote the final equal sign, a wave of giggles erupted.

"Which of you started the whisper chain?" Claire turned and raised her eyes to the back of the room where the oldest sat. Seeing Joe standing inside the door with a crate, she dropped her chalk, causing more snickers.

"Miz Claire is all flustered to see her beau," Dominque joked, causing a ripple of laughter from the students.

"I hope it's a good fluster." Joe smiled. "Don't she look fine when her cheeks match her hair?"

All out hoots and chuckles filled the room as Claire made her way down the aisle to Joe.

"If you make me lose my post, so help me, Joe Walker, I'll—"

"I brought the delivery from Miss Loretta." He lifted the box higher. "And it ain't too light seeing as how it's filled with books."

"Books!" Nanette squeaked. "Miss Claire got us more books!"

Catching their excitement rather than the fear of a lost job, she placed a hand on Joe's back and nudged him up the aisle. "Children, I'd like you all to meet Captain Joe Walker from Dauphin Island."

"Good afternoon, Captain Walker," they chorused.

"I seen him come here on Friday and walk her to the dock," one of the older girls whispered none too softly. "I done told my aunt and she said it's about time Teacher married as she's getting old. Said a girl not married by sixteen is trouble."

Claire ignored the words but felt her face grow hotter.

"Right here please." She pointed to the floor between her desk and the first row of benches where she'd played a game of marbles with the students on her first day to help the littles get over their fear of the "redheaded witch."

Joe placed the crate where indicated, loosened the top with his jackknife, and took a step back.

"Gather 'round, children." Claire settled on the floor and the youngest immediately fell to their knees across from her. "Do you remember Mrs. Eleanor Davis who brought us the globe last month? This special delivery is from her daughter, Loretta. She's engaged to be married to a Buffalo Soldier who fought bravely in Cuba. She'll be moving to California soon and wanted to send some of her books to us rather than leave them behind."

All eyes were on her as she lifted the lid to display the handsome leather copies of adventure novels for the students to hear or read for themselves.

"We have books about pirates, far away jungles, and even one about a doctor who builds a monster of a man."

She pulled out each book and read the title before passing them around. The children petted the books and reverently flipped through the pages. Feeling his eyes on her, Claire looked to Joe once she'd passed along the final book. He sported a huge grin and she returned it with a smile of her own. The children still talked amongst themselves about the books—many poring over the illustrations.

Claire reached her hand out to Joe and he helped her stand. "Thank you. You'll never know how much this means to me—to them."

"I ain't blind, Claire. I can see the excitement in their faces. If you've done nothing else for them, you've given them a love of books. And that's something special."

Her heart raced at the words and she hoped it was true. She took his hand.

"I have to leave now." His fingers caressed hers.

"Children, what do you tell Captain Walker?"

"Thank you!" Unlike the welcome, their distracted shouts came at different moments.

"It was my pleasure."

Joe took Claire's arm and walked with her to the exit. Stepping onto the porch together, she stayed in full view of the door.

"Now do you understand why I was so disappointed to not get them each a book of their own?"

He gathered both her hands into his. "But they'll love your pretty booklets."

She nodded. "I just wish—"

"I'm making your Christmas wish come true, Claire." His crooked smile displayed all the goodness in him. "I stopped at the bookstore this morning. Mr. Lloyd there is expecting a large delivery of *A Christmas Carol* by Charles Dickens this week. I remembered that name from the books you talk about and paid for seventeen copies so he'll hold them for me. I plan to collect them Friday morning and bring them so you can distribute them along with your booklets before you come home for Christmas."

Speechless, her eyes widened as his smile grew impossibly larger. Hands free from his, she embraced Joe with exuberance.

"Kiss her!" one of the boys shouted from across the room.

"Don't you dare, Joe Walker," she whispered with conviction. "I'd lose my post."

He instead turned to the schoolroom to speak to the students. "Don't give Miss Claire too hard of a time. I'll be back Friday and better not hear of any horseplay or teasing."

***

As the week progressed, the weather grew drearier. Cold drizzle and gray skies as far as the day was long. On Friday morning, Claire pulled from her pocket the letter she'd received

from Joe the day before and reread it at her desk in the
schoolhouse while the children worked in their primers.

Dearest Claire,

*I'm sure the weather has you fretful, but don't doubt I'll arrive before
three Friday afternoon with the books. It was a blessing to see you with your
students Monday. I can tell they love and respect you. Be grateful I esteem you
and your job otherwise I would have put on quite a show for your students
when I had you on the porch.*

I love you, my feisty Irish lassie.

The one who steams the foggy bay for ya,

Joe Walker

Midday the sky was grayer than ever and the temperature
several degrees lower than it had been at daybreak. A clammy
nervousness settled over Claire when she looked out the window
at one-thirty and couldn't see across the school yard.

"When's your captain coming, Miss Claire?" Nanette asked
as Claire paced the length of the room.

"I don't know if he'll make it today. In fog like this I might
be sitting at the Mathieus until it clears."

Dominque raised his hand. "What if it don't improve 'til after Christmas?"

Claire clasped her hands together and mustered a smile. "We'll pray that it does."

"You could stay with us, Miss Claire," Ines, Nanette's sister, told her. "We ain't got much, but our mama smiles a heap more than Mrs. Mathieu ever does and I want you to have a happy Christmas."

"She won't be happy unless she's kissing her beau," Raymond joked.

Claire bit back a smile and collected a book from the corner of her desk. "Since our minds are all occupied, why don't we pass the final hour reading the last bit of *Great Expectations?* When we come back after the holiday, we can start one of the new books from Miss Loretta."

A cheer went up as the children shifted forward.

"Another log in the stove please, Raymond," Claire said as the youngest settled on the floor and the oldest moved to the front benches.

As she read the final two chapters, the children inched closer, both for warmth and the excitement of the story. Five pages from the end, the door blew open in a damp gust. Hoping to see Joe or her father there, Claire rose to her knees and frowned at the misty gale outside.

Raymond rushed to close it.

"Thank you, Raymond." She looked around the room and sighed. "Why don't we finish the story and then I'll let you all go home a little early since the weather doesn't seem to be improving."

"But your captain ain't come yet. He's supposed to check on how we did this week," one of the girls whined.

"Yeah," Raymond said as he took the bench beside Dominque. "And what if your pa can't come?"

"We won't leave you alone," Ines stated and they all nodded in agreement.

"Your families will come for you eventually, but maybe that's for the best in this fog." She smiled and settled back. "Let's finish with Mr. Dickens for now."

With the final line of the book read, the students clapped and slowly made their way back to their proper seats. Claire went to the blackboard and faced them as the door flung open once more.

Joe stood in the gloomy rectangle, a crate in his arms. Raymond and Dominque were up in an instant, Raymond taking the crate and Dominque closing the door once the captain was in.

Joe whipped off his knit cap and grinned. "Merry Christmas, one and all!"

"Merry Christmas, Captain Walker!"

Nanette pointed to the box. "Is that for us?"

"That depends." Joe winked. "Did you complete all your work this week without trouble?"

"Yes!"

He looked about the room and with a stern voice asked, "The lot of ya?"

"Yes sir, Captain Walker," was the chorused response.

"Well then, let's see what we can do." Joe motioned Raymond to bring the crate to Claire's desk and followed the boy who was nearly as tall as him to the front of the room.

"I've been praying for your safety," Claire whispered when Joe came to her side.

Taking her hand in his, he squeezed it. "I made it, but barely. It's hell on the bay and the sound will be worse. We might want to wait until morning to head home."

"Is Pa on the—"

"Your ma wouldn't let him leave the past two days. I loaded up the engine and steamed to Mobile between rushing to feed the coal, my horn blaring the whole time. Coasted in the last mile as my fire burned out."

"Joe, you sh—"

He pressed a finger to her lips, looking like it took all his control for it not to have been his mouth upon hers. "I promised to get this to you today, Claire O'Farrell. I'll never let you down when it comes to my word."

Claire didn't care in that moment if she lost her room and board because Joe came for her alone. She knew enough people on the island now to find other accommodations—though not as nice—if needed. Wanting to throw her arms about him, her better sense had her offering a smile instead. "Will you help me distribute them?"

"I'd be honored to."

Claire stacked the booklets from her satchel on the desk beside the crate. Once it was opened, she saw the pile of peppermint sticks on top of the pretty red books and laughed. "You've spoiled us all."

"My girl deserves it."

***

Joe watched Claire hand the final book, booklet, and candy to the biggest boy in the room. Some of the students were openly crying in gratitude and Claire's eyes were shiny.

"Thank you for being such eager students. And thank you, Captain Walker."

They chorused Claire's last words and a lump formed in Joe's throat as his tanned cheeks turned ruddy.

"All of you have a good Christmas," Claire said, "and I'll see you next Wednesday. I just need Raymond and Dominque to stay after a moment, but the rest of you go straight home. Walk in groups as long as you can."

The biggest boys waited near the door as the others left, the rowdy sounds fading into the heavy air.

Claire's eyebrows creased with worry as she turned to Joe. "What are we going to do about getting home?"

"We could wait until morning to see if things are better." He nodded to the stove in the corner. "I could make myself comfortable in here for the night."

"But what if there's no improvement?"

When her chilled hand tucked within his, he knew he'd do whatever she asked. "What would you like me to do, Claire?"

"You got yourself to Mobile and back to here. Allow me to help you return the rest of the way. At home we can be fogged in until after Christmas without worry."

"It's thicker than molasses out there and if something happens, your parents would kill me for being fool enough to travel in it and put you in danger."

Claire took her carpetbag from under her desk and packed her now empty satchel into it before handing it to Joe. "You just tell them your stubborn girl made ya do it."

But we might not make it to tell them, he wanted to say before the surge of following through with her wishes drowned the horrific possibilities. *If Claire wants to get home, I'll get her there!*

"Then let's get going." He helped her into her coat, putting it right over her shawl, and took her elbow.

At the door, Claire looked to her final students. "Thank you for chaperoning. I'll see you next week."

"Do ya need us to walk to the dock?"

"No, Raymond, but thank you. Y'all get on home."

Dominque joined his little sisters waiting on the front stoop and herded them toward the path. Joe paused long enough to don his cap, and then put an arm around Claire as they set out.

On the boat, he tucked her bag under the wheelhouse bench and led her toward the hull. "I need to show ya the engine in case you need to feed the coal. Would ya be willing to do it?"

"I'll do anything to help get us home."

They descended through the open hatch, Joe leading the way.

"Watch your step, Claire. The ladder's slippery."

At the bottom, he turned to wait for her. In the cocoon of the hull lit only by slats holding back the dying engine fire, Joe put his hands on Claire's waist as she took the last few steps. He pulled her to him, nestling into her mist-beaded hair and kissing her neck.

"I want you to know I love you because there won't be time for sweet talk once we're underway. It's gonna take both of our eyes, ears, and smarts to get us safely home."

She nodded and angled for his mouth.

Her lips on his never ceased to thrill him. Once he set his heart solely on Claire, he denied his natural yearnings for what he hoped would culminate in the Sacrament of Matrimony with her. It had been over a year for him, but the touch of a woman wasn't something easy to forget. And Claire in his arms was another temptation altogether. She was finally his and felt more than willing to indulge.

Joe fingered the buttons on her coat before stepping away. "Let me show you how to feed the engine before we get ourselves in a heap of trouble."

She laughed and then concentrated on how he opened the engine door and shoveled coal from the storage box into the fire pit.

"Just make sure it latches before you walk away. We don't want sparks jumping out." He wiped his hands on his pants to remove any coal dust before taking her arm.

Once they were in the wheelhouse, Claire kissed his cheek. "Allow me to sit forecastle. I'll shout to you if I see anything."

"This fog swallows sound quicker than a snake bites. You'd have to use hand signs." Joe taught her a few easy signals to differentiate another ship, rocks, or land as well as noise should she hear another horn or bell. "And if we see Sand Island Lighthouse, we'll know we missed the island."

Fear darkened her green eyes when he meant to be funny.

"I won't get us lost in the Gulf, Claire, but be careful out there." He set his knit cap on her and tugged it low about her ears. Then he pulled one of the cork flotation vests off the hook on the side wall and helped her slip her arms through it. "Stay seated, especially if you see something. I don't want you knocked overboard."

The minutes stretched on in the gray expanse. Joe blasted the horn at regular intervals, eyes sweeping the shrouded horizon beyond Claire's huddled form. When he reckoned they were beyond Cedar Point at the tip on Mon Louis, he steered more east and ran to check the fire. Back in less than a minute, he muttered a prayer under his breath and steered in a true southerly course, dropping their speed.

It was almost four o'clock and no land had been spotted. Fearing the jetties in the sound closer to the island, Joe slowed to a crawl.

A minute later, Claire straightened. Her hand waved denoting a noise and he cut the engine. Then she leaned over the starboard railing.

"Claire, get back! It could be rocks! Claire!"

Whether she heard him or not, he didn't know. She gestured to the water and shouted but only the word "man" reached him before she jumped overboard. Heart plummeting to his stomach, he pulled a hard right rudder on the stalled boat to turn the propeller away from Claire and slow it further.

Snatching the coiled rope from the wall, he ran to the railing. Claire swam in the gray water toward a man clinging to a chunk of wood.

As the boat drifted closer, he saw it was Mr. Williams, one of the local fishermen who led the harsh feeling against the O'Farrell family that summer and the island drunk.

"Claire! Claire don't touch him! He'll pull you under even with the vest! Stop!"

She turned a few feet from the wreckage, bobbing in the choppy water, and looked to Joe.

"Let me throw you the rope and you give it to him, but stay out of his reach!" He shouted.

Nodding, she raised her arm and caught the end of the rope as he anchored himself on deck.

"Stay two feet away, Claire! Toss it to him and tell him to put it around his middle. Then hold the line closer to the boat and I'll pull ya both back!"

Joe held his breath as he watched her fearlessly approach Mr. Williams. The man lunged at her in a fit of panic but she swam toward the boat and he lost his grip on the wood.

"Catch the rope, Mr. Williams! Joe will bring you in," she called.

Not if you drown my girl! Joe's anxiety boiled with fear.

Half a minute later, Mr. Williams had an arm through the loop and Claire held on to it six feet from him. Once she was against the side of the boat, she shifted away from the rope.

"Pull him up first, Joe! I'm fine."

"Like hell you are! Soaking wet in those heavy things!" But he knew better than to try to reason with her and hauled the slug over the railing of his ship.

"Walker," Mr. Williams panted. "I thought I was dead out there. That O'Farrell girl is a bit crazy to try to save me like that."

"Get down to the hull and sit by the fire." He barked the orders as he lowered the rope to Claire.

Expecting to hoist her dead weight onboard, he found Claire practically climbing the rope herself, using her feet on the side of the boat to help.

"Woman, you'll drive me mad by the time I'm twenty-five!" And then he kissed her hard enough to practically bruise her blue lips. "You need out of those clothes."

Stealing a quick look to see that Mr. Williams had gone to the engine room, Joe led her to the wheelhouse as he removed the flotation vest and wool coat. She trembled with cold, unable to help as he tossed the shawl and cap away. He went at the buttons down the front of her gingham dress.

"J-j-joe." Her teeth chattered.

"No time for modesty. You need dry clothes and heat. You got clothes in your bag?"

She gave a jerky nod as he peeled the dress and petticoat from her. Grabbing the first thing he felt inside the bag, he pulled out her flannel nightgown and immediately rubbed her hair with it, then her arms and torso. If he hadn't been frantic to dry her, Joe would have marveled in seeing the thin cotton cling to her skin, the feel of her lean body beneath his hands.

When she was no longer dripping, he retrieved a calico dress from the bag and helped her into it. Then he took his own coat and situated it on her before tugging her into his embrace. He kissed her freckled face all over until her skin heated.

Gazing down at her, he imagined the sight of her jumping overboard. "I want you for my wife, Claire Marie O'Farrell, but don't ever do a fool thing like that again."

"Did you decide that before or after you saw me in my undergarments, Joe Walker?"

"Last winter, though I didn't know when I'd ask you until this Thanksgiving." He held her chin, stare intense. "Well, are ya gonna accept me?"

"Let's get home before I answer. I want to be on island soil when I accept my future husband."

Joe let out a rebel yell and filched another kiss.

"You gotta get us home first, and don't be too full of yourself just yet. I'm not giving up my students during the school year."

"Summer weddings are right nice. And that'll give me time to build a house on the lot I finished clearing this week."

It was her turn to initiate a kiss. She kept it quick. "Get my boots and stockings off. I'll tuck my legs underneath me when I take my post."

He dropped to his knees to do her bidding.

"That's where you should have been when you asked me, Joe, but I'll forgive you if you get me home."

"You're a redheaded cantankerous cuss, Claire, but that's just what I need to keep me in line." He took his captain's hat from a hook on the wall and placed it on her damp hair before buckling on the vest once more.

"I love you. No matter what I say, don't ever change."

He brought Claire to her post. "It looks a mite cleared to the west, like the setting sun is trying to burn through."

"I hope so," Claire responded.

Hurrying to feed the engine and check on Mr. Williams, Joe found both steady enough. He walked the deck once more to see if he could make out any details through the fog in the now twenty-five foot visibility.

After several minutes of steering south, Claire shouted.

Rising faintly beyond her pointing figure, the masts of the docked island fleet rose like welcoming hellos. Coasting in the final stretch, Joe made quick work of mooring his boat. He scooped Claire into his arms and ran ashore. Setting her on the first patch of sand beyond the planks he fell to his knees.

Gazing at her freckled face looking even sweeter with his coat tucked around her, he grinned. "Will you marry me, Claire Marie O'Farrell?"

He would have bottled her smile if he could have. "Yes, Joseph Walker, as long as you remember I'm crazy enough to jump ship for someone no matter if you tell me not to."

"You heard me?"

"I know the difference between a man and a rock, even when the man's as hardheaded as one."

He stood square before her. "I'll never try to stop you from helping someone again, but I'll always be there to pull you back to safety. No matter who you help, it'll be me who's blessed by your presence the most."

~~~
~~~

"The Portrait of Eliza Melling"

A Washington Square Secrets/Malevolent Trilogy/ Possession Chronicles Short

Sean Spunner paused before a gilt mirror in the ornate entry of the rebuilt Battle House Hotel. He adjusted the seam of his old skeleton costume over his left shoulder. Repurposed from the 1904 masquerade, it was Sean's fourth occasion wearing the skin-tight suit. The last time had been over five years previous when he helped kidnap Alexander Melling for a bachelor party. Pleased his regular hours at the gym kept him physically fit at the age of thirty, he gave himself a half-smile as he pulled a black mask over his eyes.

The elaborate ballroom was decked out as a haunted forest for the 1910 Halloween Flirts ball. The familiar feel of the creepy surroundings pricked at his memory. The forest, half composed of canvases depicting pine trees, were painted by his love for the 1905 ball when she crafted all the scenes for the graveyard theme.

Eliza.

Eliza Rose Melling.

The woman of his dreams.

Sean's fiancée, taken from the world five winters ago, was the reason he came to this dance every year since he escorted her. Staring at the towering pines expertly detailed with craggy bark and shimmering needles, he couldn't help but finger one of the canvases that Eliza had touched. *Created!* A bolt of energy flowed up his arm. It reminded him of the excitement he felt whenever he was in her presence. The pleasure they shared with each contact. Eliza had been his match in every way.

Seeking to quiet the ghost in his mind, he looked about the room for a familiar face. The crowd looked younger than ever—mostly those in their teens during their first year out in society. Spotting one of the gym regulars, Sean made his way to Chuck Brady dressed as a jester.

"Brady!" Sean's hand slapped the young man's colorful silk-clad back.

"Spunner." He passed him a flask. "Nice skeleton suit."

Sean took a swig and grinned. None of the people in attendance would know the significance of the Mystics of Dardenne skeleton suit—worn to their masquerade the year they were raided and many of their guests were hauled to the police station for immoral behavior.

"The room is full of fresh faces tonight." Chuck lifted his pointed hat, exposing his wavy black hair to two young ladies passing beside them. The girls—one gypsy and one fairy—leaned together and giggled before continuing on. "Take one of those first-timers out on the dancefloor, Spunner."

Sean laughed and passed the drink back to Chuck. "I know those two from the cathedral and I can honestly say I'm twice their age."

"Don't exaggerate."

"I'm the father's lawyer of that gypsy and remember him talking at the Aethelwulf Club last fall that he was debuting his daughter at fifteen to get her to stop complaining about not being able to attend balls. And the one with her is the little sister of my best friend's wife. I know for a fact she hasn't graduated as I've dined with her at supper parties."

"Then why are you here, old man?" Chuck took a shot from his flask.

"Memories, I suppose." Sean plucked a leaf off a potted ficus and rubbed it between his fingers before going for the refreshment table. He gathered a sampling of shrimp before taking a seat against the wall in defeat.

I shouldn't have come.

He closed his eyes and focused on the music. The string quartet made him envision gliding around a similar dancefloor with Eliza—hands roaming her curves.

I should have stayed home rather than resurrect these memories.

But Sean knew if he was at home, he'd be staring at her painting. It had been almost five years and he still ached for her.

He thought he'd dreamt the tap on his shoulder, but it happened again. "Mr. Spunner? Wake up, please. I'd like a dance with you. It's ladies choice."

"I wasn't asleep." He looked on Sadie Marley with a slight touch of nausea when he opened his eyes.

She giggled and stepped back, her fairy costume shimmery in the dim light. "You were daydreaming at least. Come on."

Sean looked at her outstretched hand and did his best to let her down softly. "Miss Marley, I really wasn't planning on dancing tonight."

"Then why did you come, Sean Spunner?" *The question of the night.* "We've had supper at John's house enough times to be on a first name basis. I'm Sadie, in case you forgot."

"I remember, Sadie. And thank you for the invitation." With a slight smile, he accepted her hand—the gentlemanly thing to do. He never felt like such a fool as he did following the lead of the sixteen-year-old to the dancefloor and was glad none of his old friends were there to witness how far he'd fallen.

When he took her in his arms to waltz, it was as awkward as it was half a lifetime ago when he had to practice dancing with his cousin before her first cotillion. Sean breathed a sigh of relief when the score was over.

"I look forward to telling John that I rescued the oldest man in attendance from being a wallflower. I 'll see you at the next supper party." Sadie giggled before walking away.

He inwardly groaned and headed for the punch bowl. The liquid was blessedly spiked with a liberal amount of whiskey. Sean stood at the table and refilled his glass twice before claiming a chair on the edge of the dancefloor.

The quartet switched out with a ragtime band. Half the young crowd left the space as the others immediately started to cakewalk. Those that watched from the sidelines took interest in one couple in the middle of the floor. People began to crane their necks and lean in to get a better look. Curiosity got the better of him. Sean joined the ring of spectators closing in on the dancers. The guy was a fair-headed chap in a Union Army costume but the young lady, garbed in a simple black witch's dress, captivated him. It was probably the combination of her dark braids and womanly curves, but Sean could only see Eliza. She would have kicked up her heels and shimmied like a woman set loose as well.

He made his way to the edge of the crowd when everyone clapped and stared as the couple passed. A fleeting glance from the young woman showcased her piercing blue eyes. They didn't have the violet tint like Eliza's, but it was enough. He knew if he didn't leave, he'd make a fool of himself before long.

He stumbled out of the Battle House and collapsed in his automobile until he caught his breath. Firing the engine, Sean willed his hands to quit shaking as he removed his mask. John Woodslow, his best friend, had a fine house a few blocks west so he headed there. Shadowed figures were silhouetted against the parlor drapes as the doctor and his wife hosted a Halloween party, which Sean respectfully declined an invitation to. Looking back, he realized he should have accepted. He knew John's wife—ever the thoughtful hostess—would have paired him with a lovely young woman that was probably a better match than her little sister of any of the other girls at the masquerade.

But then Sean would have missed seeing Eliza's trees—and her double in the form of the dancer. Truth be told, Eliza was a double herself. He'd only loved two girls in his lifetime and both were taken from him in most horrific ways. His first love, thirteen years previous, was another dark-haired beauty with blue eyes and womanly curves on her still budding frame. Yellow fever took the first, a horse riding accident the second. Dare he chance a third attempt?

He thought he wanted to.

John might complain about his wife, but Sean knew his friend was happy. He worked long hours at the hospital and enjoyed relaxing at home, whether with his family or hosting friends. The doctor still came to the men's club a few times a month, but he didn't stay too late and never divulged any indiscretions.

John's well-settled in life and love and it's high time I was too!

Sean drove down Government Street and stopped in the middle of the road before the Mellings' mansion. All was quiet, the widows closed—no lights or laughter. Not that there was ever much joy within those walls save for the impish fun of Eliza and her brother, Alexander. Now it was a gilded prison for widowed Ruth Melling, just as Sean's house was to him. And he wanted out.

He doubled back several blocks and parked in the drive of his towering Federal style home he'd purchased to impress the Mellings. Its flat, imposing brick façade did little to welcome him when he returned, but he couldn't give up the place he shared the ultimate closeness with Eliza for the first—and later the last—time.

Sean grabbed a bottle of brandy from the credenza in the parlor and stalked up the stairs to the master suite.

"What good is a master suite when one lives alone?" he asked aloud as he plopped into the armchair beside the fireplace.

He drank straight from the bottle and stared up at the self-portrait Eliza painted for his Christmas gift in '05. Tendrils of her nearly black hair skimmed her ivory back, bared to the viewer as she clutched a purple silk sheet to her glorious chest. Bright eyes and playful smile taunted him over her shoulder from the frame above the mantel.

"I promised I'd never forget you when we were parted." He took another drink. "I've kept my end of the bargain nearly five years. Is it enough?"

Eliza shook her head, causing her hair to ripple across her flawless back. "Never, Sean Spunner. You're my greatest passion and I must remain yours."

Sean's heart lurched as her figure stood, turned toward him fully and stepped out of the painting. With a fluid grace, she floated to the floor like a falling magnolia petal. She kept hold of the sheet, but like her form, it was barely there—a hint of purple clasped to her generous breasts. Her blue-violet eyes were misty with intrigue.

Standing before him, she smiled triumphantly. "You look like Alexander in your bone suit, drinking brandy and lamenting his lost lover."

He pressed against the back of the chair to get as far away from her as possible. "You're not here."

"I am, my darling." She lowered the sheet and cold air tickled his face as she leaned closer. "And in my natural glory."

Sean licked his lips and pointed to the painting, trying to ignore the ethereal form he could see the mantel through. Hiding his fear, he lashed out in anger. "Go back! I can't speak to you and you most certainly should not be speaking to me."

"My likeness is still there." Eliza motioned to the framed painting. "I stand before you in my current form. Am I as beautiful as you remember?"

Goose flesh pricked his arms beneath the costume. He wanted nothing more than to touch her—to feel her giving flesh beneath his palms—but the terror of what he might *not* feel overcame his impulse to caress.

"You're everything I remember, Kitten."

When she moved to climb into his lap, Sean jumped to his feet. He skirted around—through—the phantom and shivered as he glanced back from the door. The apparition drew closer.

"Stop!" His knuckles strained around the bottle.

Miraculously, Eliza obeyed, though she always preferred to give orders rather than take them.

"If you insist on haunting me, please get some clothes on. It's cruel for you to flaunt what I can no longer have."

Eliza laughed and shimmied in a provocative sway. That dangerous smile—the one his Mystics of Dardenne brothers all warned him about—flashed across her pretty face as she tugged the purple sheet around her. "Have you had anyone since me, Sean?"

He took a swig from the bottle and stalked to the hallway.

"Have you?"

He turned. The opaque figure now wore the royal blue Regency gown Eliza dazzled in at the Halloween Flirts ball they attended together. Her hand trailed her décolletage as she eyed his tight suit with an appreciative leer.

"You haven't!" She shrieked with cruel laughter.

Sean hurled the brandy bottle and it smashed on the wall behind her.

"I loved you with my whole heart, Eliza Rose Melling. Our six months together was the best in my life. Please don't spoil those memories by your actions tonight."

Sean stopped at the credenza downstairs and poured himself a glass of Irish whiskey, hoping it would somehow negate the anxiety over his dead fiancée following him around his house.

"That's what you need," Eliza said with a soft voice. "Go back to your roots rather than my brother's antics."

He took a shot and readied another. "I'm beginning to think Alex had the right idea all along."

"Staying drunk to numb the pain?"

He spoke forcibly around his trepidation. "Trying to replace the loss with other intimacies."

"You wouldn't dare, Sean Spunner! You loved me too much." Eliza's eyes were wide with fright, kissable lips downturned, and body—though not solid—held stiff with indignation. "It took you over seven years to open your heart after your first love died. I demand that long, at the very least."

"What I felt for that girl—"

"Winifred." Eliza sneered. "I know all about her now. There are some benefits in death. We had a nice heart-to-heart about you. Well, after she nearly clawed my eyes out for what I— never mind. She was a little hellion, I bet."

"She was a young woman grieving her family when I knew her."

Eliza's hand shifted over her bosom once more. "I bet you were more than ready to hold her close in her despair. And it appears your preferred type was patterned after dear little Winnie. For fifteen, she sure had some big ones. Not to mention her sky blue eyes and dark hair. I feel positively used after meeting her. I'm not one to settle for being a stand-in."

Sean set his glass on the table and choked on bitterness. "You pretentious Melling! But for all your bluster, you're jealous of a girl who's been dead more than twice as long as yourself."

Not knowing how else to get away from her, Sean went for the stairs.

Right on his heels like a January wind, she followed. "But you were so sweet with her. She told me you kissed her on the lips on her deathbed. Kissing a girl with yellow fever is mighty heroic, Romeo. Weren't you afraid to die?"

Gripping the banister, he turned and unleashed his fury. "I was ready to die after watching the life leave her beautiful face! Weeks before she grew ill, I knew I was going to wait for her and told her cousin as much. Winnie was the sweetest, bravest girl I've ever met. Wild, yes, but that made her all the more wonderful. She'd climb a tree on a whim without thinking twice, hanging upside-down though her knickers and ripped stockings were showing and her aunt would holler at her for it."

Eliza *tsked* and twirled a lock of hair around a finger. "Must you always fall for the naughty ones?"

Sean's knuckles went white around the handrail. For a moment, Eliza flickered solid and he almost sprung at her—to slap or kiss, he didn't know which.

"You were the naughtiest, Eliza."

"I should hope so." She gifted the notorious Melling smile of venom and charm before flying past him into the master suite.

"Get out of my room!"

Still grinning, she pointed to her painting. "Obviously you want me in here."

He slammed the door and knelt at the hearth in hopes a fire would chase the chill—and the ghost—from his bed chamber.

Eliza drifted about his room as he stoked the flames. "If you have a chill, you know I can warm you."

"You can do nothing for me in your current state."

"Oh, I bet I could." She perched on the side of his bed and motioned to the sketches she'd given him during their courtship—framed in a neat grouping at eye-level on the side wall. "How often do you sit here to look upon me while you work yourself into a frenzy to find release?"

Ignoring her, Sean locked himself in the bathroom and started a shower. He lathered and scrubbed in an attempt to wash the thoughts away and bring a bit of sobriety to his night. If he'd drunk too much, perhaps Eliza would leave as his mind cleared.

He opened the shower curtain and grabbed for a towel.

"You're still a fine specimen, Sean Spunner, though I thought it was a cold shower you're supposed to take to cool impulses." Her voice came through the steam trapped in the space.

Tucking the towel about his middle, Sean glared into the fog until he caught the outline of Eliza—now draped in a white nightgown. "Have you no shame?"

"None." She smiled and maneuvered closer. "But don't ask questions you know the answers to."

He shook the water from his brown hair and went for the door. Eliza raised both hands in front of Sean's chest. Trailing her hands over his abdomen, she followed each muscle. His bones ached and his teeth chattered.

"I'd draw you if I could, Sean." She looked ready to devour him. "I might have to settle on tracing every line on your body with my tongue."

"You'd kill me." He shoved through the mist. After a vigorous rub down with the towel, he pulled on his robe and stepped into his slippers.

"You've trembled before me and said those words before, but it was no hardship as I recall. You wanted me to put you out of your misery. Don't you remember the night you brought me here after the Halloween dance?"

"Every day, and that's my problem." He dropped into the armchair and tossed another log into the fire.

"We warmed each other well." She sighed as though lost in memory. "These pictures are quite a scandalous collection. No wonder you haven't taken another lover. You couldn't bring a woman here with my nude sketches on display, not to mention the painting."

Sean stalked across the room, pulled the largest drawing from the wall, and returned to the fireplace. Pausing a moment to look upon the framed image—presented when he stayed overnight at Seacliff Cottage the first time—he remembered opening the envelope that held the sketch of his fantasy woman. He had even shown it to Deacon De Fiore who was a regular guest of the Mellings when they were across the bay. Now his dream girl was a nightmare he needed to exorcise.

With deliberate swiftness, he raised the frame and smashed it upon the mantel's edge.

"Sean!" Eliza screeched.

He tore the paper from the broken glass and threw it into the fire.

"You can't destroy me!"

"I've carried your memory long enough, Eliza Rose."

"No!" Her nearness sent ice down his neck. "You still need me."

"You're attitude tonight is making it easier to leave you behind."

"You used to love my sharp tongue. Besides, what will the maid say about this mess?"

"My housekeeper has complained about these for years. I'm sure she'll be more than happy to clean the glass off the floor to be rid of the 'unholy pictures'." He turned back to the corner to retrieve another one.

"Are you trying out for sainthood?" She kept her voice firm, but she winced when he broke the frame.

"I'm no saint, Eliza, but I do try to behave these days."

She laughed. "Once a Dardenne, always a Dardenne, as the guys used to say."

He shook his head as he watched the corners of the paper curl and burn until the image of Eliza's bare chest was no more. "That's true for some, but not all. I've matured since you last saw me. I no longer seek flings."

"Because once you have a Melling, you can never go back."

"You're as arrogant as your parents." He fed another sketch into the fire.

"Father approved of you. He wanted me to have a love-blinded dupe for a husband so you wouldn't inflict me with whorehouse diseases. But I think if he saw how you've behaved all these years, he'd lose what respect he had for you in standing up to Mother like you always did in my behalf." She looked at his gaping robe and smiled. "You're as handsome and fit as ever, but much too soft for George Melling to respect."

"I was never soft for you, Eliza."

She laughed and danced around him. "I had you just where I wanted, but you didn't have quite enough backbone to go completely against my parents."

"Because I didn't want to elope to the Smoky Mountains?" He tossed the last sketch into the flames.

"And don't forget refusing to join Melling and Associates because you didn't want my father's wrath upon your uncle's firm."

"We got through all that and enjoyed the holidays and New Year's Eve. We were going to spend a long weekend at Seacliff Cottage before—"

"That weekend at Seacliff was never on my schedule. I had my alternative plan set in motion."

Hairs rising on his arms, Sean stared at the devil masquerading as his lost love. "Another—what do you mean?"

Eliza shrugged. "You wouldn't get me away from my parents so I found someone who jumped at the chance."

Feeling his heart about to break as it had when he heard the news of her accident, Sean gripped the bedpost. "Who?"

"He loved me, you know. How could he not with my play of seduction and all the time we spent together across the bay." Her poisonous smile was back. "Mother adored him, much more than you. I bet she would have eventually accepted us, though with you she would have always kept a wall up because you crossed her one too many times. After my accident, she refused to hear your name spoke in her presence—did you know?"

Staring at her deadly eyes, he made no sound.

"You might have watched your first love die, but my lover watched me fall and carried my broken body home."

"Damn you to Hell, Eliza Rose! I was true to you even before we courted, but you … you were just what the guys said you were! You had me fooled but God saved me—and the deacon—when he took you from this life."

He found not an ounce of beauty when he looked upon her features. As though she felt the shift in him, Eliza switched clothing from the nightgown back into the Regency apparel. Sean shook his head and went for the mantel.

Eliza screamed.

He reached for the painting. "Will it destroy you if it burns?"

"No, but you'll regret it in the morning." Her voice was soft, coaxing. "You burned the sketches. Wait until you wake and decide if you can do without the painting as well."

Sean grunted, not wanting to agree that he already felt the loss of his collection.

Her arms wrapped about his waist but her coldness didn't penetrate the robe. "I did love you, Sean. Part of me still does."

"You were all I wanted," he whispered.

"We had fun together, but I had to get away from my parents. Blame my hatred for them rather than any lack of feeling for you."

Sean shook his head and stepped away. "You ended up just like your father—using people to your benefit without thought of how they're left when you walk away."

Eliza laughed—bold and loud—and glowed a rosy pink on her see-through cheeks. "I suppose I did. The Melling taint. I put poor Alex to shame, don't I? He never could measure up to Father's standards. I'm glad he finally put Father in his proper place, even if I wasn't there to witness it."

"He was a great friend."

"Was?"

"He … when your father … the fire at Seacliff after the hurricane."

"Alexander Randolph Melling!" she shouted with glee. "You did what I couldn't do—you escaped our hell with your life!"

"He's not—"

"My brother never crossed over."

"But he was said to have perished in the fire."

"He's another manipulative Melling, my darling. Don't underestimate us." She did a kissing motion at Sean's face and motioned over the mantel. "Will you keep me around another night? It is Halloween, after all. Five years ago was exquisite."

Sean bit back a chuckle. "Will you go and never return?"

She nodded.

"Promise me. And turnabout so I can make sure you aren't crossing your fingers."

"You know all my games now, Sean. I promise not to haunt you." Eliza slowly turned, her splendid gown fading to nothing so she was left naked when she faced him once more. She winked. "But you still haunt my memories, Sean Spunner. You were the best—every time. Think of me—for another year or two at least. I couldn't stand to be second fiddle to a fifteen-year-old the rest of your life."

"I won't be in a rush to replace you—of that you may be sure."

Eliza rose off the floor. "And dear little Winifred. Whoever you find needs to be better than both of us together. You deserve an exceptional woman."

"Go, Eliza."

"And don't overlook her naughty side. You must have a touch of the debauched to satisfy your inner Mystics of Dardenne." She blew a kiss. "I love you, Sean. Remember me on your lonely nights."

He looked his fill at the heavenly figure before she stepped back into the painting. "And I love you, Kitten."

Fingering the canvas at the lowest glossy curl on her back, he smiled. "You were a minx to the end, but that was one of the reasons I loved you."

Sean stumbled to bed, dropping his robe and slippers on the floor before passing out. He stirred to life shortly after eight in the morning. His gaze immediately fell on the blank space on the wall by the bed.

Eliza—gone.

He sat up and looked to the hearth. Eliza's painting hung slightly crooked and a scattering of broken glass and frames were all over the floor.

But she was here.

Robe and slippers tugged into place, Sean crossed to the scene of destruction.

"It's a new day, Eliza Rose Melling," he said to her cheeky likeness before lifting the frame off the wall. "And a new season for me. Our time was wonderful, but I must say goodbye."

He opened his closet and shoved the portrait into the farthest corner.

"Rest in peace, wherever you reside."

~~~
~~~

"Grace Shadowed"

A Malevolent Trilogy /Washington Square Secrets/Possession Chronicles Short

John Woodslow walked into the back parlor of the Aethelwulf Club, eyes on the graying man amid the dark paneled walls.

Dr. Stephen Moore stood and extended his hand, his bulk towering over the younger man. "Dr. Woodslow, it's a pleasure to meet with you."

"Thank you for arranging the time, Dr. Moore." John firmly shook the offered hand. As soon as they were settled in matching leather wing chairs, a butler poured them each a snifter of brandy. Dr. Moore offered a cigar. John accepted, pleased the older doctor didn't hold back his hospitality before the subject at hand was broached. "Thank you."

When the room cleared of all but a gentleman reading The Daily Register under the corner lamp—newspaper concealing his face—Dr. Moore smiled.

"Well, John, I'm sure you've guessed why I wanted to meet with you. I know word is out that I'm seeking a partner in my practice."

"Yes, Dr. Moore. And I'm honored you thought of me."

"You come highly recommended, having graduated top of your class and doing well in your early years at the hospital, but I have reservations. That's why I wished to meet in an informal setting with you first. I don't want you to get your hopes up too high, young man."

At twenty-six, John was hardly inexperienced, though he knew a doctor over forty would see him as green. "I'm happy to put any of your concerns to rest, Dr. Moore."

"I'm pleased to hear your willingness, but I'm afraid the matters at hand could sully your reputation in the medical field if they prove to be true."

John felt the color drain from his face and glanced nervously at the hidden man in the corner. "I can't think what you might have heard that would sour you toward me."

"Mystics of Dardenne membership for one." Dr. Moore's grin shone more amused than disappointed.

The butler came into the doorway. "Telephone call for you, Dr. Moore."

"I know you understand what life as a doctor is like, but you must excuse me, John. I'll return as soon as possible." Dr. Moore stood and took his hand with the Dardenne handshake.

John stared after the doctor as he left.

Across the room, the newspaper lowered to reveal a smirking Rupert Lyons. "Gave you the old handshake, did he?"

"How did you know?"

Rupert laughed. "You look as though you've seen a ghost and my stint as secretary of the society afforded me the opportunity to peruse the books. I'm happy to report Dr. Moore's years as a member gave a grand showing, even given our record as most debauched. He was head Dardenne in eighty-one when—"

The butler returned to top off the brandy glasses on the side table between the doctors' chairs. Rupert raised his own tumbler and the man saw to it before leaving.

"Then why is he no longer a member if he never married?" John asked.

"Not many Dardennes hold membership for longer than half a dozen years. Those who don't marry tend to step down or are run out well before they turn thirty. We'll get our letters of resignation after this carnival season, with or without a bride to walk down the aisle."

John sucked on the cigar and blew smoke rings as he took a mental tally of the eligible debutantes in the city. Grace Anne Marley always seemed brighter than her peers. Unfortunately, he'd heard too much about her loose ways from other Dardennes to take her seriously.

"Now that my purchase of the Mellings' law firm has been finalized, I'll be staking my claim by New Year's Eve," Rupert warned. "The hurricane in September seems to have all the men in the city on the move. Better choose fast if you want prime pickings. Study the ladies at the Stuarts' Christmas party tomorrow and call dibs before Sean or one of the others step up."

Rupert raised the newspaper as Dr. Moore returned.

"Sorry to keep you waiting, John." He took his former seat and swallowed a shot. "Now, as I was saying, you're at the age of settling down if you wish to remain respectable in society. In order to keep the esteem of my patients, I can only bring in a partner who's in good standing socially. If you'd like to entertain an offer, I insist you revoke your membership and find a respectable wife. There seems to be too many scandals hanging over the Dardennes and debutantes these days, but maybe that's more to do with that gossip magazine than an influx in wanton behavior. That Kate Stuart…" The doctor took another swig. "Whoever chains himself to that firecracker will be in for a treat."

***

"Grace Anne!"

Sadie's shrill voice carried up the stairs to where Grace Anne sat as she fixed her hair at the dressing table. She turned as her sister careened to a stop in the bedroom.

"Grace Anne, you have to help me! It's a matter of life and death!" Anything and everything was a dramatic episode to the twelve-year-old.

She put a hand on Sadie's quaking shoulder. "It can't be all bad."

"But it is! Come to the back porch and see for yourself. Alice and I had to rescue it from her brothers."

Grace Anne groaned. If the Beauchamp boys were involved, there was no telling what mess her sister had gotten herself into. "Judith is picking me up in thirty minutes and I still need to powder my nose."

"You know I wouldn't bother you on a party night if it wasn't important. And we need to move fast before Cook or Nanny notices and tells Mama and Papa when they get home."

She sighed, but followed her sister's blonde pigtails down the front staircase. At times like these, Grace Anne resented being the oldest and having a nine year gap between her and Sadie. Esther, the sister between them, took ill in the yellow fever epidemic nearly a decade prior and didn't survive. Sadie was too young to remember but their parents took years to recover from the loss. Five-year-old Marie wasn't born until 1901, four years after Esther passed away. The three remaining sisters were too spread age wise to be bosom friends and Grace Anne felt more like an aunt than a sister to them.

They exited the house through the dining room and met Alice Beauchamp on the patio. The solemn-faced girl held a rope attached to a mangy brown dog that was knee-high to her. Its matted fur had an odor of the sewer from ten feet away.

"Alice's brothers were tormenting him."

"Of course they were! That beast isn't fit for human companionship." Grace Anne thought of her beloved dog, Flora, who disappeared after she was sent out of town when Esther took ill. She returned to a home devoid of her dear sister and collie.

"It's not his fault he's dirty!" Sadie said with indignation. "Those boys were pulling him through the alleys like he was a tin can on a string. We had to save him, but Alice can't keep him with her brothers around. If you could hide him in your roo—"

"Absolutely not!" Grace Anne crossed her arms over her blue gown. "I don't have time for a filthy mutt, especially with Carnival season upon us."

"But if we get him clean, we could give him to Marie for Christmas. Mama wouldn't say no to a present, especially one so cute."

"He's hideous!"

"He's not so bad. And once he's washed and brushed he'll be even sweeter. We've never asked for a dog before, so Mama never told us no. It'll be the first—"

Grace Anne's chin went up. "I had a gorgeous dog with silky fur. She was the smartest thing this side of Government Street. Esther and I played with her every afternoon and she slept at the foot of my bed each night. There can never be another dog like Flora in this house."

"Please, Grace Anne," Alice said with pleading brown eyes. "I can't hide him from Nanny in my room and if we let him go Richard will kill him."

"That brother of yours is a hooligan, but not a murderer, Alice." Both girls continued to stare at Grace Anne—the dog joining in with sad eyes. "I won't let you bring him inside in his current state."

"We'll wash him out here and brush him real good. We'll work fast before Nanny brings Marie down for supper. I only need to keep him in your room until Mama comes home and it's too late for her to say no. Please, Grace!"

"If he soils *anything* in my room—"

"He'll be good as gold," Sadie promised with a smile. "Come on, boy."

The two girls led the dog toward the garden spigot, the poor thing limping behind them.

"That dog's lame," Grace Anne called after them.

"He's just tired is all," Alice said. "My brothers wore him out."

The mantel clock chimed through the open door and Grace Anne hurried back to her room to finish preparations for the Stuarts' Christmas party. She wanted to be sure to look appealing enough to catch the eye of one of the handsome bachelors—preferably Dr. Woodslow.

***

John trudged up the front walk of the Victorian monstrosity on Government Street and handed his hat and coat to the help as soon as he was in the door. After the obligatory greeting to Mr. and Mrs. Stuart, he journeyed through the evergreen swags for the sitting room where the younger crowd gathered and forced a smile for the host's daughter.

"It's always good to have a doctor in the house," Kate Stuart simpered as she took in the fit of his black tuxedo. "You are looking especially well tonight, Dr. Woodslow."

"Thank you, Miss Stuart." Unable to find something to compliment her on—other than her well-endowed chest beneath the tight gown—he stopped his greeting at that.

When he tried to continue into the room, she put a hand on his arm. "We seem to have more ladies than gentlemen in attendance tonight. Would you be a dear and spend a little extra time dancing so none of our guests go without?"

"Of course, Miss Stuart."

"It would, after all, be beneficial to you as well. I know Dr. Moore is set on partnering with a family man."

The hurricane might have put an end to *Snitch*, but magazine or not, Kate was still on top of the gossip game. John nodded to her, hoping she'd release him from her clutches soon. "We're all approaching the settling years."

"Just don't settle for anything short of the best, Dr. Woodslow." She angled toward his ear. "I assure you there are plenty of virginal ladies within these walls tonight. There's no need to be a Davenport with your choice."

"Well said, Miss Stuart." John smirked at the thought of Alexander Melling's ex-fiancée now joined with the most respectable man of their age group in the city. As he helped himself to a glass of eggnog, John wondered if it were possible to find a debutante whom a Mystics of Dardenne member hadn't deflowered. He didn't want to sink himself so low as to court a first year deb, but which lady in the room hadn't felt the groping hands of a Dardenne at a masquerade or entertained more? Probably only Kate Stuart herself as no man would dare attempt anything on that predator.

Thomas and Sean waved him over to the corner. Sipping his drink, he ignored their attempts at conversation as his eyes roamed the sea of colorful gowns across the room. Grace Anne Marley's hour-glass figure filled her royal blue dress perfectly, her golden hair framing her heart-shaped face like a halo. Her nose was a little too sharp, but those lips made up for it. If it weren't for the fact that Sean and several others had boasted about kissing her, he would have declared himself to her when they danced at The Point Clear Hotel the weekend before the hurricane.

Rupert joined them.

"Did you do it?" Sean asked.

"I have her father's permission." Rupert grinned.

Sean slugged Rupert and laughed. "I don't envy you that prize, Lyons."

"What?" John looked between the two.

"Did you not hear anything we were talking about?" Sean gave him a scowl before continuing. "Rupert asked Mr. Stuart's permission to court Kate."

John choked on the eggnog, sputtering until Thomas slapped him on the back—which, thanks to Thomas's boxing hobby, nearly sent him face-first onto the Oriental rug.

Rupert leaned closer once the coughing subsided. "She may be a frigid bitch, but I know where to get what I want. Even though Consuela left town this autumn, there are plenty more to choose from. And what better way is there to avoid being gossiped about than by marrying the source of the chatter? Kate is all about saving face. She'd never speak ill of me to anyone."

Though impressed with Rupert's business plan for marriage, John couldn't get over the idea of marrying a woman he had no desire for. Life was too short for that. He wanted respectability *and* love. He'd be too busy with work to see to a woman at home and then seek release elsewhere. It was already rare he entered the red light district outside of carnival season. His lack of time and energy was to blame because—unlike his lawyer friends—his job was physically demanding and took more hours from his day.

A few minutes later, a string quartet began playing across the hall. Rupert offered his arm to Kate and they led a procession to the ballroom. As couples paired off, John ditched his tumbler on the credenza and approached Grace Anne.

He bowed before her. "Would you do me the honor of this dance, Miss Marley?"

With a beguiling smile, she dipped into a curtsy that showcased her décolletage. "It would be my pleasure, Dr. Woodslow."

Keeping his hands in respectable locations as they waltzed, John couldn't help but stare at Grace Anne's perfectly bowed pink lips. At least they weren't red from use like they often were at gatherings. Maybe tonight he'd be the one to bring color to those succulent petals.

"Have you had a pleasant December thus far, Miss Marley?"

"Yes, though my hands are full at the moment. My parents are in Birmingham for a week and my younger sisters always manage to court trouble, especially the middle one as she's old enough to go about without Nanny."

John smiled down at her, happy to hear she wasn't overly strained with the care of rambunctious children—for he wanted a few of his own one day. "Nothing too troubling, I hope."

"She brought a mangy dog home," Grace Anne blurted, showcasing her manners weren't as refined as some of the other ladies.

John laughed and enjoyed the way her eyebrows pinched together as she flashed a quick frown.

"It's not only that," she continued. "Sadie expects me to keep the dog hidden in my room until Christmas. She wants to give it to Marie, our youngest sisters, so our parents can't turn it out."

"Would they turn out a helpless puppy?"

"It's not a puppy, Dr. Woodslow. It's a dog. A filthy little beast it looked too." Grace Anne's cheeks turned rosy.

"Do you not like dogs?"

"I have nothing against them. I had my own as a girl." Grace Anne shuddered and a shadow crossed her face.

John instinctively held her closer. "What is it, Miss Marley?"

Her eyes widened and she appeared to blink back tears. "Nothing, Dr. Woodslow. But that creature was not fit for proper living in the state it was in."

The song came to an end and he took her by the elbow, not wanting to let her go. "May I escort you to the refreshment table?"

"No, thank you. You've been most kind."

He reluctantly watched her leave. Heading for a tray of wine being brought around the ballroom, John found himself reaching for a glass at the same time as Dr. Moore.

"While it's good to see you dancing with an eligible young lady, please keep in mind that one's father has had his fortune less than a decade and she was unfortunately linked with Lucille Easton as recently as two years ago."

John felt his cheeks go red and smoothed a hand over his slicked back hair in desperate need of a trim. "Miss Marley was on a European tour with her family when the scandal happened. I hardly see how that impugns her character."

"Those young ladies were dearest friends, were they not?"

"I cannot say." John kept his gaze on the doctor's. "I haven't a younger sister or connection to either of them other than through Edmund Easton, who was just as shocked as the rest of us over the fall of his sister."

The knowing look in the older doctor's eyes was one of amusement as he patted John's back. "Choose wisely, Dr. Woodslow."

***

Grace Anne stood with a chattering Judith McGowan—her companion for the night—but all she could think about was the feeling of being in John's arms. It had been three months since she'd spoken to him. The previous time was a September night across the bay during the celebration for Alexander Melling and his Yankee fiancée, Beatrice Kirkpatrick. The New Yorker was elegant, but no match for how he and Lucy must have looked together. Having missed her best friend's first relationship and its aftermath, Grace Anne resented her European travels. If she had been home, she could have kept Lucy from losing her head over a smooth talker like Alexander. But she was pleased to know her dearest friend was now settled with a gentleman. Frederick Davenport had always been kind to Grace Anne when she was playing at the Eastons'—even before her father's lumber business took off during the Spanish-American War.

Kate joined the group emanating a surprising glow.

Hoping to keep Kate focused on her own affairs rather than sniffing out news about Grace Anne's dance partner, she focused the conversation on her. "Do you find Mr. Lyons to be a good dancer, Kate?"

"Of course he is." She checked the time on the pocket watch on her necklace, as though down-playing the excitement in her voice.

"He's nowhere near as fine as Alexander Melling was," Judith said. "He was a scoundrel, but the best dancer in town, though Frederick Davenport is light on his feet as well. Is he here tonight?"

Kate snorted back a laugh. "My parents wouldn't invite that trollop he married into our home. Becoming Mrs. Davenport doesn't make a lady out of a fallen woman. Poor F.L.D. will turn into a hermit from lack of invitations this Mardi Gras season."

"Still," Judith said, "Mr. Lyons isn't as good a dancer as Mr. Davenport."

"He's a thousand times more functional on the dance floor—and other places I bet—than the ancient man you keep making eyes at. And he asked me to call him Rupert." Kate turned away from Judith with a sneer.

"Mr. Smith is a seasoned businessman," Judith retorted. "What's a twenty-year difference anyway? If he doesn't last long, at least his money will. Rupert Lyons is nothing but an upstart lawyer with well-connected relatives."

Kate turned back, her watch lifting from her chest with the quick motion. "Haven't you heard, Judith? Rupert bought the newly renamed *Lyons*, Melling, and Associates. He now owns one of the longest established law firms in the city."

Judith's torso hardly moved within her tightly strung corset, but Grace Anne could tell she huffed for breath. "But he's still a crooked nose cad like the rest of his friends."

Rolling her eyes, Kate went for the hall.

"Have you danced with Rupert Lyons?" Judith asked Grace Anne.

"Unfortunately."

"See! He's nothing to get worked up over, especially compared to a man like Frederick Davenport. Kate can say what she wants about Lucille Easton, but that girl has to have something we don't to land a man like that with her reputation."

Grace Anne held her tongue, refusing to speak of her former best friend though she knew Frederick had loved Lucy since childhood. He was the type of man to remain loyal, no matter what.

"But that Dr. Woodslow," Judith continued. "He's nearly as fine to look at and seems smitten with you tonight, Grace Anne."

"Do you think so?" She cursed the eager tone in her voice when Judith responded with a toothy smile. "I mean, he is handsome, but I—"

"He's coming this way."

Grace Anne felt the blood leave her face and forgot how to breathe as John came to a stop beside her.

"Are you all right, Miss Marley?"

Managing to nod, she gazed up at John, focusing on his strong jaw as she wondered what it would feel like to kiss him.

"She does look pale, doesn't she?" Judith took a step away. "Why don't you take her to get some air, Dr. Woodslow? The veranda can be reached through the dining room."

Judith winked at Grace Anne as John led her toward the hall. The brisk night air kept the party indoors, but Grace Anne was no stranger to dark locations. She'd often gone off with dance partners to show them the kissing skills she'd perfected from her time toying with chauffeurs and the brothers of her friends.

John stopped beside a trailing bougainvillea, the white railing and columns behind him a striking contrast to his black tuxedo and the dark vine. His touch lowered from her elbow, caressing her white gloves until he held her hand. "Are you well, Miss Marley?"

If it wasn't so chilly, she would have melted at the sound of the concern in his voice. "I'm only worried about that stupid dog and what mess might await me at home."

His grin was charming even in the dim space. "I'm afraid I can't help you much with that."

Still holding her hand, she half wished he'd steal a kiss like his friends always did—but the other half was glad he didn't if it meant he respected her. Or maybe he had no interest, though Judith was seldom wrong when it came to what men wanted. Testing her sway over him, Grace Anne tilted her head and pursed her lips ever so slightly.

John squeezed her hand. "Has anyone told you that you're a beguiling figure, Miss Marley?"

"No, Dr. Woodslow," she whispered.

"But surely they must have, with all the men—"

Grace Anne yanked her hand free and stepped back. "Just what do you mean by that?"

"I didn't—"

"Surely you don't think me dim-witted enough to believe there's no accusation when a man referrers to *all the men* in regards to a lady? Just what do you think all these men are doing?"

"Kissing you, Miss Marley," he said with shame. "What man could resist your perfect lips?"

"Surely you can, Dr. Woodslow. We've been acquainted several years now and you've yet to do more than dance a few times with me. Are you morally stronger than the other suitors you accuse me of being fresh with or am I beneath your appeal?" Her hands were on her hips now.

Cheeks ruddy, John met her glare with a soft gaze. "Neither of those things. Please forgive my poor word choices."

She shook her head, not wishing to think about John knowing all of her exploits—however innocent they seemed at the time. "Please excuse me, Dr. Woodslow."

***

The next morning, John stood between Rupert and Sean on the cathedral portico. The three bowed to the widow in black when Mrs. Melling walked by, but soon returned to their whispered conversation.

"And you didn't even kiss her?" Sean looked incredulous.

John shook his head.

"There's definitely something wrong with your approach if you didn't get any action from Grace Anne," Rupert smirked. "The only deb more willing than her is Judith, though she's mellowed a bit now that she's working the older crowd. Mark my words—Judith will be on the arm of a rich widower before Fat Tuesday."

Sean laughed. "And she'll be back on the market within a decade. As long as she keeps those measurements, she'll have no problem scoring another pay day."

"Excuse me, gentlemen." Rupert straightened his tie and descended the steps, offering his arm to Kate when she entered the churchyard with her family.

John cleared his throat and looked at his friend. "How far have you gone with Miss Marley?"

"It's been two years, but it's not something to forget." Sean laughed and slapped John on the back. "Relax, Woodslow. She's not like my Eliza. She's more than willing to kiss, but she's no pushover. I know for a fact she's slapped Thomas and a few others who went for a feel though they'll deny it and claim they won the prize."

He smiled as the woman herself entered the gate. The three Marley sisters with their varying shades of blonde hair were a bright spot amid the Sunday crowd. Grace Anne held the hand of the youngest tucked into her own and the middle sister—the one causing her trouble—followed behind them. On the portico, they paused as Grace Anne removed their mantillas from her reticule. Watching the motherly sight of her pinning the head coverings on the girls spurred John to action.

Reaching the door nearest them, John held it open for Grace Anne with a bow. "Good morning, Miss Marley."

"Good morning, Dr. Woodslow." She gave a shallow nod and went through the door without a smile, though the middle sister turned to stare at him.

Sean came to his side. "What *did* happen between the two of you last night?"

"I fear I made a muddle of things when I alluded to all the men she might—"

Sean laughed. "I knew you weren't as smooth as Easton, but of all the things to say to a woman, that's the worst!"

"Think she'll ever forgive me?"

With a hand clapped on his shoulder, Sean led him into the cathedral. "What girl could resist a Dardenne? Give her time."

But did he have time with Dr. Moore seeking to fill the role of a partner? And would Grace Anne be acceptable in the older doctor's eyes?

****

After Sunday supper, Grace Anne came to terms with what she hoped to avoid. Staring at the chocolate brown dog that followed her around whenever she was in her room, she could no longer pretend its limp wasn't increasing. A whine even accompanied it every few steps. Seeking to provide a bit of relief for the creature, she sat at her desk. The dog immediately settled at Grace Anne's feet. Reluctantly, she reached down and rubbed behind its ears. Her hand then trailed down to the dog's back, fingers threading through the long fur that was softer than she expected.

After hearing Nanny bring Marie down the hall from the bathroom to the nursery, Grace Anne slipped out of her room to the telephone in her father's study on the main floor. She waited while the operator looked up the number and connected her to the other extension.

"Dr. Woodslow's residence," the voice of a housekeeper or cook came across the line.

"Is the doctor available?" Grace Anne asked.

"Yes, ma'am. May I ask who's calling?"

"Grace Anne Marley."

She twisted a finger around the cord of the earpiece as she waited.

"Miss Marley?"

"I'm sorry to bother you, Dr. Woodslow, but there's a medical issue in my house. I was wondering if you would be able to examine the patient."

"I'd be delighted to, Miss Marley. Is half an hour soon enough?"

"That would be perfect. Thank you. I'll leave the front door unlocked. You may let yourself in so my sisters aren't unnecessarily disturbed. I'll wait for you in the parlor, just to the left upon entering."

"I'll be there as quick as possible, Miss Marley."

Grace Anne said goodnight to Marie and made sure Sadie was settled in her room with a book before collecting the dog. She bundled it in a blanket to carry the poor thing downstairs so no fur would mar the front of her red Sunday dress. After putting the blanket in the corner, she sat in one of the armchairs. Grace Anne was pleased her coldness to the doctor at the cathedral that morning didn't affect his willingness to help.

Five minutes later, John silently stepped into the parlor carrying a black bag.

"The door, please, Dr. Woodslow." When he closed it, she stood. "Thank you for coming so promptly."

He grinned and smoothed a hand over his dark-blond hair that showcased a schedule too busy to visit the barber as often as his friends. "I'm happy to be of service, Miss Marley. I do hope you'll forgive my fumbling words."

Her cheeks heated at him bringing up the unladylike behaviors he alluded to the night before. "Let us speak no more of it, Dr. Woodslow. Are you ready to see the patient?"

"Of course. Which sister is ill? They both looked to be in the peak of health at Mass this morning." He turned for the door. "Or is it one of the help?"

Grace Anne crossed the room to him, the dog jumping from its blanket to follow. "Here, Dr. Woodslow. See how he limps?"

John watched the dog for a few seconds before staring at Grace Anne in disbelief.

"Sadie thought he was simply tired from being strung about by the Beauchamp boys, but it's only gotten worse." She pointed to the floor. "The dog, Dr. Woodslow, or have I grown a second nose that I'm not aware of?"

"I am no veterinarian, Miss Marley. I have been schooled and trained to work exclusively with humans, not animals." His handsome face set in a grimace of indignation.

"Then I suppose I should have called Dr. Hughes. I remember he always gave Flora a checkup when he came to examine me or Esther."

John's face softened before a chuckle escaped. "I'll have to remember that if I move from the hospital to doing regular house calls. Kindness to an animal would be the best way to the heart of an uncooperative child."

It was Grace Anne's turn to take a defiant stance. "First a wanton and now an uncooperative child. Never in all my life have I been subject to such uncouth accusations!"

"You misunderstand me once again." He set his bag on the nearest chair and moved toward her.

She crossed her arms and sidestepped. "Don't try to take it back. I know perfectly well when I'm being insulted."

"I'd never wish to insult or harm you, Miss Marley." His hand settled on her shoulder. "I'm forever saying the wrong things because you make me feel like a school boy before your beauty. My brain runs through a heap of jealous thoughts and my heart beats quicker than my mouth can run. Forgive me for falling under your spell."

A smile of relief found her lips. "You don't think ill of me?"

"Never, Miss Marley."

With a flood of relief, Grace Anne's arms were about his neck, hands playing in the hair that grew over his stiff collar as she angled for his mouth. Pleased John could be bold, she reveled in his taste as his arms encircled her waist. She pressed against him and enjoyed the surge of delight their bodies together brought her.

As though taking her motion as an invitation for more, John's hands roamed her back until they settled on her hips with a kneading motion that made Grace Anne's body tingle with passion. The kisses turned ardent and he worked his lips to the red ruffle at her throat.

She gasped. "Dr. Woods—"

"Call me John, Gracie." He kissed his way back to her lips, planting one there before pulling back enough to look her in the eyes as he ran a thumb across her cheek.

***

Maybe he did wrong by calling her by a pet name before Grace Anne even asked for him to call her by her given one, but it fell from his lips as natural as azaleas blooming in March.

"John," her red lips curved prettily as she whispered, "I don't know what you've heard, but please know I've never allowed a man to hold me like this."

He shushed her with a finger on her mouth—which urged him to lean in for another taste of her sweetness. "As long as I'm the only one you give your kisses to from now on."

Her hug was tight and the feeling of her bosom pressed against him was nearly too much. "I've had my eyes on you a long time, John Woodslow. Every time I practiced kissing, I imagined it was you. I hope I didn't disappoint."

"Let's not start in on that again." He laughed and stroked her arm in an attempt to erase all the stories he'd heard about her. "But you're wonderful, Gracie. And I've been watching you as well."

At their feet, the dog shifted and whined.

"Oh, the poor dear!" Grace Anne bent to retrieve the dog.

"It appears you've taken a liking to him since you cared enough to phone a doctor. Or was that a ruse to get me here for a kiss?" He winked as she blushed.

"He's really much better looking since Sadie and Alice cleaned him up. I believe he has a bit of terrier in him. Of course he doesn't compare to my old girl. Flora was twice this size and her coat was long and silky."

"Set him down a moment so I can see how he stands." John stood back and noticed the way the dog favored its front right paw. He motioned to the blanket. "Is it all right to use it to examine him on?"

Grace Anne quickly spread it over the settee and knelt on the floor beside the dog she'd placed on the blanket.

John got his bag and joined Grace Anne, retrieving the necessary supplies from the case before angling the side table lamp to shine on his four legged patient. Slipping the metal band for his head mirror over his hair, he adjusted the disc so he could see perfectly through the center hole with his left eye. He chanced a look at Grace Anne—the brightness of the reflected light making her creamy complexion glow. He wished the dog wasn't in pain, for he wanted nothing more than to hold her once more, but he silently blessed the mutt for bringing them together.

"Hold him steady, Gracie."

She leaned over the dog with one arm, its affected paw tight in her other grip. John angled closer and the gleam of the mirror immediately caught something in its light. Carefully spreading the fur between the pads of the paw, he licked his lips and held his breath before gingerly touching the object. The dog whined and tried to wince, but Grace Anne held him firm.

"What is it?" she whispered.

"Looks like a piece of glass." He took the scissors in hand. "Let me trim some of these hairs and get a better look."

Trimming done, John turned to Grace Anne. "Would you like to see it through my head mirror?"

"No." She shuddered and buried her face in the dog's coat. "Please hurry and get it out."

"I assume you had no romantic notions of nursing if you can't even bear a bit of glass in a dog."

"No, never. I tend to faint at the sight of blood."

"And yet you've set your sights on a doctor," John teased.

"I might change my mind," she said as she took a coquettish glance at him.

He filched a kiss from her before she could protest. "Don't you dare, Gracie. You're even more amusing than I imagined."

"I shall add amusing to the ever growing list of insults you're unintentionally labeling me with."

"Will I forever be sticking my foot in my mouth around you?"

"I hope so, for it would mean I'll see you again."

John returned her smile before focusing on the task of removing the inch long piece of glass with a steady hand.

"I need alcohol," he said upon removal as he held a clean cloth to the paw. "I've got him."

Grace Anne hurried across the room to a decanter set and returned with two glasses. "Do you always celebrate after a successful operation?"

John laughed so hard he dropped his hold on the cloth. Grace Anne set the drinks on the coffee table and paled at the sight of the bloody linen. Turning to her, John took the nearest tumbler and brought it to her lips. "Drink it quick, my dear. It'll set you to rights."

She downed the whiskey and coughed. John continued to chuckle as he held her upright with a loving arm.

"How old are you, Gracie?"

"Twenty-one last September." Her cheeks were now rosy with health.

"Forgive me for adding another vulgarity to my ever growing list, but how did you manage to make it to twenty-one when you're delightfully naïve about so many things?"

Rather than watch the spark of anger in her eyes, John turned his attention back to the dog. After pouring the contents of his glass over the wound and applying pressure for another minute, he wrapped the paw with fresh bandages from his bag.

"There." He sat back on his heels. "I can honestly say that's the finest paw I've ever tended. Now, do you think I could get a drink I'll be able to enjoy this time?"

***

After his Monday morning rounds in the hospital, a visitor waited for John in the doctor's lounge.

Dr. Moore snuffed his cigarette in the nearest ashtray. "Did I not make myself clear, Dr. Woodslow?"

"Sir?" John closed the door behind him and prayed no one would enter until the conversation was over.

"About that Marley girl not being the right sort of doctor's wife for my partner. I was leaving a house call at the Powells' across the street after ten o'clock last night and saw her accompany you out onto her porch. I know her parents are out of town and—"

Indignation over the reproachful tone regarding the woman he loved surged through John. "I may be on staff at the hospital, Dr. Moore, but I have been known to take house calls when the need arises. I'll have you know Miss Grace Anne Marley assisted me in a medical procedure for someone in her household. She bravely sat with the patient to offer comfort while I removed a glass splinter from a limb. Then she helped with the sanitation of the wound afterward. If that doesn't sound like a doctor's wife, I don't know what actions would."

"Well…" Dr. Moore puffed his cheeks with a flustered exhalation. "There's still the issue of her friendship with Lucille Easton."

"Perhaps you don't know because you weren't the physician who attended the families, but Miss Marley lost a sister during the yellow fever epidemic of ninety-seven along with the Eastons' three children, all close in age to Lucille. The two bonded in their grief, Dr. Moore, because they both had heartaches not many other children could relate to." John was pleased to have learned that information himself the previous night during a quiet chat over coffee while the dog convalesced on the sofa. "They shared books and daydreams like well-bred girls do in their tender years. They never went about wantonly on the town or any such nonsense you seem determined to believe of Miss Marley because of her childhood friendship with another girl in mourning."

Dr. Moore smoothed his suit jacket as he stood. "It seems you've taken this all to heart, Dr. Woodslow. I'm happy to see you're thinking things through, but do remember the citizens of Mobile don't always know the intricacies of a person's personal life. They only know what they've seen and heard. When they choose a doctor they want respectability."

"As you've said yourself," John said with a smile, "I'm doing well at the hospital. Patients who find themselves within these walls are often too far gone to care what the gossip was about a physician or his wife from years back. They only care that the hands are capable. And the board of directors will see the statistics of those cared for and medical achievements when selecting a head surgeon."

The older doctor laughed. "You're intelligent to the end, Dr. Woodslow. I wish you the best."

"Thank you, Dr. Moore." He offered his hand.

"And she's a vivacious young lady. Just the type to satisfy a Mystics of Dardenne member."

"Was there no one sprightly enough in your day, Dr. Moore?"

"Only one," Dr. Moore said with a smile. "Another Dardenne may have taken Ruth down the aisle, but I got to her first."

***

Grace Anne entered the parlor Monday night, her shadow directly behind the train of her tea gown. While she carried the dog up and down the stairs when it needed to go out, Shadow made fine progress for short trips around her room that day. Settled into the corner of the settee, the shaggy dog curled on the rug beside her.

John let himself in a few minutes later. His grin lit the room and Grace Anne found herself rising to meet him. The dog came directly behind her and John dropped to a knee to look him over.

"If I'm going to come in second to patients, Dr. Woodslow, I'll have to rethink allowing you to court me."

"Well Miss Marley," he said with his drawling charm as he looked up at her, "I'd say seeing our patient is doing well is a cause for celebration. We make a good team, you and I. Another dose of alcohol is just what the doctor orders if all is well, but first I need to inspect the wound."

She motioned to the folded towel on the settee with an air of superiority.

Standing, he took her by the waist and kissed her hard. "And today someone had the nerve to tell me you wouldn't make a proper doctor's wife."

"Yet another insult!" She tried to squirm away, but he held fast.

His warm lips were at her neck, breath in her ear before he whispered. "You may be certain, Gracie dear, that I praised your bravery and comforting abilities when you worked diligently beside me. I hope you'll do as well tonight and we're able to enjoy another conversation afterward."

Feeling completely adored within his arms, Grace Anne pressed her mouth to his and threaded her fingers through his unruly hair.

"Is my sister paying for house calls with affections?" Sadie asked from the doorway.

Grace Anne turned to the door. "Of all the—"

"Come now, Miss Sadie. You know better," John said as he approached the girl in her nightdress. "Your sister and I have a connection deeper than the dog. I respect her too much to accept payment for tending to someone within these walls—human or otherwise."

"Grace Anne said Shadow's better. Is he truly?"

"Shadow is it?" He smiled and looked from Grace Anne to the dog at her feet. "So they've both taken a liking to each other enough to earn a fitting name. The only way to know for sure is to check the wound. Miss Sadie, would you care to be my assistant when I remove the bandage?"

"Yes, please!" Sadie took the doctor's hand.

"But only if you promise to go straight back to bed as soon as Shadow's tended," Grace Anne added.

"Yes, yes. Anything!"

John motioned them toward the settee and set about arranging his supplies. He pulled a bottle of clear alcohol from his bag. "So I'm not accused of using up your daddy's good whiskey on a dog."

Grace Anne placed Shadow in her lap and allowed Sadie to hold the affected paw over the towel so her sister had full view of the happenings instead of her.

"No sign of infection and the swelling is significantly less than it was yesterday," John declared. "It appears your big sister is a better nurse than she expected."

Sadie giggled and then John poured the alcohol over the wound. The dog whined but held still until the paw was wrapped once more. Then Shadow licked John's face before jumping down and lying at Grace Anne's feet.

"Go on to bed now, Sadie," Grace Anne said gently.

The girl stopped beside John as he repacked his medical bag. "Will you have to see Shadow again? Our parents come home tomorrow and he's supposed to be a secret."

"I most certainly will make inquiries over my patient. I've grown rather fond of Shadow and wish to speak to your father about bringing him to my house in the future."

"But I wanted to give him to Marie for Christmas!"

"That dog has chosen your big sister, Sadie. Don't give Shadow to anyone else because I aim to take care of them both."

Sadie caught on with a blush and giggled. "Yes, Dr. Woodslow. Goodnight, and thank you for helping Shadow."

Once they were alone, Grace Anne extended her hand to him. "Do you really mean it, John?"

He pressed his lips to each knuckle. "With all my heart, Miss Marley. I'll declare my intentions to your father tomorrow evening and ask permission to escort you to Christmas Mass and Order of Mayhem's New Year's Eve ball so all of Mobile will know the best kisser in the city is off the market."

"Will you ever learn to pay me a compliment without shaming?"

"I'll keep trying, Gracie, if you can keep on forgiving me."

"I'll do my best, but you better pray Shadow's sore foot is the only wound you'll need to heal between us." She tugged him to the settee beside her. Their kiss broke when Shadow jumped into Grace Anne's lap. She rubbed the dog's ears and looked to John with a playful smile. "You may keep company with some scoundrel friends, but Shadow will protect me. He'll not stand by and allow my heart to be broken."

His arms were about her waist, a smolder in his eyes that promised a lifetime of passion. "You could do no better in life than with a faithful dog and loving husband. And you'll always possess my heart with your enticing ways. Though please remember, I am good with stitching if the need arises."

~~~
~~~

"Safe Embrace"

A *Fortitude*/Possession Chronicles Short

Claire Walker snuggled closer to her husband, eager to share his warmth in the predawn hours. Glad to have a few days of freedom with the entire family—Joe had the Sabbath off the day before and no scheduled runs from Dauphin Island until after Ash Wednesday—Claire relished the extra time in his arms.

Joe rubbed a hand across the back of her flannel nightgown. "Ain't it a shame my body won't let me sleep after sunrise when I don't have to take a boat out?"

"You and me both." Claire rested her cheek on his shoulder.

He smoothed the loose tendrils of hair off her face. "I can think of another way to spend the time."

"Save me from your unruly plans, Joseph Walker." She playfully nudged him.

Joe caught her wrist. "Don't feign shock, you redheaded cantankerous cuss. We've got four young 'uns that prove you're none too pious with your husband—not to mention all the other times in between."

Claire muffled her laugh against his chest. "It's good just lying together in the quiet."

"But it can be even nicer when we're working toward a common goal." He opened a few buttons on his long johns.

Soft footsteps padded overhead as they kissed. Joe groaned his annoyance as a solid *thunk* announced their youngest had jumped off the ladder from the loft he shared with his big brother.

Claire, once again tucked within Joe's arm, saw the outline of their nearly three-year-old son stop in the bedroom doorway.

"Whatcha need, Abraham Jeffrey?" Joe's voice was gruffer than necessary.

"Ain't ya getting up for work, Pa? Emmett told me to leave off when I woke him."

"Get yourself here." Joe opened his free arm and Abraham bound across the dark room, jumping on the bed beside his father. "You've got the soul of a captain if I ever saw it in one so young. You want a boat in my fleet one day?"

"Yes, Pa." He settled in the crook of his father's arm. "I'd be a heap better than Emmett. He sleeps too much."

"You won't be a lazy captain?" Joe teased.

"No, sir. Kade and I get up early so we're ready for captaining and fun."

Claire laughed at his earnestness but knew it was true. As soon as Abraham and his bosom friend Kade Campbell had learned to walk, they ran the island like a pair of wild boars. Had Abraham been her first child, she didn't think she'd have been willing to birth another for fear of being worn to nothing by the time she turned twenty.

"You'll be on the boats quicker than you realize, Abe, but not today," Joe said. "Tuck in for a few with me and your ma."

Abraham squeezed himself between his parents like a wriggling worm but soon dozed off.

"He's the best there is at preventing things, ain't he?" Joe whispered. "He always did love snuggling. I think you spoiled him too much with it as a baby."

Claire smoothed their son's straight red hair—the same as her own. "Can you blame me? It's the only time I had more than a minute of peace once he was mobile."

"The poor thing will be hanging on women once he's of age, seeking arms that'll make him feel as secure as yours." Joe tweaked her nose. "You've done set him up for failure, Claire Walker. There ain't another girl with arms as strong and loving as yours."

"I've been praying for Abe since the day he was born. I know God's preparing someone for him."

***

They managed another hour of rest before the lightening sky was too bright for Abraham to ignore. Joe caught him in a bear hug when he went to spring out of bed.

"Get your boots and coat, then go out to Ma's chickens and gather the eggs."

"Yes, Pa."

"And no jumping 'round once you've got 'em. We want all the eggs for a nice breakfast."

"Yessir!"

"Close our bedroom door on your way."

Abraham was gone quicker than a summer storm arriving, the door slamming behind him.

Joe laughed and knelt over his wife. "Now where were we before that hellion joined us?"

Their next kisses were overrun by the sounds of the girls tromping to the outhouse upon waking.

Joe collapsed upon Claire in defeat. "Why'd we have so many?"

"Because the Lord knew we needed three extra sets of eyes looking after Abe."

Joe rolled to his side and tugged her closer. "And I just wanted to give you a good lovin' on Valentine's Day since I ain't got flowers for ya."

Claire ran her hands over his shoulders. He was still in his prime at thirty-three, and she knew they'd be partners for decades to come. Joe wasn't the type of man she read about in romance novels, and she'd learned not to expect extravagance, but he was thoughtful and kind in all the right ways.

"Extra time with you is the best gift, Joe. But we can try for some of that other tonight."

"That's my feisty island girl." He kissed her. "You rest a bit longer while I get these mites in line for the day."

Though she would have preferred to rise, Claire decided to follow Joe's request when she saw the determined set to his jaw as he dressed. He paired an azure shirt with his brown trousers and buttoned on leather suspenders. The room was light enough to see the shine in his eyes made bluer by the shirt when he leaned over her the next time.

"Rest as long as you like." He left her with another deep kiss before the rumble of his commanding voice to the children filled the house.

Mary Louella, who had nearly three years on Abraham, came in a minute later with a fresh pitcher of water for the washbasin. "Mornin', Ma."

"Good morning, Mary." Claire smiled over the resemblance Mary and her oldest brother shared with their father, from coloring to blue eyes. "Sounds like Pa's working you all good out there."

"Clara Jane's got the biscuits in the oven and is cooking the eggs. Emmett's setting the table. Pa wants you to have a day off."

"You're all excellent helpers."

The six of them ate breakfast at the table Joe built the year they were married. When the morning cannon sounded from Fort Gaines, Abraham shot to his feet and saluted in memory of the soldiers who died protecting the island during the Civil War. They continued the meal, but from then on Abraham had a mischievous glint in his hazel eyes.

As the children cleared their dishes, Maggie Campbell came to the screened door on the back porch.

"Come in, Maggie!" Joe called. "Ain't it a bit nippy to bring Tabitha out this early?"

Maggie stepped in, a protective arm about the four-month-old she had swaddled to her chest in a tartan wrap. "She stays warm enough against me. I'm sorry to bother you so early."

"We slept in today." Claire joined her friend near the stove, noting the anxiety in her brown eyes. "What's going on?"

"Douglas got word from an early boat that Uncle Simon's headstone is ready. He's determined to collect it today since everything in Mobile will be shut down the next two days for Mardi Gras and Ash Wednesday. I don't want him going alone, but he doesn't want the children on the bay in this weather."

Though only a year younger than Claire, Maggie had a later start in life. Claire had been married over a decade, but the Campbells had only celebrated three anniversaries thus far.

"I don't blame him with your littles," Joe said as he stood from the head of the table. "How 'bout I go along and bring the oldest three with me? You're welcome to stay here while we're gone."

"Yes, please do. I'd enjoy the visit," Claire said. "We don't often get idle days."

Maggie agreed and returned home to give word to her husband. Joe and ten-year-old Emmett secured their boots and outerwear while Clara Jane packed a picnic lunch with the help of her mother.

When the Campbells arrived, Abraham immediately took Kade's hand and the boys ran out the door.

"Get your boots on!" Joe hollered after him. "Ma don't stand for you outdoors without 'em this time of year!"

As Abraham dashed back inside, Douglas Campbell—one of the captains from Joe's fleet—came in with a smile amid his red beard.

"Thanks for helping Maggie," he told Claire in a whisper. "She's been melancholy since Uncle Simon passed and worries too much about me."

"Those with tender hearts are apt to do that, Douglas."

"Aye, and Maggie's heart is the most generous of all." He turned from Claire and took his wife's hand. "You enjoy your day. We'll be home well before supper."

Douglas kissed Maggie goodbye. When he went for the door, Joe came to Claire's side.

"Now I gotta put on a good show so you don't feel neglected." Joe's merry eyes drank her in before he had her in his arms. "And I was lookin' forward to being with you all day."

"We've got tomorrow, Joe, but hurry back."

***

From the rocking chairs on the front porch, Claire and Maggie oversaw Abraham and Kade digging trenches around a stick fort in the yard. The two boys bent close as they worked their hand shovels through the damp earth. Kade had his great uncle Simon's old pipe in his mouth and Abraham swatted it.

"My troops blow up the fort!" Kade bopped his friend on the head with the pipe.

"I rally the forces!" Abraham countered with a shove.

Rocking a bundled Tabitha, Claire cuddled her friend's baby and enjoyed the fresh scent of infancy after handling the dirt and muck associated with an active boy the past few years.

"Miss Claire!" A shout came from the road.

She passed the baby to Maggie and stood as Darla Beauchamp raced into the yard. The only daughter of the island midwife was level-headed at seventeen, so it alarmed Claire to see her distraught.

Meeting her in the middle of the yard, she took the girl's hand. "What is it, Darla?"

"My family's gone to Grand Bay for the day, but Mrs. Collier sent word her grandpa's in poor shape. I'm supposed to stay at home to keep an ear out for Miss Megan next door as she's due any time, and I don't know the first thing about nursing old men."

Claire patted her hand and smiled. "It isn't so different from caring for a baby, but I'd be happy to check on him."

Darla's face relaxed and she exhaled. "Thank you, Miss Claire. I best get back home."

"I'll watch Abe so you don't need to bring him," Maggie said when Claire climbed the porch steps. "I'll bring him home with us if you don't mind."

"That would be great, Maggie."

Since marrying Joe, Claire had often assisted Virginia Beauchamp with births and newborn care. In addition, her time as a volunteer nurse during the Spanish-America War made her seem as a medical expert to their neighbors. Besides helping when she could, Claire also secured free transportation to Mobile on one of her husband's boats when the situation was beyond home remedies.

Claire collected her bag of rudimentary medical supplies and a green knit cap for Abraham. "You keep this on when you're playing outside, Abe. I'll see you at Miss Maggie's as soon as I'm done helping the Colliers. You be good and listen to her, all right?"

"Yes, Ma."

Kade tossed a rock at the pile of sticks, and both boys laughed at the destruction.

Claire kissed Abraham's face, the dirt streaks hiding his freckles, and she waved goodbye to Maggie.

She was able to provide relief to Mr. Collier by helping loosen the congestion in his chest and propping the bed at an angle better suited for his breathing difficulties. Claire watched his situation for over an hour after he settled. Satisfied there was nothing else she could do for the elderly man, Claire dropped her bag at home and walked to the Campbells.

Maggie stepped onto the porch, wiping a hand on her apron. Tabitha was swaddled her to chest once more, nursing from the comfort of the cocoon. "That didn't take too long."

"No, but there isn't much to do besides make him comfortable at this point. Did Abe give you any trouble?"

"No worse than normal." Maggie laughed then gazed about the yard. "I told them to stay put when I went inside to take the bread out of the oven. They must have run to the back."

The women walked around the little house. Claire saw the empty yard and her heart sank.

Maggie shifted Tabitha off her breast and closed her shirt. "I wasn't inside more than three minutes."

Bleats carried through the palmettos and scrub that shielded the Campbells' lot from the next. Claire turned for the narrow footpath. "Maybe they ran over to see the goats, but my parents are in the city for the day."

Crossing the yard she'd grown up in, Claire scanned the chicken coop and roaming goats on her way to the backdoor her father always left unlocked. "Abe!" she called as she walked through the house. "Abraham Jeffery Walker!"

All the rooms were empty, save a lounging cat in the front room window.

"They're not in the yard," Maggie said when they met back on the kitchen porch. "I'm sorry, Claire. I should have made them come inside with me."

"It's not your fault. Nothing can stop those two once they get an idea. You go toward town and I'll head to the shore. Let anyone you pass know the boys have gone missing."

Claire passed no one as she took the trails through the pines. At Alligator Lake she remembered a night a dozen years earlier when her younger brother went missing. Claire had found him up a tree beside the pond with a lost goat, but she shivered at remembering Kevin's fear of alligators eating him and his beloved pet. Fortunately it was too early in the season for the massive reptiles to be about since the weather hadn't sufficiently warmed.

"Abraham! Kade!" she hollered as she made her way east along the Gulf of Mexico.

One of the men who worked as a deckhand for Joe ran out from the forest. "Miss Maggie told us what happened. We've got men going in every direction, Miss Claire. We'll be sure to find your boys. I'm headed west."

"Thank you, Michael." Claire quickened her pace when he turned the other direction.

She walked close to the tree line and called out the boys' names several times a minute. Trying not to visualize her youngest in mortal danger, Claire kept her mind on her footing in the pale shifting sands.

The image of the boys building and then destroying their stick fort kept coming to her. Abraham and Kade loved to play soldiers. Many Sunday afternoons, Joe and Douglas took them to Fort Gaines at the eastern tip of the island and allowed them to run the tunnels and battlements. One time, the Colonel in charge of firing the cannon twice a day let the boys assist in the evening shot.

Claire broke into a run.

Soon the brick fort came into view. The drawbridge was down. Like a beacon of doom, Abraham's green cap lay on the weathered planks stretching across the trench. Claire snatched it to her heart and paused in the mouth of the entry.

"Abraham! Kade!"

The courtyard was empty of life. Running for the nearest tunnel entrance, Claire's booted feet struck the stone floor with an ominous sound. The dank air penetrated her wool coat as she ran the length of the hall, glancing in the open rooms as she passed them. Pausing at the juncture where the next side of the pentagon-shaped fort began, she shouted their names again.

"Ma!" A far-off cry echoed.

Claire ran to keep the terror from freezing her. The cries came louder as she reached the ammunition magazine corridor.

"Ma! Help!"

Breathless, she rushed through the arched doorway. Her eyes settled first on the sight of Kade Campbell sitting astride a field artillery cannon. His teeth clenched the pipe between his smiling lips. Beyond him, Abraham was pinned to the brick wall by the cannon's muzzle. Tears smudged his dirty face.

"Ma, please help."

"How in God's green earth did you—"

"We're blowing up the enemy!" Kade bounced on his perch, causing the cannon to shift a fraction closer to the wall on the uneven ground.

Abraham yelped.

Claire snatched Kade from the weapon and set him back a few feet. "Kade Gabriel Campbell, you better stand there until I tell you to move."

Taking hold of the carriage shaft with both hands, she heaved the wooden beam backward. The ancient wheels creaked and splintered in protest beneath the shifting weight.

Abraham took a heaving breath with the extra room. "Mama!"

"Hang on a second more, Abe." Claire readjusted her hold, ignoring the way the wood ate at the skin of her palms as she tugged against the slight incline on the floor she worked against. The next heave took all her strength. When Abraham was able to slip out from his pinned position, Claire collapsed.

Abraham ran to her. "Sorry, Ma! Don't feel bad. I sorry!"

Once her body steadied from the exertion and fright, she opened her arms and cuddled her son in her lap. "I'm not hurt, Abe. Just tuckered out from worry and having to move this iron beast."

She kissed his freckled cheek that mirrored her own, not minding the dust from his adventure.

"Love you, Ma. Thanks for saving me."

"I love you too, Abraham Jeffrey, but please follow directions next time and never run off." Claire straightened and took his hand, holding her other toward Kade. He shyly approached and she squeezed his hand as she smiled to show she wasn't mad. "Come on, Kade. You both should know you aren't big enough yet to leave home without someone."

"You here now, Miss Claire." Kade tugged on her arm. "We go see lookout posts!"

"Your mother is worried sick, Kade. We're going home."

Before they reached town, a search party found them. Claire sent the men ahead to find Maggie with word for her to meet them at her house.

***

More than an hour later, the boys were fed, washed, and tucked in for a nap on the loft bed Abraham typically shared with Emmett.

Claire stirred her coffee and looked across the kitchen table at Maggie. "So much for a relaxing day."

Maggie kissed Tabitha's brunette hair as she rested in her arms. "I hope this one's less trouble than Kade. I don't know how you juggle four."

"Lord knows the only way I'm dealing is because Abe's at the tail end. But maybe it's better you got your spitfire first while you're still young enough to handle him."

Her smooth complexion filled with smile lines as she laughed. "I might have aged a decade when they were missing."

Minutes later, Joe, Douglas, and the three oldest Walker children arrived. Clara Jane immediately wanted to hold baby Tabitha, and Joe pulled Claire into a hug.

"What's this I heard on the docks about the boys running off? I'll tan Abe's backside if needs be."

"He's had enough of a fright for one day."

Joe's blue eyes narrowed, but there was a flicker of amusement in the corner of his mouth. "You done spoiled him, ain't ya? Loved on him so good he'll expect a big production every time he's a hellion."

Claire frowned before replying. "So long as he doesn't go about stealing kisses from girls before they can freely give them, he'll turn out just fine."

"I married a cantankerous cuss." Joe's crooked grin lowered to her lips for a firm kiss. "And it's the smartest thing I ever did."

Laughing, Claire turned to the Campbells. Douglas held his wife in an amorous embrace. On the table were a bundle of hothouse roses and a jar of face cream.

"Those gifts are why Douglas was in an all-fired hurry to collect the headstone." Joe's bristly chin tickled her ear. "He wanted to buy something special for Maggie on St. Valentine's Day without her expecting it. You sorry you didn't catch a romantic fool who brings flowers and fancy concoctions?"

Claire's hands trailed Joe's solid middle and over his shoulders until she linked her hands behind his neck. "I don't need special gifts when you love me like you do every day."

"That's right fine to know before I give you this." Joe pulled out a book he'd had tucked in the back of his waistband. "Mr. Lloyd told me this was the newest sensation among the ladies in town."

Claire ran her hands over the green hardcover—*Where Birds Sing* by Olive Kent. "You know I love her books. They're half what Loretta and I write about in our letters. Thank you!"

"I can't let the Scotsman show me up on a day like today." He tucked a strand of her hair behind her ear. "I love ya something fierce, Claire."

Their kissing rivaled the Campbells' affections and cleared Emmett, Clara Jane, and Mary from the room.

"When you come up for air, I need to thank your wife for finding my boy," Douglas said.

Joe nearly crushed Claire before letting go. "She's feisty as is, but if I give her a new book, she can't keep her hands off me."

"Hush your mouth, Joseph Walker." Claire nudged him away. "You know I don't need a book for an excuse to love on you."

He grinned. "Nearly eleven years of marriage and you ain't run off yet. Either you're too lazy, or I'm doing something right."

"If I only knew back then wh—"

He cutoff her words with a pinch on her backside that made her jump.

"So help me, Joe, I'll get you for that!"

"If you ever need me to show him the higher road, let me know," Douglas told Claire.

Joe straightened his suspenders with a proud air. "Don't go on trying to beat your boss now, Campbell."

Maggie stepped forward and lightly punched Joe in the stomach. "I'd do it myself if you ever mistreat Claire."

Joe's cocky grin doubled. "It seems we've got ourselves a couple of feisty women."

"Aye," Douglas replied. "They're the best type to have."

In the doorway, Abraham's carrot top peeked around from the front room.

"And the feisty ones give birth to even more spirited souls." Joe rushed to the door and grabbed Abraham, lifting him until he was eye level. "Why'd you give your ma and Miss Maggie trouble today, Abe?"

"We had to fight the enemy!"

"And did you get 'em?"

"Yessir! We got 'em good, but I got squished."

Joe laughed but then forced himself to sound gruff. "If I ever hear 'bout you leaving without permission again, I'll put my belt on you, ya hear?"

"Yes, Pa. I'm sorry."

He hugged the boy to his chest and reached an arm out for Claire. "You're both cut from the same cloth, but this boy's got it double with my bits inside him too."

She nestled into her husband's embrace, pleased that her family was reunited with no catastrophes to mar the day of love.

~~~
~~~

"Revelry's Requiem"

A Chateau Rouge/Possession Chronicles Short

Co-written with Jolie St. Amant

New Orleans

1911

Carnival season was in full swing in the lounge area of the Chateau Rouge. Every night was a party at the hotel, but the revelry of Mardi Gras added a whole new level of lewd debauchery. Women danced with wild abandon wearing dresses that exposed creamy shoulders and raised the hems of their gowns to show way more skin than was socially acceptable as they kicked up their heels. In the center of the melee was Ivy, shimmying to the rhythm and smiling at her new lover, Valentino. Shivering when he raised one dark eyebrow and smiled, it was a silent promise of tantalizing things to come later in the evening.

As the most talked about bordello in the French Quarter, Chateau Rouge had the best girls. Members were among society's elite—the movers and shakers of New Orleans. Many deals had been made in the hotel's card room, with a pretty girl on either side of each gentleman.

Every evening started with the women coming down the hotel's staircase, decked out in the latest fashion. The men watched as they glided into the lounge, hoping to get some time with one of their favorite "girls". Ivy had been preferred by many until she had met the handsome musician, Valentino De Fiore. She had taken one look at him and had decided instantly that he would be hers. His passion matched her own, their affair had been a whirlwind.

When the song ended, Valentino set his violin down and rushed to join Ivy on the dance floor. He enveloped her in an embrace that left her breathless, his lips devouring hers as his hands slid over her small waist.

"Drinks?" Ivy asked when they finally came up for air.

"Yes, *amore mio.*"

"I will be right back," she ran a finger across his collarbone within his unbuttoned shirt and smiled when he trembled.

While she left to retrieve the refreshments, he took a seat in a lounge chair plenty big enough for two. When she returned, she sat on his lap. He took a sip from his drink, set it on the side table, and trailed a hand up her thigh.

She turned in his lap to straddle him. Taking his face in her hands, she traced kisses along his soft neck. Her hunger for him almost taking over, she scraped her long teeth over the spot where his pulse thrummed just below the surface. The fast rhythm only encouraging her for more.

"Ivy…" the stern voice of Alcide coming from off to the side, effectively ruined the moment. "You know the rules."

She rolled her eyes, "Never in the lounge."

"Perhaps," Valentino said, "we should play some more music. Ivy, would you please do me the honor of accompanying us for a song?"

"I would love to."

"That is a grand idea," Alcide said before leaving to attend to his security duties.

Valentino held Ivy's hand as they walked to the piano area. To get Winston's attention, who currently had his head buried in the ample bosom of one of the girls, he picked up his instrument and played a few notes.

Hearing the music, Winston slowly raised his head and grinned at the woman, "Later, my beauty."

He took a seat at the piano, while Ivy and Valentino sat on top of it. They began a lively tune, kicking their feet to the rhythm while they sang.

***

Father Claudio De Fiore hopped on the streetcar with a group of passengers, a suitcase in one hand and his black bag of Holy relics in the other. The trolley was crowded compared to the train he rode that evening from Monroe. He smiled and motioned an elderly lady onto a bench as he leaned against a pole.

After the short ride, he stepped onto the banquette in the French Quarter. A charged atmosphere greeted him with shouts and loud music from a nearby bar. Claudio had learned about the wickedness that occurred during Mardi Gras in Mobile and Carnival season in New Orleans was not something the priest wished to experience. But his cousin had begged him to visit so he could brag about his success in the Southern city firsthand before returning to Italy.

Chateau Rouge wore a crisp gray façade, decorative wrought iron balconies servicing the three floors above the entry. Claudio received a few choice looks from passersby before a doorman stepped aside for him.

The pale blue, cream, and gold Grecian style could not disguise what Claudio had learned to recognize as dark spirits within a beautiful setting. Whispering a prayer, he passed his bag to the hand with the suitcase so he could do the sign of the cross. The women sitting on the couches in the lobby stared at him—the men with them nervously adjusted their collars.

Touching the cross he wore about his neck, he approached the desk.

"*Bienvenue.* Welcome to Chateau Rouge … Father."

He met the azure gaze of the brunette behind the desk and pushed aside his thoughts of Eliza Melling. "*Grazie, signorina.* I am here to meet Valentino De Fiore."

An amused laugh escaped, her words cutting it short. "Excuse my candor, but I don't think a confession will save our young guest."

Claudio met her red-lipped smile with one of his own. "That does sound like my cousin. I am here on a social visit not business, though I am always happy to assist in that regard. I am well versed in blessing buildings."

Her laugh shifted the loose hair bun on the back of her head. "That will not be necessary, but thank you, Fath—"

He offered his hand. "Claudio De Fiore. Do not feel you need to use my title if you are not of my faith."

She accepted his handshake with her small, cold grip. "Josephine Jacobson, owner of Chateau Rouge. Valentino did set a reservation for a Claudio De Fiore, but do not feel pressured to stay if my establishment is not to your liking."

A door across the lobby swung open. Ragtime tunes being pounded out on a piano filled the elegant space, accompanied by the high keen of a violin. A couple danced through the lobby to the beat that quieted when the door swung shut. As they came to a halt by the elevator, the man's hands roamed down her hips.

The proprietress cleared her throat. "The merrymaking in the lounge, if you couldn't tell, is supplemented by your cousin this evening. He has made himself very much at home during his stay in New Orleans."

One of the men on a couch stood and kissed his companion's hand. He gave a curt nod to Claudio and a mumbled farewell to the owner as the sounds from the bar surged into the room once more. A middle-aged man gave chase to a feisty redhead. They bypassed the elevator cage and went directly for the stairs. The second man in the lobby took one more look at Claudio before rushing out the front door.

Claudio watched the retreat with an amused smile. "It appears my staying in your establishment has the potential for being bad for your business. If you would like to ask me to leave, I will understand."

Smiling, she shook her head. "Do not worry about me, Mr. De—"

"Claudio, please."

"Claudio. Business will be the least of my concerns this Carnival. Besides, it would be next to impossible for you to secure a room anywhere else in town this week." She took a key from the rack behind her desk and held it out before him. "You are most welcome. Your room is on the fourth floor, number 408. Valentino's room is across the hall."

Claudio squeezed her hand in thanks as he accepted the skeleton key. "*Grazie, signorina.* I assume I can find my cousin through those doors after I place my bags in my room."

"Yes, but I can have someone bring them up for you if you would like to go straight in."

"No, but thank you."

The quaint room overlooking the courtyard showcased more classic lines and colors like those found along the Mediterranean Sea. After setting his luggage on the bench, Claudio removed the St. Benedict's crucifix from his smaller bag. He kissed it and fell to his knees in supplication—to protect himself and his cousin for what evils lurked within the walls of what he now knew to be a bordello. He retrieved the Holy water and salt to bless his room. Then he slipped the wood and metal crucifix that had saved him and his friends within cursed Seacliff Cottage into the pocket of his cassock.

When he passed through the lobby, he looked to the front desk. A man clad in all black stood beside the proprietress like a demon in men's clothing. They both watched the priest so he smiled before stepping into the gaiety of the bar.

The dark paneled room was alight with swaying bodies, chatter, the clink of glass, and music. The upright piano was played by a man with garters over his white sleeves and a jaunty straw hat set crooked on his head. Valentino perched on top of the tall piano, legs kicking to the ragtime song as he fiddled along. Beside him, a buxom brunette in a skirt much too short for the frigid temperatures outside sang in a clear voice.

Claudio made his way across the room, creating a trail of silence before he stopped beside the piano.

"Claudio!" Valentino jumped to the ground and embraced him with one arm as he kissed his cheeks. "Why did you not leave off the coat and collar before joining me?"

His eyes swept the bar's occupancy before answering. It was lessened by half a dozen men from when he entered. "Why did you not inform me where you were residing?"

Valentino ran a hand through his chin-length, black hair and grinned. "I can assure you this hotel is better than the one the orchestra put me in when I first arrived. I found Chateau Rouge my second week here and moved in immediately." He set his violin and bow on the now silent piano and helped the singer to the ground. "*Cogino*, meet Ivy. She has the voice of a songbird."

Her gray eyes were as arresting as her figure, but Claudio felt the danger she presented before touching her cold hand. She leaned in for kisses—the hallmark of Valentino's seductions always included making his women accept and give Italian greetings.

"I have never been so close to a priest before. You smell delicious."

"It is lovely to meet you, Ivy." Claudio's hand went into his pocket to rub the crucifix. "It appears my vestments in a brothel are more inspiring than a Sunday sermon."

"Such weaklings! They need to be content with their actions to enjoy them fully. No regrets, no guilt." Valentino waved a dismissive hand before banging it on the piano. "Begin, Winston, I want music while I drink with *mio cogino*. Did you not bring vacation clothes, Claudio?"

He narrowed his eyes at the twenty-year-old. Ivy placed a hand on Claudio's shoulder and ran it down his sleeve—bringing back memories of his lost love, Eliza.

"You're about the same size as Alcide." She smiled and turned to Valentino. "Surely the head of security would loan a few things for the cause of protecting the guests from their own beliefs."

Valentino's bravado faded with the mention of the man in charge of security. "You better handle that, Ivy."

"Happily." She nipped his neck before sashaying out of the bar.

"Is she not glorious?" Valentino nudged Claudio toward the now empty section of stools along the far counter. "I can no longer remember the names or faces of those girls in Mobile. Mere children compared to Ivy. She is perfect. I hope to join her for eternity."

***

When Ivy didn't see Alcide at his normal post where he could see both the lobby and the lounge, she assumed he would be in the office area with Josey.

She could hear their voices murmuring behind the closed door.

"We must keep an eye on the priest. His presence here can put us in great jeopardy," Alcide said.

"Should I call on Selena?" Josey responded. Selena was the oldest vampire in town, and thus the person who attended to all problems pertaining to mortals.

"I do not think that is necessary. Yet. I will keep my eyes on him. And his cousin." The last word said almost like a curse.

Ivy's eyes widened when Alcide mentioned Valentino. To be put on Alcide's watch list was never good. She was tempted to listen more, but she knew it wasn't appropriate. Besides, being caught listening to a conversation with Josey and Alcide would get her into serious hot water with the two, and she was not willing to risk that.

"Come in," Josey responded after Ivy knocked. She entered the room and stood in front of Josey's elegant antique desk.

"Miss Josey," she said in greeting, then nodded to Alcide who stood across the room. He carved a red apple with a small knife. It was an interesting action for a man who typically did not concern himself with human actions such as eating.

"Valentino's cousin is visiting."

"Yes," he nodded, then waited for her to continue.

"Well, see, he's a priest, and he didn't bring anything else to wear besides his robes. We were wondering if you might have some things he can borrow. He sticks out here like a sore thumb."

Alcide raised a black eyebrow, "You don't say?"

"It may be a good idea," Josey said. "His presence has already caused quite the stir here. If he blended in, it might work out for the best."

"Very well," Alcide said, then crooked a finger at Ivy. "Come with me."

Ivy followed him to his suite on the fourth floor where the important people stayed. She hoped to have her own room there one day, but hadn't acquired that status yet. She was lucky now because she stayed with Valentino. As they walked, there was no conversation because Alcide did not make small talk, nor did he have patience for anyone who made the attempt to engage him in thus.

He unlocked the room with his special skeleton key—adorned with a black heart—and pushed the door open to allow her to enter first. She had never been in his lair, and the decor was just as intimidating as he was. The room was black. The walls, the window dressings, the furniture. He waved a hand and the candles in the votives mounted in crystal fixtures flared to life. Their flames cast eerie shadows all through the room. The room smelled of sandalwood and something darker.

"Wow!"' Ivy breathed as goosebumps raised on her arms.

"This way," he gestured for her to follow him down a dark hallway. Anyone with sense would be apprehensive, but not Ivy. She was far too fascinated. She was sure he could hear her heartbeat reverberate around the room as she walked down the hall.

If his living room was intimidating, his bedroom would make one's knees weak. A giant four-poster bed took up most of the room, the black canopy creating a gothic room-within-a-room. And not somewhere even Ivy would want to venture into.

He opened the door to his closet and began pulling out clothes. He gathered several suits that would be acceptable for daily wear.

He nodded, "These should be sufficient. Advise him to send the clothes to housekeeping when he is finished. Be sure he informs them that they are mine."

"I will. But, Alcide, what about the ball?"

"Ivy ... Selena will not like this. He is an outsider."

"He's family Alcide. Valentino's family."

He raised a dark eyebrow, "He is potential trouble. But, for now, I will send something appropriate. Ivy, if he causes any ... disruptions ... he will be dealt with. And there will not be anything I, or his God, can do to save him."

Ivy scoffed, "It's just a Mardi Gras ball, Alcide. What could possibly go wrong?"

He shook his head morosely, "There is much for you to learn, yet. This world is new to you. Please do not let your innocence be your undoing. Or someone else's."

Ivy gathered the garments close to her, "Thank you Alcide, I'll be careful. I promise." She turned to leave the room. She halted for a moment when his raspy voice said softly, "It is not you that I am concerned about."

***

Claudio stared at the suits laid across his bed. How could he decide which to wear when they all reeked of death? Turning away from the collection of black articles, he stalked to the dresser to retrieve the aspergillum. Flicking Holy water over the clothing, the priest allowed his irritation to display on his face with a scowl as he recited the words to cleanse the man's tainted fabric. Claudio would never have traveled to New Orleans for his cousin were it not for the fact he was lonely in Monroe since his best friend returned to Alabama two months before. Gone was his chess opponent, as well as the conversations and confessions the men enjoyed several times a week during their four years in Louisiana. Losing Alexander Melling's companionship hurt Claudio as much as when he lost Eliza five winters ago. There was no doubt the Melling siblings were well-versed in causing pain.

Claudio winced as he tugged on the black suit. His cousin was just as gifted in that regard. The weeping women he left across the globe were testaments to his cruel game of seduction. Though this time Valentino appeared to have been caught in a siren's spell.

"May we teach him a lesson between the two of us," he whispered as he stepped into the hall.

After a few minutes of waiting, Valentino exited his room wearing a look of dazed satiation along with a crisp tuxedo.

"Have you no self-control?" Claudio snapped. "Thirty minutes was afforded to change, yet you—"

A stupid grin filled his face. "I cannot help what she does to me, *Cogino*."

"Which is what exactly?"

Valentino laughed and fell against him as though drunk. "I do not know, and that is part of the beauty of it! I rejoice in it— this splendor of love! I want it always and will have it."

Claudio gave a dry laugh. "You never want something longer than your contract lasts."

***

Ivy surveyed the handiwork of the young girl the hotel used to assist with hairdressing. She fluffed the dark curls that were left long and flowed down her shoulder. A golden barrette held the hair in place.

"You did well, Marie." She reached into the small purse on the vanity and handed the girl a few silver coins.

"Thank you, Miss Ivy," she said beaming.

"You're very welcome."

The girl nodded, still smiling and left Ivy alone in the room.

Ivy poured a glass of champagne and walked out onto the balcony. With her right hand, she brushed the train of her gown away then rested her arms on the railing. She looked up into the night sky, seeing the fat, full moon. Valentino would be there soon, along with his cousin. They were all going to Claire de Lune, one of the best restaurants in town. Ivy hoped Valentino would behave. He had already drawn enough attention at Chateau Rouge. Selena's attention could be deadly. As she was the owner of the Claire de Lune, it would be hard to avoid her.

When the men came to her door, she took Valentino's arm as she tasted his lips. "We'll grab one of my friends on the way out for Claudio to escort to supper."

"No, please." Claudio followed them to the elevator. "I am used to dining alone. Being with the two of you will be pleasant enough for me."

"I told you, Ivy." Valentino smirked. "Even without the robes, my cousin has no natural male urges left inside his priestly body."

They stepped into the lobby and Ivy ran a finger across Claudio's lapel. "We'll see about that. We're dining at Claire de Lune, a place where even your archbishop enjoys dining."

A cab drove them to the few blocks so they arrived at the restaurant fresh. The roadster pulled to a stop in front of the Claire de Lune. Valentino exited first, then extended a hand to Ivy. More than a few heads turned their way as they walked into the restaurant, Claudio following at a respectable distance.

The host greeted them with a smile, "Your table is ready, Miss Ivy."

"Thank you, Maxwell."

The trio followed the tuxedo-clad man through the white topped tables lit by candlelight that sparkled off of the fine china and silverware. Soft music played from a quartet situated on a small dais in the middle of the room. They stopped in the back of the restaurant in a VIP room. It was secluded and intimate, a favorite for the patrons and employees of the Chateau Rouge.

Valentino stopped in the entryway, "We need a table in the main room, please."

Ivy touched his arm, "*Cher*, this is the best table in the house."

"But, it is so…quiet. I require a table in the main room where everyone may see me."

"Well, sir," the host said. "We have no tables available at this time. However, if you would like to wait, I can seat you at the first available."

"Good. We shall wait at the bar."

"That sounds like a grand idea," Ivy said.

The three took the remaining seats and placed their drink orders.

While they waited, Valentino looked around. "This place needs more passion. I wish I had brought my violin so I could play a few songs. Clare de Lune would love me!"

"As we all do," Ivy said, reaching out to play with a wayward strand of his hair.

He reached out to pull her close for a kiss and Ivy leaned out of his reach. She slapped his hand playfully. "This is not the Chateau Rouge, Valentino. We must have a modicum of decorum here."

"Decorum," he scoffed. "That's not for people like us, *amore mio*. We are special. Chosen. All three of us—even my *cogino* here, chosen by God."

He grabbed his goblet of wine and raised it into the air, clearing his throat. "Ladies and gentlemen of the Clare de Lune, I am the violinist Valentino De Fiore! I have played in concert halls in cities all over the world, and there is no place as grand as New Orleans! I would be pleased if you would come and see me perform. I can even be found accompanying the fine pianist at the Chateau Rouge."

The restaurant went silent. Ivy, who was always pale, turned a shade of gray when he mentioned the hotel. Although the Chateau Rouge was a popular location in the French Quarter, it was unwise to draw undue attention, it could even prove to be dangerous.

"Valentino," she whispered, shaking her head.

"What is it, *amore mio?*"

"You don't understand."

"Understand what?"

"I cannot explain here. Could we leave? We can have a fine dinner at the hotel." She tugged on his jacket.

"We are just getting started. Aren't we, *Cogino?*" He looked over to Claudio. "We need to show my cousin a night on the town!"

The flames on the candles danced as a cold wind blew through the room. Ivy exhaled a breath, her hand falling away from Valentino's jacket.

A regal blonde approached them with such a sense of elegance, one would swear she was royalty. She stopped in front of Valentino, who for once, was silent.

"Good evening," she said, nodding to Valentino and Claudio. "My name is Selena Prosperie, I am the owner of the Clare de Lune."

Valentino reached out a hand in greeting. Selena glanced at his hand and ignoring it, looked him in the eye. "I provide a setting of elegance that my customers have come to expect. It is my job to see that atmosphere is maintained. If it is revelry you are looking for, I can suggest other places more to your liking."

Ivy tugged on his jacket again, "I am sure we will find a place."

Valentino looked at Selena again, and opened his mouth to speak.

Claudio took Valentino's elbow and stood between his cousin and Selena. "We apologize, *Signorina* Prosperie. I fear my cousin is too eager to show me the highlights of your fine city that he forgot where he was for a moment. We mean no offense."

Ivy looked between the two, noticing the priest fingering something in his hand. A crucifix!

Selena looked to it as well, a smile softening her hard stare. "Thank you for understanding." She nodded and took a step back to signal their expected departure.

As the three turned to leave, Selena stopped Ivy with a touch on her arm. "I expect to see you in my office tomorrow night, directly after sundown. Bring Josephine with you."

Ivy blanched and lowered her head, "Yes, Selena."

"Now, go along. This boyfriend of yours has done enough damage for the evening. See that he and his cousin return to the Chateau Rouge at once."

Ivy hurried to catch up with Valentino and Claudio.

"Why did she not appreciate having a world-renowned musician in her establishment?"

She pasted a smile on her face, "It's nothing against you, Valentino. Let's return to the Chateau Rouge, shall we? There will be a party going on there."

He kissed both her cheeks. "That sounds like a grand plan! Back to the Chateau Rouge we go!"

***

When Claudio followed the lovers out of the hired automobile in front of Chateau Rouge, Ivy's grey eyes flashed intriguingly at him before she attached herself to Valentino. The red evening gown played off her lips that looked as though they would drip blood with their lush color. She smiled at him sweetly and mouthed the words "thank you." Claudio nodded to her acknowledgement of his help in defusing the situation with Selena Prosperie—who he was certain was as dangerous as she was beautiful. Were all gorgeous women in New Orleans harboring unholy secrets?

Inside the lobby, Claudio met the dead glare from the head of security. This time, he could not muster a smile.

Valentino swept Ivy into his arms and deposited her at the center table of the lounge with a flourish. "Stay. My cousin will guard you until I return with my violin."

Ivy grabbed his hand before he could turn away. "Wait, please. Claudio must be starved. Let's eat before you turn to music. You cannot forget your cousin's needs."

Claudio took the chair diagonally across from the woman and smiled. "*Grazie, signorina.* I have to admit that without food, I will soon be forced to retire."

"Then food, music, and love making it shall be!" Valentino declared. "We need—"

Ivy interrupted his shouting command with a kiss. "Allow me to order at the bar. I'll be back in a moment."

If he wasn't so concerned over the state of Valentino's soul, Claudio would have admired the way Ivy was able to handle his cousin. Smiling, he watched the young man follow the hypnotizing movements of his current lover. "Will you play *'Boccherini'* for me tonight, Valentino?"

He took the seat opposite and shook his head, long hair brushing his cheeks with the movement. "I do not play Vivaldi unless paid handsomely. You, *Father* De Fiore, cannot afford me to play your antiquated baroque tunes. I had enough Vivaldi in Mobile to last me years! If it was not for the Tchaikovsky and Paganini, I would have gone crazy in that town."

"And in New Orleans?"

"Here I have the French influences of Chopin and Debussy, coupled with the locals' lively tunes. And Ivy. The songbird and I create beautiful music together. We shall be celebrated for our music and attractiveness forever."

Forever. Eternity. Valentino had never before looked beyond his current contract in whatever city he found himself in. What hold did Ivy have over him with these eternal plans?

The platters of blackened fish with seasoned rice and vegetables were excellent—Ivy's choice of wine an exquisite match. It was the broken conversation concerning a masquerade in two nights that concerned Claudio. He could tell it was of great importance to Ivy though she appeared reluctant to speak of it before the priest. Valentino's questions involving some sort of ritual seemed to aggravate her the most.

"This all sounds most interesting," Claudio said to ease an awkward silence at the table though the bar sounds continued around them. "I shall be most curious to learn more. It appears the carnival festivities here are different than what I learned of in Alabama."

Ivy fingered the corner of her napkin. "Alcide promised to provide a tuxedo for you. Someone will come tomorrow for a fitting, but if you don't think it proper for a man such as yourself to parade about masked, we can surely find you entertainment elsewhere."

Valentino took her hand. "Do not lose your nerve, Ivy. You know I sent for Claudio to be here this week especially for my moment of glory."

She bit her lip and nodded.

Valentino clicked his tongue and fished his key out of his suit pocket. "Fetch my violin, Ivy. It will bring you to a better mood to hear me play and then I shall remove the remainder of your cares within my chambers."

Surprisingly, she did as he asked. As soon as they were alone, Claudio pressed Valentino for answers.

"What is this plan you have in conjunction with the masquerade?"

His head tipped back with laughter. After drinking the rest of his wine, he held his cousin's gaze and grinned. "I shall be known from now until forevermore as the greatest violinist of all time! Sarasate and even Paganini himself will be forgotten as the years roll by. My name—my very face—will be immortalized as I take my place as the true master, an undying flame in the music world."

The new heights of his cousin's inflated confidence nauseated him. Possibly it was the undercurrent of dark power that he could feel but not name that soured him the most, but Claudio suffered through only thirty minutes of music and drinks before he excused himself for the night.

Locked in his room, he immediately stripped the borrowed clothes from his body and sealed the door with blessed salt and prayers. Clutching St. Benedict's Cross, he curled in the bed and willed himself to sleep.

A short time later, noises in the hallway roused him. Claudio lay in the darkness repeating the sign of the cross as he gripped his relic. In an attempt to block out the fevered procreation that pounded against the wall while moans split the night air, he prayed aloud for Valentino—and himself. He must not succumb to the memories of his violet-eyed beauty. Her scent and taste must be repressed though the sounds brought him back to the hours he had spent in her arms. He should not feel the softness of her curves nor crave the forbidden pleasure of ultimate release after five years.

"God help me," he whispered. "Take the agony of losing Eliza Melling from me. I cannot keep enduring the pain. If I am truly forgiven, please take the ache once and for all."

Cries of ecstasy shouted and moaned from across the hall, but it didn't sting.

A slamming door—a distant groan of submission.

The sharpness in his loins transformed into a dull ache in his chest.

Emptiness filling with hope, charity, and complete surrender.

"I am yours, Lord. Eliza's life was given to see it so."

The granted sleep was restorative. Claudio woke with the sun, dressed in the second borrowed suit, and left Chateau Rouge. The morning stroll to clear his lungs of the dank spirits that surrounded him within those deceptively pretty walls fed his soul. The *café au lait* and *beignets* boosted him as well.

***

The chimes signaling a customer roused Madame Vivian from her back room. A tall man dressed in a sharp black suit walked through the store, casually looking in the display cases filled with various treasures curated from all over the world.

"*Bienvenue,*" she said softly in greeting so as to not startle him.

He looked up, his brown eyes connecting with hers. She felt his intense faith. But, also a pain that haunted him though his friendly greeting was capped with dimples of a deep smile.

"Good morning. You have some interesting items in your store."

Vivian smiled in return. "Yes, we do. It is called *Enchanteé* for a reason."

She stepped closer to clasp the hand he offered. He smelled of sandalwood and spice. Intriguing. She knew that scent well.

"Are you staying at the Chateau Rouge?"

"*Sí.* How do you know?"

"Your suit. It belongs to Alcide Santiago."

He looked at his outfit with a slight frown. "*Sí,* do you happen to sell clothing? I would love to return his things."

Vivian grinned. "Nothing in your size, I am afraid."

"I am here to visit my cousin who is staying at Chateau Rouge. As a priest, my presence in the vestments made the other guests uncomfortable."

"I can see how that could happen. You must be a special guest if they afforded you the luxury of Alcide's closet."

"My cousin, Valentino De Fiore, has taken quite a liking to a woman there named Ivy."

"Ah, so *you* are Valentino's cousin!"

"You know him?"

"I know everything about the Chateau Rouge."

It was his turn to look surprised. His eyes filled with questions that Vivian could not and would not answer. "So, Father, what brings you to *Enchanteé* today?"

"I was merely taking a morning walk through the Vieux Carré. I happened upon your shop and felt compelled to come in."

"We are always glad to entertain our visitors. I take it you would not enjoy a card reading today."

He smiled. "No, but thank you. I am intrigued by these rosary beads." He gestured to a long set of small dark beads attached to a carved cross by a fine metal chain.

"Ah, the bone beads. Those are quite special. They belonged to a casquette girl, Angelique. Are you familiar with the history of the casquette girls, Father?"

"No, I am afraid not."

"In 1728, a group of girls of marriageable age were put on a ship and sent to New Orleans from France. They were escorted by a member of the Prosperie family and taken in by the Ursuline nuns upon their arrival until a suitable partner could be found. Angelique was one of those girls. She formed quite the friendship with the woman who escorted her. Madam Prosperie also encouraged the girl to work on her art, as she was very talented."

Vivian stopped for a moment and retrieved the rosary from the case, holding it out to the Priest. "When a husband was found for Angelique, they were wed and resided in a house not far from here. Unbeknownst to the nuns, the man was an alcoholic and abusive. One night, in a fit of rage, he shoved her and she tumbled down the stairs. She died, so young.

"Madam Prosperie was enraged. She appeared at his home the next night. What happened after that was only whispered about from servants' gossip. But the man was never seen again. Some of the belongings she had ended up here, including that rosary. It's been here since but I only placed it on display today. If you ever meet Selena Prosperie, she is a descendant of the family. Some of Angelique's artwork can be found in her restaurant."

The priest rolled the beads in his fingers. "I met *Signorina* Prosperie last evening, though I am afraid that it did not go very well. My cousin can be uninhibited at times. I would, however, love to see this art. Perhaps I will go again tonight."

"If you should go, tell her Madam Vivian sent you."

"Excuse me, but is *Signorina* Prosperie well? She seemed more than upset over Valentino's minor disturbance. Surely she is used to boisterous guests, especially during Carnival."

"You are very perceptive, Father." Vivian patted his arm. "Selena's main concern is her friends. They are her family now. Anything that causes undo attention to Chateau Rouge and its special inhabitants causes her alarm."

His caressing touch on the carved beads turned into a grip. "There has been trouble at Chateau Rouge before?"

Madame Vivian shrugged. "What do you think?"

His brown eyes narrowed. "The staff seems well equipped to deal with any issues. Then the trouble has been with *Signorina* Prosperie?"

"It is not my story to explain further, Father." They held each other's gaze for several seconds. "However, I am happy to help you however I can."

"I would like to buy this rosary."

"Very well," Vivian completed the transaction and handed him a small bag.

"It was nice to meet you, Father ..."

"Claudio. Claudio De Fiore." His dimples creased his face once more.

"Please come and visit me again. I so enjoyed your company."

"And I as well."

Vivian watched the priest exit the store. If anyone needed divine intervention, it was Selena. And the handsome priest was just the one to offer it.

***

That evening, Claudio looked down on Valentino from his stance atop a footstool while a tailor reinforced the bottom hem of the borrowed tuxedo pants. "I tell you I will be there, Valentino."

"Do you need a guide? One of the girls downstairs could—"

"Just because I have lived several years in Monroe, does not mean I cannot handle navigating a city, especially one as compact as New Orleans." Claudio smiled over his cousin's pouting frown. "All will be well. You do not perform until after intermission, so even if I go astray, I will not miss your grand entrance."

A knock sounded on Claudio's door.

"*Entrare!*" Valentino shouted from where he lounged on the floor, paying no mind that it was not his place to invite others in.

Ivy's beautiful form appeared in the opening door.

As soon as she was close enough, Valentino snaked a hand around her ankle and tugged her to the floor. Hands roaming her little black dress, the two bodies surged together.

The tailor cleared his throat and glanced at Claudio. "I am almost complete, sir."

"Thank you."

Claudio ignored the passionate kissing until the tailor was out the door. Crossing the room to the tangle of limbs, he nudged Valentino's backside with his foot. "Come, or you yourself will be late."

"My public awaits!" Valentino jumped to his feet and ran his fingers through his black hair, no concern for the woman he left behind with her dress askew.

Offering Ivy his hand, Claudio helped her stand, turning away from the expanses of skin exposed in several sensitive areas while she straightened her gown.

Valentino slipped on his own tuxedo jacket that was slung over a chair and came back to embrace Ivy once more. "*Amore mio*, please escort Claudio to the theater. Two tickets are waiting at will call."

Claudio used his most authoritative voice. "I require no escort, Valentino. I will attend the show and meet you afterward as planned."

"Having a woman on your arm is no sin, *Cogino.*" With that, Valentino and Ivy left the room.

Alone, Claudio studied the fit of the altered tuxedo in the full-length mirror. It would be pleasant to escort a lady to the orchestra performance that night, but none that were within those walls would be right. Not even Josephine, with her coloring similar to Eliza's. No, he could never attempt to play-act with someone in residency of this cursed hotel. Bordello. *Alexander would laugh at me if he knew Valentino tricked me into staying here.*

He took his latest acquisition from the dresser, pocketing the carved rosary from *Enchanteé.* Claudio knew Selena Prosperie had something to do with what was going on at Chateau Rouge— as well as the connection with Madame Vivian at the shop—and he was going to find out how it related to Valentino before it was too late.

After he descended to the lobby, Claudio stopped at the sofa where Ivy perched on the arm. "I pray you do not take offense to my refusal of your company, *signorina.*"

She shook her head. "I understand it's about your commitment to your faith, nothing against me."

He kissed the back of her hand. "*Sì.* A man would be foolish to reject your company. A fool or a priest—perhaps I am both."

"You're neither, Claudio. But let me know if you change your mind." She glanced at some of the others about the room. "There are many who would—"

He laughed and kissed her cheeks in parting. "You are too kind."

"Do you need a cab?"

"I am used to walking, but thank you."

"Be sure to watch for puddles and grime. Alcide won't share a second tuxedo. I'm afraid that one will have to service you tonight and for the masquerade tomorrow, but it can be sent for cleaning in the morning if needed."

"I will mind myself on the walk, *signorina. Arrivederci.*"

Claudio skirted Bourbon Street as he made his way to Claire de Lune. Several times he turned around because it felt as though he was being followed, but no familiar faces met his sweeping glances.

At the restaurant, he informed the host he was there to see Selena on behalf of Madame Vivian. Claudio was immediately ushered to a private office and asked to wait. He took in the space rich with Victorian furniture and red hues under the electric light before settling on a straight-backed armchair. Displayed above the fireplace was a painting of the French countryside.

Selena Prosperie arrived a few minutes later. Lean body draped in a gold silk gown and white gloves that reached over her elbows, she presented a cold shell with her unearthly beauty.

Claudio greeted her with a bow.

"I am sorry to keep you waiting, Mr. De Fiore. I was on my way out when I was told you have word from Madame Vivian."

"I am sorry to disappoint you, *signorina*. I am not here on Madame Vivian's errand but my own." He noted the way her body went rigid, as well as the distance she carefully put between them with a few mincing steps toward the door. Claudio fingered the scrolling designs carved on the beads and the delicate metal chain connecting them within his pocket. "I can only describe that I was led to her shop this morning for a purpose I do not yet fully understand."

Her lips curved into a sneer of skepticism. "I have heard things like that before, but I doubt there is anything within the store that would interest a man like you."

"And what type of man am I, *signorina*, who earns such contempt from you?"

"You are Valentino's cousin, are you not?"

"*Sí*, and I suppose that is enough for you to judge me by. You are not the first to do so, but I assure you I possess neither the arrogance nor the seductive wiles of my young cousin."

Her laugh was cruel. "I'm afraid this is something you cannot blame on Valentino."

Confused at her hostility, Claudio studied the way she tugged at her gloves. "I do not understand. Perhaps if I called at a better time we could—"

"I am not in the habit of accepting personal visits from priests." She crossed her arms as her venomous words continued. "Yes, if the archbishop comes to dine, I will pay a call at his table if asked, but I do not seek the company of those who claim to protect God's children and then do the opposite."

"I must apologize for whoever wore the vestments of my faith that wounded you—"

"If only it was me!" Her gloved hand trembled as she clutched a fist to her heart, eyes flashing red. "Pain to me I can live with—even if the one inflicting it could not."

Seeking to comfort her tempestuous spirit, Claudio ignored the possible danger of her viciousness and moved forward with a hand outstretched. "*Signorina*, I know what it is to have heartache, but there is nothing the Lo—"

Selena knocked his hand away with a motion powerful enough to send him stumbling back several steps. "I was in the process of losing my faith before I left my homeland. The betrayal here solidified my decision. I have gone nearly two centuries without the aid of God so do not expect me to fall on my knees before you tonight!"

Claudio hastily crossed himself and stared at the hand on her stilled chest as she sucked in a breath with the admission. Selena immediately advanced, her former blue eyes shining crimson with fury.

"Go, Priest!" Fangs could be seen within her snarling lips. "Forget this meeting ever happened before it is too late for you."

"I must know something first, *signorina*." Arms open in a show of peace, he held the vampire's deadly gaze. "I do not fear for myself."

"Then you're an imbecile! No man has failed to shrink before my wrath since—"

"What is to become of Valentino?"

Her laugh raised goose flesh on his skin. "He has chosen to become his own god, forsaking the one you pathetically cling to."

"How much time do I have to stop him?"

She shook her head, blonde chignon as stiff as her will. "It's too late. He's made his choice and the rituals are prepared. Now leave, Father De Fiore. My office is no place for you, especially tonight."

Catching the hint of softness in her last phrase, he gambled on the perceived weakness that she wasn't as vile as she wanted him to believe.

Claudio gave a chivalrous bow, hoping to capture his vision of escorting a woman to the orchestra and help Valentino at the same time. "*Signorina* Prosperie, I fear you do not know what you welcome with your diabolical plans. I beg of you to accompany me tonight. Attend the concert with me that I might show you Valentino's true self."

"It would be foolish for you to be in my company."

"As I said before, I do not fear for myself. In that regard, lovely Selena, I believe we are the same." His genuine smile brought a look of surprise to her face. "I know you are capable of caring for yourself, but your friends might not be as skilled. Valentino would be dangerous to them."

He saw the battle raging in her mind as she simultaneously licked her lips and leaned away. "I am overdue to feed. You are in danger every minute you stay in my presence."

Pulling the rosary from his pocket, he fingered the cross.

"Where did you get that?" Her voice snapped.

"Madame Vivian sold it to me." Claudio nonchalantly crossed the room and motioned to the painting over the hearth. "That is Angelique's too, is it not?"

Selena nodded, a faraway look in her eyes—once more their natural blue.

"My sister was taken from this life prematurely. I was sixteen when she died from fever. That was when I decided to give my life to others through service."

"A death from fever would have been a Godsend compared to the hell Angelique lived in!"

Selena snatched at the rosary, but Claudio quickly pocketed it.

"I too loved an artist who was taken from this world through the greed and sins of others. I understand the anguish and loneliness, the guilt and suffering because I did not do enough to protect her."

Inches from his face, her lips curled once more. "You can never understand."

The intoxicating sweetness of her scent, the womanly curve of her chest angled defiantly before him washed a wave of cold sweat over his body. Fingering the rosary in his pocket for strength, Claudio held her stare. "I am no man set above another, Selena."

"Prove it." Her lips brushed his cheek and her gloves encircled his neck as though she prepared to feast. "Prove your humility before I end your life."

"The artist was my lover." He kissed her cheek and leaned away to watch her startled reaction. "Our hidden love affair spanned several months and I planned to run away with her. Yes, even I once found something I loved more than God."

Her bittersweet smile brought him a semblance of peace. "Oh how the righteous fall with sins of the flesh, Father De Fiore."

"I was a deacon then, but even with my new title, I still stumble through life. We are all imperfect. Anyone claiming perfection is deceived by the devil and deserves not the vestments of the priesthood." He offered his arm. "Will you attend the orchestra with me, *Signorina* Prosperie?"

"Be careful what you ask for, Priest." She took a fur wrap from the coat tree by the door.

He helped her into the cloak and smiled when she took his arm. "Call me Claudio, a man blessed to bring the most beautiful woman in New Orleans to the orchestra."

***

Claudio and Selena were shown to a private box during the final movement of the first half of the performance. The dreamy strains of Bach vibrated to a low hum before the crowd burst into applause. Immediately after the houselights came up, a gentleman entered their alcove.

"Selena, my dear!" The gray haired man took her gloved hand without pause and pressed his lips to the back. "How good it is to see you outside of your restaurant."

"Good evening, Mr. Charbonnet." Her manner was cool and clipped. "It is kind of you to stop by. Allow me to introduce you to Claudio De Fiore."

Her hand went to Claudio's knee with an intimate squeeze while she flashed a seductive smile at him, accompanied by a wink.

Mr. Charbonnet stepped forward to shake Claudio's offered hand when he stood. "A pleasure, Mr. De Fiore. Any relation to—"

"They are cousins," Selena said before the conversation could be expanded upon.

"Splendid. I shall see you next week when I dine at your restaurant."

"Of course, Mr. Charbonnet. Goodnight."

When they were alone, Claudio shifted his armchair closer to Selena's before sitting. Her eyes darkened and her nostrils flared.

"I figured after your actions with me, word will spread about us." Claudio touched her gloved forearm and nodded to the curve of box seats stretching away from theirs. "There are many eyes on you."

Selena smiled. "I grow weary of turning away suitors. I hope you don't mind being brought into my scheme for peace."

"I am here to help you." Fingers trailed her cheek and he leaned close to whisper. "Your beauty shines, though you appear to be struggling. Do you need fresh air?"

"No, but thank you for being a considerate escort. It is past time, but I will wait until after the performance before slaking my thirst."

The orchestra returned to their seats, followed by the conductor to the center. The theater hushed until the buzz of the electric chandeliers were heard, making the thunderous praise when Valentino took the stage deafening.

"He loves being the center of attention," Claudio spoke into her ear. "He will not hide in the shadows if he is turned. You saw how he was in your restaurant last night—that was minor compared to most instances. He has no filter in his speech. He will brag to all who will listen"

Selena twisted her fingers in her lap as the crowd settled into silence. Bach's *Violin Partita #3* began, Valentino mastering the simple beauty with warmth and charm.

Claudio put his arm about Selena so he could whisper easily. "He will not be content to hide within Chateau Rouge, or even the whole city of New Orleans. His personality is one that feeds off others in a different way—he is a parasite of adoration. Ivy might hold him captive for the moment, but it will not last. He collects women in every city, leaving them with no thought when his contract is complete. Valentino is a gypsy, roaming from the highest paying client to another and sets himself as a prince wherever he is."

She gripped his hand with strength that almost caused Claudio to blackout from pain.

"Please," her voice tremored, "give me space."

With the release of her grip, she leaned against the far corner of the velvet wingchair—eyes closed. Even at rest, there was tightness in her features showcasing pain.

Your dependency on the blood of others makes you vulnerable, lovely Selena. You cannot rely on yourself all the time. You need more and I will help you find it.

Valentino's solos received a standing ovation, for which Claudio helped Selena from her chair. He shouted "*Bravo!*" but kept an arm about her as she weakly clapped.

By the time *Orchestra Suite #2* began, Selena was ashen. Claudio eased her to her feet and allowed her to gently fall into him between the back curtain and the side wall of their box. The space warm and private, Selena's lean frame cold against his length.

"Partake of me, Selena. You need strength to deal with Valentino after the performance."

"No." She tried to push away, but Claudio locked his wrists around her slim waist. Her ebbing powers were no match. "You do not understand what you're saying."

"Will it kill me?" he whispered.

"No," she replied in kind.

"Will it be painful?"

She shook her head. "I can take the pain and replace it with pleasure, but you will crave more of it."

"That is no concern for me." He caressed her bare neck and tried to ignore the press of their hips in their precarious position. "You must get relief. Take what you need to see you through the next few hours."

After a moment's hesitation, Selena pushed up his left tuxedo sleeve. She fumbled open the cufflink on his shirtsleeve and dropped it to the carpet in her shaky state. In a breathless rush, she held his forearm and kissed his inner wrist before biting down. Uncomfortableness quickly turned to exquisite … bliss! With the heavenly sounds of Valentino leading the orchestra along the baroque tunes, Claudio soared with relief until Selena laved the punctured skin with a motion that was just as profound.

Luminous eyes and fresh red stain on her lips, she embraced Claudio with a surrendering quality. "Your blood is magic."

"And your touch is divine," he whispered in reply as he willed himself not to become too familiar.

"I might only partake of Holy blood from now on."

They were back in their seats before the finale. Even under the dim lights, Claudio could see Selena's warm glow complete with a blush of youth on her cheeks. She appeared pure and whole—virginal even, if it were not for the provocative cut of her gown.

At the close of the performance, Selena clapped and shouted as though reborn. She hastily took his arm and turned for the hall. With the help of an usher, they were brought to a gilt reception room with two dozen other distinguished guests to await Valentino. Selena fingered the floral arrangements and partook of the champagne, all while linked to Claudio's arm. Smiling over his vision from earlier in the evening coming true, he happily obliged her whim of the deception of their relationship.

Several minutes later, the doors opened to the arrival of Valentino with half a dozen female admirers at his heels. He boisterously made his way around the room, shaking the men's hands and kissing all the women while collecting their praise with his ever-expanding head.

Coming at last to Claudio and Selena, Valentino laughed. "I see how it is, *Cogino*. No one at Chateau Rouge would do because you already had your eye on the biggest prize in town!"

With the mention of the brothel, the nearest guests gasped and Selena loosened her arm from Claudio's.

Valentino made use of the change and swept her into his arms for a playful hug and kisses to her cheeks. "If you have a taste for Italians, *Signorina* Prosperie, I will happily provide when Claudio is gone. I assume you will be joining us for tomorrow night's festivities? I have taken the liberty of inviting all of my new friends"—he made a sweeping motion with his hand around the group assembled—"to our party tomorrow night."

When he released her, Selena looked ready to claw his eyes out. But Valentino was already greeting the next guests, his harem trailing along two steps behind.

Claudio clasped her hand in his own. "Have you seen enough?"

"Yes, let's go," she replied.

When her private car pulled to the curb in front of the theater, Claudio escorted her out.

Ready to walk back to the hotel alone, he handed her inside. "Thank you for accompanying me to the orchestra."

"Come." She patted the bench in the enclosed backseat. "We have more to discuss."

He couldn't hide the grin that built from his joy at spending more time with her, but he tapped down the excitement of the thought of her lips on his body once more.

"You may congratulate yourself, Claudio."

Her voice was lighter than anything he had heard from her before and he relaxed into the leather seat.

"I have been swayed by a priest for the first time since I arrived on this soil nearly two hundred years ago."

"And before that?"

She took his challenge, languidly removing her gloves and dropping them beside her. "I worked with one in France. My father was a generous donor to our parish. My childhood memories are of Mass and church gatherings. One of the priests often took meals with us and became an uncle to me. Father Elijah."

"I am sure he appreciated the family time as much as you."

Her cool skin stroked his cheek. "Are you lonely, Claudio? You are so far from home. Do you ache for companionship?"

"*Sí*. I am human, Selena." He reached into his pocket and retrieved the carved rosary. He kissed the cross, placed it in Selena's chill hands, and closed her fingers around the gift. "For you to remember your faith and your friends—both the old and the new."

"Thank you." She bowed her head over their joined hands a moment. When she raised her head, she hung the rosary from the door handle and projected a composed façade.

"Hold to faith, however you can in your life," he admonished. "You are never alone."

"Do you miss her?" Long fingernails traced his lips as she leaned closer. "Do you still ache for your lover?"

Claudio hugged Selena to his chest, nose buried in her golden hair. "Not typically, though my arms often crave a woman to hold when I am alone."

"Poor, lonely priest." She laid her head on his shoulder.

Out the window, the buildings became smaller, set further apart. He gently set her back and shifted away. "Does your driver not know the way to Chateau Rouge?"

"Of course he does. He's bringing us out River Road. It's the closest location I have around here to feeling like I'm in the French countryside. My father had an estate in the country. I grew up playing in the vineyard every summer."

Hoping to bring the subject back to her pains, he took hold of the changed subject matter. "I too grew up around the vines, but in Tuscany. Their wines are the best."

"I always preferred reds." She ran her tongue over her teeth.

"And I as well."

They sat frozen in a charged stare, the roar of the motor the only sound. The tires hit a rut in the road and threw them together. Selena held his biceps, eyes appearing more red than blue in the dark interior.

Claudio inclined his head toward her. "Tell me how you came to work with the church."

"I changed the year I was twenty. The next Christmas I came home, my father found me feeding on one of the stable boys after midnight Mass. The shock of seeing me pressed to the neck of the young man and him squirming in passion was too much. He suffered a stroke. I stayed with him as often as possible as he convalesced, but after several months he physically declined further. When Father Elijah came to perform the last Rites, my father confessed to him what he saw, asking Father Elijah to look out for me, for my soul—if I still had one."

"You do." Claudio kissed her cheek. "I can feel it, Selena."

She smiled as she settled against him once more.

"Father Elijah came to me the following year to tell me about the King's plans to send virtuous young women to the colonists to establish it with families. The church helped select orphans and girls' whose parents could not support them, but Father Elijah was concerned for their welfare. He wanted a chaperone to bring them to the nuns that he could trust. Someone he knew could deal with sailors and pirates without being a threat to the young women themselves."

"A grave responsibility for one so young." Claudio reached his arms about her. She nuzzled into his chest, loosening his bowtie.

"But I did it. I completed the task and was paid handsomely for my efforts. Many of the girls became like sisters to me on the voyage. Angelique especially." Her breath hitched.

"Madame Vivian told me about her. You don't need to speak of it if you do not wish to."

"Even as I set my home here, we kept in touch. I was at her wedding—joyfully happy for her. But on my first visit to see her afterward, I knew she was not happy though she refused to speak ill of the man. I should have taken him out the day I saw the bruise on her cheek."

"We do what we can, but it is not expected of us to prevent all sin."

"But the church! They set the girls up as lambs to the slaughter for those rough men. No, monsters! The nuns should have seen how they treated the working girls and known they would not cherish the flowers sent by the King!" Selena was ashen again, trembling hands grasping at his lapel.

"The Holy Bible tells us to seek the good in others. Do not blame those of us who look forward with hope." He kissed her forehead and followed it with the sign of the cross. "Forgive those who you think wronged the girls through their good intentions and forgive yourself."

Tears wet his shirt and he held her tighter.

"Selena, you did what you could back then. Now there is a new threat to a young woman. You must save Ivy—and the countless others—from Valentino. He will expose you all. Imagine what will happen when he discovers he can make his own immortal harem?"

She nodded but he felt her weakening in his arms.

"And now you need me." Claudio eased himself to lay on the seat, keeping one arm about her.

As though taking power from the dominant stance he gave her, Selena deftly opened his bowtie and collar. Shifting below her enticingly, Claudio gloried in the pleasure of once again offering himself to a beautiful woman.

***

Selena checked her reflection in the mirror one more time before leaving her room. Her blonde hair was perfectly coiffed, a gold barrette holding it in place. She had a black and gold mask she would put in place when she arrived at the Chateau Rouge. Her ivory and black gown swirled around her body with a plunging neckline she couldn't wait for Claudio to see. She longed for the feel of the priest against her again.

Her face flushed as she thought of being in his arms the night before. His lips on hers. Of feeding, and the warmth of his blood as she drank from him. He was exquisite but would be gone after tonight.

She brushed the thought aside. There was no time for such feelings. First, Valentino must be dealt with. Then, Ivy for foolishly bringing such a threat to their world.

With a frustrated sigh, she closed the door to her quarters.

Children!

A few moments later, her driver pulled to a stop in front of *Enchanteé*. She walked into the store and waited for Madam Vivian to enter the shop area. Shortly, the woman appeared through the beaded curtain, a small vial in hand.

"This will take care of our arrogant violinist?"

Vivian raised an elegantly arched brow, "You doubt me, Selena?"

Selena smiled. "Not at all. In fact, I do believe I owe you."

"The priest paid you a visit, then?"

"That he did. Thank you."

"It was time, Selena. No one should carry around such guilt and be burdened for so long. Angelique would not have wanted that."

"You are right, Madam. As always," she reached out and enveloped the small woman in a hug, "Now, let me go deal with this situation."

"Yes, and come see me soon."

"I will, Madam. Thank you again." Selena slipped the small brown vial into her beaded evening bag.

"Remember, only a few drops. Any more than that will put him to sleep forever."

"I will show him mercy. For his family. And because the disappearance of a famous violinist in New Orleans could bring unwanted attention."

Vivian nodded, "A wise decision."

"Goodnight."

Resigned to her duty and the mess it would leave behind, Selena left the store. Her next stop was the Chateau Rouge for the masquerade.

The normal bawdiness of the Chateau Rouge was replaced with a quiet elegance as people arrived for the masquerade ball. The bordello was closed for the night, the only day it was closed to the general public. An unknowing mortal would never have a chance in a place filled with such bloodlust.

A man dressed in evening gear was waiting to take her hand and escort her from the car. Selena nodded to those she knew, vampires from all over the South. It was one of the two nights of the year they all gathered in one place. The other night being the ball on All Saint's Day, the day after Halloween, and that one was held elsewhere.

As Selena stepped into the lobby, her heart skipped a beat when she saw Claudio dressed in a freshly pressed tuxedo. His face was covered with a mask when he spotted her, but she could feel the passion beating from his heart. It was intoxicating. Had she been there for any other reason, she would have spirited him to a room on the fourth floor and taken her fill of his body and blood.

"*Signorina,*" he said in that European accent, and it made her body ache.

"Claudio," she whispered, her voice raspy with need.

He leaned down and placed a warm kiss on her cold cheek. She was distracted for a moment, but then reached into her purse for the vial Vivian had just given her. She pressed it into Claudio's hand.

"Take this. Add only a couple of drops to his drink. Do this, as I do not trust myself to not add more and end this completely."

He cupped it in his hand then slid it into his pocket. He nodded, "Thank you."

She trailed a finger along his jawline, "You may properly thank me later."

His eyes flared with desire. "I will do what I can."

He offered his arm and Selena tucked her gloved hand into the curve. As they walked through the lobby to the ballroom, she could feel Alcide watching them. She turned and looked at him, her eyes sharp. She would deal with him later as well. He had a hand in this too, letting Valentino into their midst and risking all of their safety.

"*Signorina?*" Claudio said as she stopped for a moment. She looked into his kind eyes.

If only Angelique had found such a man.

She exhaled a breath. "It is nothing. Shall we proceed?"

He smiled. "As you wish."

Selena leaned into him for a moment before addressing the reason they were there.

"We have work to do. I trust that you have contacted the nuns? With their healing herbs, they may be the only ones who could save him if the potion takes to his body too strongly."

"They are expecting us."

"If it were any other man, I would kill him and leave him for the alligators to eat in the bayou."

He patted the hand tucked into his elbow, "Thank you for your mercy."

Two white-gloved men opened the double doors as they approached the ballroom.

"So it goes, my priest. Are you ready?"

He leaned down and placed a tender kiss on her lips. "Yes, *signorina.* Are you?"

The ballroom was decked out in hues of white and silver. White fabric streamed from the ceiling to create a cloud-like effect. The tables were adorned with tall centerpieces that featured feathers trimmed with silver and each with a special masquerade mask. A single skeleton key, a Chateau Rouge trademark added to the décor. A band was on the stage playing a Viennese Waltz.

"Perhaps I may talk you into a dance before we foil Valentino's plan?" Claudio asked with an arched eyebrow.

A thrill went through her body as she thought of swaying in his arms to the beat of the music. Unable to speak, she nodded.

Selena stopped at several tables to greet people, some vampire, some human. The party had begun, as vampires and mortals reveled in their freedom. One young vamp had mortal women on both knees, taking turns feeding from each.

Ahhhh, the insatiable appetite of the young, Selena thought.

They reached the table already occupied by Ivy and Valentino. The black suited Valentino had one arm draped around Ivy's shoulder. He leaned in to trail kisses across the exposed skin from her low cut, white evening gown.

Claudio cleared his throat to gain his cousin's attention.

"*Cogino!*" he exclaimed, jumping up to embrace Claudio. When he approached Selena to do the same, she pasted on a smile and returned the hug, while inwardly shuddering under his kiss. The man was ridiculously forward.

Just one snap, and his neck would break. Just one. She looked to Claudio for patience.

He smiled at her, and like a giddy schoolgirl, she flushed and returned the grin. He pulled out the chair next to Ivy, seating her as far away from Valentino as possible and for that she was grateful. Whether it was out of consideration of her feelings or for the safety of his cousin, Selena did not know.

"I am excited that you are here to witness my glorious transformation!" Valentino held out a glass of champagne.

"Valentino, are you sure you want to do this?" Claudio asked.

"I get to spend eternity with this beautiful creature. I will never grow old. I will be just as handsome as I am at this moment for the whole world to enjoy for centuries to come!"

The band began a new song, a lively ragtime tune that had Valentino jumping out of his seat. "Come, Ivy, let's dance!" He grabbed her hand and led her to the dance floor.

"Now?" Claudio asked.

Selena nodded.

Claudio removed the vial from his pocket, and with a quick motion of his hand, allowed two droplets of the mysterious liquid to drip into Valentino's bubbling champagne.

He slipped the drug back into his jacket and made the sign of the cross. A prayer for luck? Guidance? A miracle?

When the song ended, the couple returned to the table. Flushed and overheated from the dance, Valentino grabbed his glass and finished it off.

Selena squeezed Claudio's hand under the table. Now, they only had to wait for the potion to work its magic on Valentino. It couldn't come quick enough. She took a sip of her own drink.

When the music shifted to another waltz, Claudio stood and offered his hand. "Shall we have that dance now?"

"I would love to."

He held her hand as she followed him to the dance floor then led her in a flowing movement of sensual grace. Selena took in every moment. The feel of his body against her, the smell of him, the way his heart sped up when she ran her hand along his back.

But tomorrow he will be gone.

Ever perceptive, he picked up on her sudden shift in mood. "What is it, Selena?"

"Tomorrow is coming too fast."

He pulled her even closer and time stood still as his lips moved against hers.

"We have this moment," his voice was ragged, hoarse. "Selena, I—"

"Valentino!" Whatever he was about to say was cut off by Ivy's scream.

The music stopped and a hiss sounded throughout the ballroom. Claudio and Selena rushed for the table.

Valentino lay crumbled on the floor unconscious, a gash on his head. Surrounding him were several young vampires, teeth bared, Ivy moved to protect him, her own eyes red with hunger. Valentino's blood was staining her pristine white dress.

"He just stood up," she panted. "He fell. Please, Selena. I don't know what's wrong! He only had a few drinks! You have to get him out of here!"

Claudio moved swiftly, gathering his cousin in his arms. He was quickly surrounded by a pack of young, hungry vampires. Their low growls were echoing throughout the room.

Selena pushed through the crowd, tugging on Claudio's coat, "Come with me!"

Selena led them to the back of the ballroom, to the service hallway. She closed the door, locked it, then leaned her body weight against it. Even through the heavy wood, she could hear the frustrated howls of the hungry.

It was then she spotted the small quiet, Anisette, a blind girl Josey had taken in when she'd been orphaned. She was always exploring the hotel and knew every nook and cranny of the building.

"Anisette! Lead Father Claudio out the back way of the hotel. Then, take him to the nuns. I will pay you handsomely upon your return."

The girl nodded and held out her hand to Claudio, who stood breathing heavily, his cousin and his ever-present flaws a heavy burden.

He took one last look at Selena, as if there was something he wanted to say.

"Go, Claudio. Be safe."

He nodded and said softly, "*Signorina.*" Then he followed Anisette down the hallway.

When she was sure Claudio was safe, she unlocked the door and stepped back into the ballroom. She nodded at Alcide who had stood guard at the door. She addressed the crowd of vampires. "It's all over. Go get yourselves together."

She watched as their eyes returned to their normal colors, breathing slowed, and fangs disappeared.

She went to see about Ivy who still lay on the ground. Blood tears ran down her cheek as she sobbed Valentino's name.

"Valentino De Fiore will not be returning to the Chateau Rouge. His cousin has taken him away. We will discuss this further tomorrow."

This only served to make Ivy cry even harder, her body shaking. Selena leaned down and tucked a strand of hair behind her ear.

"Alcide!" Selena called, the big man by her side in moments, "Please take Ivy up to her room. See that one of the other girls stays with her. She will have a difficult time tonight."

He nodded and cradled Ivy in his arms, carrying her out of the ballroom.

Selena watched them leave through the same doors Claudio had taken Valentino. It was then that she finally allowed the tears to trail down her own cheeks.

***

Twenty-four hours after Claudio rescued Valentino from the masquerade, he still lay unconscious on the narrow cot within the infirmary at the Ursuline Convent. Surrounded by candles, crucifixes, and a strange mix of fragrant herbs, his cousin looked peaceful in his repose though the priest was uneasy. He trusted Selena and Madame Vivian not to murder Valentino, but the use of magic was not ideal. And he had been the one to administer it.

It was the only way to free him from himself.

He had repeated that to himself all day to no avail. It was time to move beyond the suffocating weight of passivity. Standing from the simple cane chair at the foot of the bed, Claudio stopped beside the young nun currently praying over his cousin. Laying a hand on her shoulder, he waited for her prayers to cease.

"Sister Sarah, please tell Reverend Mother I've gone to the cathedral to pray. Have word sent if there is any change before I return."

"Yes, Father De Fiore."

He crossed the room, and paused just outside the door. Looking over his shoulder, he watched the nun place a tentative hand on Valentino's cheek in a caressing motion.

"Sister, you are relieved from your post!"

She jumped to her feet, wide brown eyes filling with tears.

"At once, Sister."

"Father, I—"

He took her hands into his own. Knowing she felt enough guilt, he softened his tone. "You are fatigued. Send Sister Agatha for the next watch. I will stay until she arrives. And be sure to spend time on your knees for yourself tonight, Sister Sarah."

"Yes, Father De Fiore."

"Have faith." Claudio blessed her before she departed.

As soon as the elderly nun arrived, Claudio exited the building into the crisp, midnight air. He passed the Ursuline chapel, crossing the courtyard to the guarded gate. With a humble bow, the gatekeeper opened the spiked fence and Claudio strode onto Chartres Street with one hand gripped around his rosary.

Cassock billowing about his legs, he made his way down the cobblestones to avoid the drunken pedestrians on the banquette, but rather dodged piles of horse dung and smelly puddles for three blocks instead.

As soon as he was through the heavy doors of St. Louis Cathedral, he crossed himself and whispered a prayer in his native tongue. After lighting a candle for Valentino and a second for Selena, he made his way down the silent nave. His hands trailed the rounded edges of the pews as his eyes looked heavenward. The arched ceiling reminded him of The Cathedral of the Immaculate Conception in Mobile, and he smiled to think of his friends there.

"Sanctus. Sanctus. Sanctus," he whispered as he approached the altar. *"Dominus. Deus. Sabaoth."*

Rather than entering the holiest of spaces, he knelt on the steps and clasped his hands in supplication and pled for forgiveness in harming his cousin.

"Help him heal, O Lord. Allow the punishment to be mine for tampering with unholy magic in order to save my cousin from a greater sin."

Twenty minutes? Thirty? Claudio did not know how long he prayed, but his legs were unable to support him once he was done. He fell prostrate onto the altar floor, arms outstretched in complete surrender.

When he at last stood, he did so as a humble servant. Crossing himself, he whispered a final covenant. "In the name of the Father, the Son, and the Holy Ghost, I will always help those you place in my path. Thy will be done—no matter the cost."

As though the city went to sleep while he prayed, Claudio journeyed toward the convent on the deserted banquette with a pace to match the stillness of the night. Two blocks away, a lone figure cloaked in a purple cape stood beneath a gas lamp.

Selena's blond hair shone bright with the yellow illumination. "I thought I'd never see you again."

Smiling, he cupped her cheeks, his olive skin dark against her lily whiteness in the shadowed street. "I will come to you whenever you need me, *signorina*, but Valentino still sleeps. I will not leave town until he awakens."

"Then I shall pray he sleeps through one more night."

He rested his forehead on hers and absorbed the carnal sensation of her breathing him in. "Do you need me, Selena?"

She shifted closer, teeth scraping his chin. "You are a gift from God, Claudio. I need to taste your benevolence once more."

Holding hands, she steered him around the next block and down an alley. Opening a wooden gate, she brought them into a courtyard lush with evergreen bushes. Selena's intent face and the tinkling of a fountain were all Claudio registered until he felt the damp bricks against the back of his cassock. Selena's hands on his shoulders pinned him to the wall.

Claudio unfastened his collar and spread his arms in an imitation of his prone position on the alter floor. "Partake of your sacrament and know that God loves you."

"And the man, Priest?"

"You are in my heart, Selena. I will see to your needs tonight."

"All of them?" She licked his throat and opened more buttons.

"*Sí*, all of them."

Claudio's silent smile twisted into a moan of pleasure as the fangs pierced his neck. Unlike the other times, Selena didn't allow him to float into a sated lull. His body was kept alert to everything—the feel of the cold silk of her dress, her open mouth beneath his jaw, and the loosening of his vestments. Claudio knew life would never be the same, but he mentally thanked Valentino for bringing him to New Orleans. Selena needed him as much as his cousin did. And no matter what she took from him, to Claudio it felt the farthest thing from a sacrifice.

~~~
~~~

"Natural Selection in Life and Love"

A Malevolent Trilogy/Washington Square Secrets/Possession Chronicles Short

Sean Spunner removed his hat as he entered the Davenports' foyer on the first Friday in December, 1912. Welcomed by the party's hostess, he smiled at the attractive redhead and bowed over her extended arm to kiss her hand.

"Thank you for the invitation, Mrs. Davenport."

"You're most welcome, but please call me Melissa. I've been with Freddy over half a year. We can dispense with formalities."

"In that case…." Sean's hand slid to her elbow and he kissed her cheek. "You look ravishing in that peacock gown, Melissa."

"I am glad you're here, Sean." She smiled and placed his hat on the credenza. "There's a friend of mine I want—"

"Spunner!" Chuck Brady hollered.

Sean looked from Melissa to the younger man making his way through the crowded hall. He stepped to the side to greet Chuck, bracing for the hefty thump he knew would come from the heavyweight boxer. Not a weakling himself in his middleweight division, Sean held his own with his average height and toned physique. Chuck, on the other hand, flashed his stature and strength with youthful exuberance as he clapped Sean on the back so hard he would have stumbled into Melissa if he hadn't taken a solid stance.

"Spunner, my Rachel's got a cousin in town for Christmas and wants to introduce you. She's a cute girl."

Sean pressed his lips together, trying to think what to say to get out of the matchmaking scheme. He had no interest in a woman labeled "cute". At thirty-two, he craved maturity and substance. An ample bust wouldn't hurt things either.

Melissa stepped between the friends. "I'm sorry, Chuck, but I counted on Sean to help with one of my friends tonight. I'm sure Rachel's cousin would be better-suited to one of the men closer to your own age."

Chuck's laughter blurted through the din of chatter. "Davenport got himself a fine one, didn't he? I'll leave you to the aging population, Spunner. If you decide to flirt with a lady without a cane, let me know."

Melissa's warm brown eyes followed Chuck's retreating form before looking back at Sean. "I hope I didn't overstep my role as hostess."

"Not at all. Thank you for saving me."

"I welcomed Rachel and her cousin when they arrived with Chuck." She tucked her arm through the crook of Sean's. "The young woman is pleasant, but based on what I know of you, she wouldn't be to your liking."

"We've only met a dozen times, Melissa."

"But we've talked at length at the last two parties and I'm a keen observer. Investigating people goes hand in hand with being a travel writer."

Intrigued, he led her into the nearby dining room where the furniture had been set aside and the gramophone played lively tunes. He settled beside Melissa in chairs lining the wall, doing his best not to look at Henry and Darla Adams as they Turkey Trotted across the hardwood floor.

"And what do you believe about my preference in women? For all you know, I could be happily set in my bachelorhood."

"You never pay any attention to the twittering ladies who flock to contestants after a tournament, you seem more than impressed with the Adamses relationship, and I learned you were once engaged last decade. The young woman you were pledged to shared several likenesses with Darla Adams, but I think it goes beyond her looks. Darla is mature for her age—a career woman. You admire that over the flounces of the females your younger friends surround themselves with. You want a woman with a strong mind that will challenge you in the evenings, not to mention a solid figure to keep you satisfied in bed."

Sean laughed. "Are all New Yorkers as outspoken as you?"

"I know how to speak my mind without worrying about offending Southern sensibilities, if that's what you mean. But it's not just New Yorkers."

"Davenport is a lucky man."

"I'm glad so many came tonight. Freddy loves parties."

"I've never seen him happier than he has been since you came to Mobile. Where is he?"

"In the parlor, last I saw. Now about my friend—"

"I'd like to give my thanks to the host before being paired off." Sean squeezed her hand and stood. "I *am* looking for a match, Melissa, but I won't settle for anything less than what Frederick found in you."

He stopped at the credenza and helped himself to a tumbler of whisky before making his way to the parlor. All the Davenports' friends were there save one couple—the Mellings—but Frederick's ex-wife and her husband were probably watching his daughters while he and Melissa hosted the party to kick off the month of Christmas.

Sean slung back his glass and refilled it before scanning the crowded parlor for Frederick. Edmund Easton and Thomas Charles were across the room. Both were boxers and former Mystics of Dardenne brothers, but had settled into married life well enough. After his first months back at the gym, Edmund appeared to have thrown off his whoring habit, but maybe it was more of reduced circumstances than a complete turnaround. His roaming eyes settled on anything with shapely proportions, even with his wife standing two feet away.

Frederick Davenport was with a group Sean knew by sight—a few newspaper reporters and shopkeepers. All their attentions were upon a woman that a reporter's shoulder blocked all but the top of a brunette chignon from Sean's view.

"Marie Curie sharing the Nobel Prize in Chemistry must be seen for what it is—an advancement for women in science. We've come too far in recent years to allow men to shove us back into Victorian parlors and petticoats." The voice was soft but firm and very much Yankee, though not like Melissa's New York accent.

"Well stated, Ms. Fernsby," Mademoiselle Bisset said. The robust form of the French dress shop owner turned to Frederick. "Mr. Davenport, pray excuse me, but I must find your wife. I heard she's in a most exquisite gown that did not come from my store."

Frederick laughed. "I hope to speak with you again before you leave, Mademoiselle."

Sean stepped into the vacated space to see who captivated the group. Though petite in height, the outspoken woman was curvaceous in all the right places. Fresh faced but mature, Sean assessed her to be in her mid-twenties. She wore not a flashy gown like the society wives in attendance but rather a functional azure dress. The buttons down the side of her bust further drew his attention to her shapeliness, but it was her arresting sky blue eyes as they narrowed at him over her glass of eggnog that he focused on.

"Spunner, you made it!" Frederick shook Sean's hand and motioned around the circle. "I think you're acquainted with everyone except Mobile's newest resident, Ms. Fernsby. She began teaching Science at the Girls' High School this fall. Ms. Fernsby, Sean Spunner with Finnigan and Spunner Law Firm."

She smiled up at him and offered her hand. "Hello, Mr. Spunner."

"Welcome to Mobile, Ms. Fernsby." He kissed the back of her hand.

She withdrew, frowning. "I'm afraid I'll never get used to the liberties Southern men take in the name of chivalry. I offer my hand as an equal and expect it to be embraced as one. Any lips on my skin are to be there by direct invitation only."

Sean reddened and the others chuckled.

"And how many men have been lucky enough for that invitation, Ms. Fernsby?" the reporter asked.

She offered a sardonic smile. "More than you need to worry about, Mr. Powell. Please excuse me."

The other men watched her walk away with amused grins, but Sean wasn't ready to lose her company.

"Ms. Fernsby, I beg your pardon."

She turned to him in the hall, the blue of her dress brightening her almond-shaped eyes under the electric light. "Yes, Mr. Spunner?"

"Forgive my unfamiliar manners. I assure you I meant no offense."

"But offense was taken. As a lawyer, surely you respect that actions have consequences and justice must be served by those victimized." Her impertinent chin lifted.

Sean managed to keep his mirth to a slight curl of his lips. "And what can I do for the scales of justice to be leveled between us once more, Ms. Fernsby?"

"Prove you can be a gentleman without taking advantage by dancing with me." Her sly smile cut almost as deep as her sharp tongue—and he craved more.

***

Hattie Fernsby couldn't help but tease the man Melissa praised. Happy to have found him before an awkward introduction could be orchestrated, Hattie relished the control it gave her over the presumed match by her friend. Melissa often spoke of Sean's quick wit and she eagerly tested it.

Sean bowed, golden eyes mischievous under his wave of brown hair. "Ms. Fernsby, would you do me the honor of sharing a dance?"

"You may have *one*, Mr. Spunner but I'm afraid you'll need to wait until a traditional tune is played. I don't Turkey Trot or know any of the new dances," she admitted as Darla and Henry Adams pranced across the room.

Sean smirked as he looked down at her from his half-foot advantage. "That's rather depressing, Ms. Fernsby. A modern woman should be well-versed in the newest dances, especially when females are losing their jobs for doing them in public dance halls during their time off while their male partners suffer no consequences. That's not fair, is it? Where is *their* justice?"

"I'm surprised a man like you takes notice of the lack of freedom women have."

"I assure you I am *very* interested in women, though only one at present."

Hattie bit back a smile as a new song with a Latin beat began.

"Your dance education begins now, Ms. Fernsby. Follow my lead and keep moving." Sean took her right hand and his other went snug around her waist as the length of his firm body pressed against her front.

A gasp escaped Hattie as the sensual dance began and she looked away from Sean's smug grin. The host and hostess entered the room and the Adamses were shown up by the Davenports' tango.

"With a bit more practice, you'll be gliding as easily as Melissa, Ms. Fernsby."

Hattie stumbled and Sean pulled her even closer, her chin jutting into his chest. Over his broad shoulder, she caught Melissa's gaze, who flashed a smile of encouragement. Soon the dizzying tune stopped and an old-fashioned waltz began.

"You survived the first lesson, Ms. Fernsby. Would you honor me with this next dance as well?"

She took a half step back and nodded.

He settled into a stance for the waltz. At ease with the familiar pattern, Hattie relaxed enough to recognize Sean's elegant moves. Remembering Melissa told her Sean was a friend from Freddy's gym, she understood he needed to be light on his feet in the boxing ring. Curious to the state of his form beneath his suit, Hattie's left hand roamed from his shoulder to feel the thickness of his biceps.

"Why, Ms. Fernsby, I'm offended." Sean brought them to a halt amid the other couples. "I did not ask you to dance to be groped."

Caught off-guard, her face heated as the other dancers had to alter their course to prevent bumping into them. "I meant no harm."

"Still, an offense was made. You owe me restitution." His mouth was set in a sensual pout but his eyes were merry.

Playing his game of revenge, she looked up at him with a humble countenance. "What may I do to set things right?"

"Come to the porch with me."

Happy to escape the curious stares of those in attendance, she hooked her arm through his. "Lead the way, Mr. Spunner."

"Please, call me Sean."

"All right, Sean."

His triumphant smile served to make him look younger than what Melissa informed her was his age of thirty-two. A six year difference wasn't too much. It could even be said it was the perfect difference between a male and female as men matured slower.

On the porch, Sean saw her seated on the bench swing before taking the other end. He tilted toward her to converse easier over the dance music coming from the open window.

"Now, Ms. Fernsby, I—"

"You may call me Hattie if I'm to call you Sean."

"Miss Hattie, no matter where things go from here, you have brightened my evening."

"After I called you out for kissing my hand?"

"Especially for that. Not to mention your suggestive touch while we danced. I'm happy to settle your curiosity." He made quick work of the buttons on his jacket, slipped it off, and held his shirtsleeve to her. "Touch all you want."

"*This* is your restitution? For me to do what you found so offensive?"

"Only if yours is the same." He winked.

"I merely wished to feel if you were muscular. There appears to be a large ratio of boxers to businessmen here."

"But many are both, Hattie. Boxing is a great hobby. Use your scientific powers to deduce how strong it keeps me." He lifted her right hand onto his arm. "Explore away."

Never had a man been so forthright. Usually a line or two was exchanged, and then the man moved along to a woman who offered more of a physical show. "But then you will expect to kiss—"

"No, though I hope you will request my lips pay a return visit to your delectable skin at some point in the future. What is your scientific guess for that happening?"

His eyes gleamed in the shadowed porch light like the purest amber, playful as a cat.

She spread her fingers around the thickness of his forearm before traveling over his elbow and biceps. "The data is showing favorably for you."

"Was that before or after you felt my muscles?"

"Before." Hattie managed to speak as her laughter quieted and she clasped her hands in her lap. "Your company is refreshing."

"And you, besides pricking my soul with your cleverness, are the first woman to touch me like that since…." They stared at each other, a soft smile on his lips that Hattie felt reflected on her own. "I'm afraid I need to return to the party. Our lovely hostess wanted to introduce me to a friend of hers, hoping I'd entertain her. A great loss for me because no one can be as good company as you, Hattie."

"Unless Melissa double booked your companionship for the party, you may stay here. She's been talking you up to me for weeks and was pleased to finally introduce me to you tonight, though Freddy unknowingly took that honor."

Sean crossed his arms. "You've had the advantage over me from the beginning, haven't you?"

"It appears that way." Her smile brought his back around. "But you should be pleased to know you've kept up with me like no man before."

"Are you keeping score?"

"Always. Men interest me very much, though only one at present."

Sean's chipped-tooth grin was infectious. "I could spend weeks like this and never tire. Tell me of yourself, Hattie. Where did you move from and why?"

"Boston, born and raised. I needed a change of pace after my mother died. My father's family has been in Boston for generations, but my mother's parents were Irish immigrants during the famine."

"My mother's family was Irish. I was raised by uncle and aunt after my parents died. All of us our Catholic, and you?"

"Baptized, but not much of anything these days. It's been nearly a decade since I've attended Mass." Noticing the downturn of his mouth, she pounced. "Don't tell me a sharp-witted lawyer like yourself attends regular Mass and confession."

"I try for Mass at least bi-weekly—even when I was a scoundrel—and need confession as much as the next man."

"Or woman." She raised a challenging brow. "I would have loved to have crossed paths with you in your scoundrel days."

"Those times are far in the past, though a sharp woman like you brings it all back to me." His face softened as memories clouded his vision.

Hattie laid a hand on his knee. "What was her name?"

"Eliza," he whispered without pause. "Next month will be seven years since she died."

Hattie noticed the moisture glistening in the corner of his eyes and squeezed his knee. "Melissa told me you were once engaged. I would love to hear about her if you want to talk."

"She was the Fourth of July, Mardi Gras, and New Year's in one explosive package—all reckless passion and fantastic dreams." Sean gave a dry laugh. "I thought my experience over her eighteen years readied me for her, but Eliza Melling bled me dry. I gave her everything within my power, but it wasn't enough."

***

Sean closed his eyes, embarrassed to look upon Hattie after spilling his heartache in the first hour of their acquaintance. He rarely spoke of Eliza. Why would he break that silence with someone he just met?

Within the Davenports' house, a ragtime tune poured from the dining room window. Hattie's warm hand remained on his knee, a friendly gesture—bold and comforting.

"Forgive my reminiscing. I'm sure you would rather be with your friends. Allow me to escort you inside." Sean shifted to stand.

Hattie tightened her hand on his leg. "Yet more chivalrous ideals from a Southern gentleman. I assure you, Sean, when I want to return inside, I will—with or without you."

There was something about her—the smallness of her stature and the clarity in her blue eyes coupled with the elvish smile—that created the illusion of frailty. Sean's instinct was to protect her, but he knew she would resent him for attempting anything.

Sean placed a hand over hers. "I'm glad to hear that, Hattie. Your company is most enjoyable."

Smiling, she released her hold on his knee and turned to clasp her fingers through his. "Do you mind?"

"Not at all." He stroked her dainty wrist with his thumb.

Hattie shifted closer, allowing their hands to settle between them on the swing. "Thank you for bringing me out here. It's much easier to talk."

"And my thanks to you for accepting an invitation to join me in a secluded location."

"Will my reputation be sullied?"

"You will not be gossiped over for this rendezvous. I've been known as an old wallflower for years."

"Good." She sighed. "I can't afford to lose my job. I used most of my savings to relocate and don't wish to return to my father or beg one of my brothers for a place in their households while I scrounge for work. Teaching jobs in Boston are scarce. There are too many teachers and not enough classrooms, especially for science."

He gave her hand a gentle squeeze. "Why science and not literature or history or—"

"Something more suitable for a woman?"

"Don't put words in my mouth, Hattie." *I'd rather have something else in there.*

As though she heard his thought, she blushed. "I've been fascinated by the natural world since childhood. I was not welcomed to play with my brothers and spent hours observing any wildlife I could find. Things like how wind affected water, the subtle changing of the shadows, and nature in general, but no one took my questions seriously. Girls shouldn't be dismissed for their curiosity."

"Your ideals are admirable, your search for justice commendable."

"And how were you as a child? Did you bar girls from playing boys' games?"

"I welcomed them. Both at home with my cousin and during events at this house. The Eastons lived here back then—all ten of the children. Davenport was a close friend to one of the middle sons. They hosted the best battles in the yard. Come see!" He stood and drew Hattie after him, hurrying down the front steps and across the lawn to the base of a live oak. "Can you make out the board between those branches?"

"Yes."

"Sometimes the Easton sisters would play with us—Lucy most often. Whoever it was became a scout. I always made sure she climbed up first so I could see her knickers."

"Why you little cad!" Hattie dropped his hand.

Sean laughed. "I told you I was a scoundrel, but I wish I could say that was the worst of my infractions."

"Tell me the worst," she whispered.

"I was a member of Mystics of Dardenne for seven years," he trustingly declared.

"And what's that?"

"The most notorious Mardi Gras society—secret, of course. All bachelors with too much money, alcohol, and drugs but little in the way of common sense or decency."

"Scandal for the scoundrel?"

"I never got caught and confessed every vice at each opportunity."

She stepped before him, her buxom chest nearly brushing his middle. "And what would you do to me if we were alone like this a decade ago?"

"Are you welcoming my lips?"

Before she could fully nod, he cupped her face with a hand while the other reached around her back to steady her as he pressed in. He felt her smile and trailed his hand from her jaw to neck. Whether he was on his second or third kiss, Sean didn't know. It all blended into a heady rush of desire he hadn't felt in years. Her lips brazenly parted with a welcoming flick of her tongue. Hands trailing her back, he tried not to devour the deliciousness of her rum-infused mouth.

Hattie was right there with him as he brought them into the shadow of the oak, lowering her to his lap on a wrought iron bench. He continued to caress her as their heaving breaths mingled while they tasted each other.

The front screen door snapped shut and they broke their kiss.

"I thought Spunner was out here," Chuck bellowed.

"Try the kitchen!" another voice replied. The door slammed again.

Hattie kissed Sean once more before standing. "You've proven to be no wallflower, Sean."

He put an arm about her waist, gently tugging her against him. "I'm sorry if I went too far."

Hattie fingered his lips and smiled. "Never. I just can't be caught in a compromising situation. Against my better judgement, I pledged a code of conduct for my personal life when I signed on with the Girls' High School. I need this job."

"There aren't any school officials at the party." He accompanied her across the lawn.

"I've learned this city loves gossip. I like you, Sean, but I have to be careful." She stopped at the front door and turned to him. Sean did his best to memorize the tender look on her countenance. "Please stay with me the rest of the evening. Give me as many dance lessons as you'd like, but keep me out of dark corners. Will you do that for me?"

"I'll do anything you ask, Hattie."

***

A week later, Hattie sat at her school desk during lunch and nibbled a sandwich. A crisp breeze blew through the open window, nothing like the cold in Boston that time of year. She was alone by choice because she needed silence to better recall the magnificent hours she'd spent with Sean the Friday before. They had danced and talked until they were the last guests, then took a final cup of eggnog with the Davenports. She had informed Sean she would contact him, but she'd kept silent all week. Having lost her head over a man before, she couldn't risk that with her job in the balance. It was best to stick with daydreams when it came to Sean Spunner and his delectable lips.

On Sunday, she almost went to the Cathedral of the Immaculate Conception for late Mass. Not keen on revisiting the rituals of her youth when all she wanted was a glimpse of the man, she instead telephoned Melissa and they took a meandering stroll along the bay.

Another week passed much the same as the previous— dreaming about Sean whenever she wasn't teaching.

On Thursday, December 19, Hattie readied for her final class of the day. The students filed in and took their seats. She barely had a decade on her students age-wise, but Hattie took charge and lifted a shoebox of fossils she brought from home.

"Ladies, I have a special treat for you today. As I stop by your seat, reach your hand in and retrieve one of the items nestled in the cotton padding. I want you to quietly study your specimen and record as much about it as possible in your journal—size, shape, texture, and so on. All the scientific data you can muster from an observation. Then everyone will report to the class what they have in their possession before you exchange them among yourselves to see the variations."

"Oh, Ms. Fernsby!" The curly haired brunette in the front row clutched her fossilized shell to her chest. "It's a—"

"Please hold your enthusiasm, Rosella. Take notes and there will be time to talk later."

With all fourteen girls on task, Hattie settled at her desk with a shark tooth in her palm. She ran her thumb across the serrated edge while thinking of Sean's chipped tooth that had heightened their playful kissing session. Few things in life brought her greater joy than giving her students what she was denied—an authority figure who loved science and believed each student was capable of success with the subject—but Sean's attentions were high on her list as well.

When observation time was over, Rosella begged to go first. She spiritedly shared information about the fossilized spiral mollusk. Twenty minutes later, the students completed sharing about shells, conifer cones, and shark teeth. Then Hattie reminded them about their lesson from the day before about how fossils were formed before sharing the history of the specimens.

"I collected these when I was your age. My family used to camp on Martha's Vineyard each summer. We'd travel all over the island, but my favorite part was Gay Head. It has the most beautiful clay cliffs and aqua water, not to mention a plethora of fossils."

"Aren't fossils what led Charles Darwin to believe in evolution?" Rosella's dark eyes shone.

Surprised that some her age would know about the controversial figure, Hattie smiled. "You're exactly right, Rosella. Darwin studied fossils, rocks, plants, and animal samples that he collected during his global journey on the HMS Beagle when he was only twenty-two—younger than me."

"Who's Charles Darwin?" another asked.

"He was a famous British naturalist during the previous century. His scientific studies led him to believe in evolution of species—that nature causes plants and animals to adapt to the world, that only the strongest survive. Natural selection."

"He thought humans evolved from monkeys," Rosella declared.

A few girls giggled but more gasped. Then the whispers began.

"That's blasphemy!"

"My brother looks like a monkey."

"God created man—my Sunday School teacher says so."

"Please settle down." Hattie stood silent until the room quieted. "Charles Darwin had his opinions, as we are all entitled, but now is not the proper forum to debate the merits of his theory. Be sure to finish reading the chapter on sediments tonight. I look forward to showing you my second collection tomorrow. Please return the specimens on your way out, ladies."

Rosella stood by Hattie's desk, looking over each item as it was added to the box. "Thank you for showing them to us, Ms. Fernsby."

"Stay after a moment, if you can."

"Yes, Ma'am."

As the last student filed out, Hattie motioned to the opened box. "Pick one to keep, Rosella. I know you will take good care of it. I want you to have something to remind you about discovery."

Rosella smiled and bent over the open container. "You're the best teacher, Ms. Fernsby. I can't talk about Darwin's theories with anyone at home."

"Or in class, I'm afraid." Hattie sat in her chair behind the desk. "Darwin's concepts have the potential for trouble."

Rosella looked up. "I'm sorry."

"Don't be. Whenever you wish to talk about evolution or anything else, take lunch in here or stay after class. I'm happy to discuss topics beyond our textbook with willing students."

"I'll remember that." She pulled the mollusk shell from the box and cradled it in her hand. "I'd like the one I chose. Thank you, Ms. Fernsby."

"I'll see you tomorrow, Rosella."

Hattie closed the box and collected her coat. Crossing Government Street, she walked south until she reached the boarding house on the far end of a residential area. She switched out the fossils in the box with ones from her display case, preparing for the next day's lesson before settling with a book about the Amazon while waiting for the dinner bell.

The supper table was usually interesting with the mix of the house's inhabitants—teachers, sailors, and sales clerks. On any given night, there were as many as a dozen souls around the table, including the landlord couple, Mr. and Mrs. Grimes. That evening, there were only five: two other female lodgers who occupied the first floor rooms next to Hattie and the owners. Not wanting to be lumped into spinsterhood with the aging teachers across from her, Hattie made up her mind to telephone Sean after school the next day.

"Thank you for another good meal, but I'll be taking supper out tomorrow, Mrs. Grimes," she said after dessert.

"Another party invitation, Ms. Fernsby?"

"No, I am ringing up an acquaintance."

"Remember the rules, dear. You were out much too late the other week, though the Davenports are respectable. Take special care of who you associate with."

Rules.

Codes of conduct.

I'm a grown woman in charge of my own destiny!

"Yes, Mrs. Grimes."

After a restless night, Hattie buttoned on her nicest blue linen day dress and donned her gray capelet. She journeyed through the chill morning to Barton Academy with her box of fossils. Pleased with the thought of finally talking to Sean, she hummed the tune that had played when he taught her to Turkey Trot, hoping he wouldn't be sore over her prolonged silence.

As soon as she was through the front doors, her name was called.

The secretary stood in front of the office. "Mr. Gentry needs to speak with you."

"Allow me to place my things in the classroom and—"

"He said it was urgent, Ms. Fernsby."

Hattie sighed and knocked on Mr. Gentry's door. She balanced her things in one arm as she turned the knob at his sharp call of "Enter!"

"Ms. Fernsby, have a seat."

Not a fan of the man who over saw both the girls' and boys' higher education, she managed a tight-lipped smile and carefully sat in the chair before his desk.

He met her gaze with brown eyes hooded by fuzzy eyebrows. "Ms. Fernsby, you have been released from your contract with the school. You can pack your bags and head north because I doubt any school in the state of Alabama will hire you after your outrageous behavior."

"I don't understand. What have I been accused of, Mr. Gentry?"

"Accused? No, there are more than enough witnesses to prove it happened. You may return after the close of the school day to remove your personal items from the classroom, but you must leave the property before students arrive."

"What is it people say I did?"

"You taught about evolution in your final class yesterday, Ms. Fernsby. Darwinism is not allowed in our schools, as you well know. Three of your students went home and spoke of this progressive education you are forcing on their impressionable minds and I fielded telephone calls all evening from angry fathers. I thought the first must have been mistaken, but after the others, I had no choice but to promise your expulsion from the school system."

"I didn't teach evolution, Mr. Gentry. One of the girls brought up Charles Darwin an—"

"There is no referencing that man under this roof! Now please leave, Ms. Fernsby. Do not return until after four o'clock or I will call the police."

Hattie strode from the room with her chin up. Numb with the encroaching weight of her predicament, she headed for the only place she could think of.

***

"Mr. Spunner, there's a woman here to see you." Ms. Keller said from his open doorway.

Sean looked up from his morning coffee and half-read newspaper. After seeing his secretary without glasses for over a year, Sean had to admit the new specs somehow improved her appearance—correcting the unfortunate squint that had marred her otherwise unremarkable face. "Does she have an appointment?"

"No, but she looks distraught. I think she might be in trouble."

Disappointed his lazy Friday was interrupted, Sean's second thought was maybe it would quicken the passing of time that had all but came to a stop two weeks before. "Send her in."

"Yes, sir."

Sean stood from his padded chair behind the mahogany desk, buttoned his suit jacket closed, and made sure his tie was straight. As he crossed his office, a burdened Hattie accompanied the secretary into the room.

"The door, Ms. Keller," he snapped in his eagerness.

His secretary closed it when she left. Before questioning Hattie's worried countenance, he swept her box and bags onto the nearest chair. Then he took her in an embrace that squeezed the breath from her.

"Hattie, dearest! I was beginning to think you came to your senses about me and I'd never see you again." He kissed her forehead. "But the concern on your face shows you're here for help."

"I'm sorry for not telephoning. Over supper last night, I made up my mind to do just that after school today."

"There's nothing to forgive now that you're here." He lifted her chin and planted a kiss on her lips. Seeing the unease in her typically glittering eyes, he smiled. "Now quit being a stoic feminist and tell me your troubles so I can help."

Sean saw the flash of annoyance before she began crying. Arm about her, he led her to the leather sofa along the far wall where he sat close and rubbed her back.

"Hattie, you're safe here." He leaned his head to hers, inhaling the marvelous scent of soap and woman as he nuzzled against her neck. Coming to his senses, he removed a handkerchief from his pocket.

She accepted Sean's offering and wiped her nose. "It's already too late. I've lost my job."

Hattie's sobs returned. Sean's first thought was no more blasted code of conduct. He wanted to show her how he felt about her without fear of repercussion, but settled on offering a sympathetic ear.

"Start from the beginning and tell me what happened."

"There's no point. I'll still be out of work."

"Hattie, dearest. Look at my office. I can't furnish an establishment like this without being a successful lawyer. I may have been a scoundrel in my youth, but I brought my uncle's firm out of obscurity the past few years. I'm well versed in the law and backroom deals. If there's a loophole in what happened to you, I'll find it."

She sniffed and her gaze lingered on the carved trim of the shelves lining the opposite wall, the collection of law books that filled them. The Turkish rug met her stare next as she fingered the soft leather of the sofa's arm beside her.

"Why on earth are you interested in me, Sean? You should be with society's elite, not a teacher living in a boarding house."

"Because you're the most extraordinary woman I've ever met. Yes, I loved two others before you, but they were girls. You, Hattie Fernsby, have gained my fondness for the woman you are. I haven't stopped thinking of you since the party. The only reason I didn't rush to you the next day was because you asked me to wait for your outreach. You've tortured me severely, but you haven't lost my affection in our days apart."

A blush covered her cheeks and she smiled so that it reached her eyes a moment. "I've also thought of you every day, but it will do no good with me being forced to leave town."

"Have faith in me, dearest, and tell me everything."

Her chest heaved with a sigh. "Mr. Gentry wouldn't listen to my story, he only spouted off what he'd heard and dismissed me, saying he would call the police if I returned before the students went home."

"Don't tell me he found out about our time at Freddy's house?"

"Worse."

"What is worse than a code of conduct breach?"

"Charles Darwin." She narrowed her eyes. "And if you have the nerve to ask if I'd been kissing him, I'll call off every daydream I've had about you."

Sean laughed. "Kissing a corpse? Do think better of me than that. Darwin has been dead decades now. I may not be a scientist, but I am well-read. You must know it's against the law to teach Darwinism."

"Yes, and I didn't. I brought in a box of fossils I've collected to go along with the lessons in the textbook on sediment and fossil formation. Rosella, my brightest student, mentioned Darwin collected fossils and the others wanted to know who he was. I briefly explained how he got his start as a naturalist and the most basic of his theories so the others had a point of reference. Nothing more. I even held Rosella back after class and let her know we could not discuss Darwin or his theories in class and she apologized. But apparently a few girls mentioned to their families what was said and their fathers telephoned Principal Gentry. He promised them I would be dismissed from the school system."

"Franklin Gentry?" Hattie nodded and he laughed. "Leave it to me."

"How?" She asked as they stood.

"Loopholes, Hattie, and you're coming with me. But first, I need to do something before you're officially under a code of conduct clause again."

Sean took her in his arms, gazing down at her for a signal of acceptance. Her eyes widened, bright blue above her rosy cheeks before nodding. Caressing her back, his hands roamed to her hips as he leaned down to meet her enchanting mouth with a deep kiss. Hattie fervently returned the attention and he lowered her to the sofa, a knee next to her middle and an arm braced on the cushion beside her head.

He tasted her lips and kissed the swell of a glorious breast atop her dress. "It's been so long," he breathed the words.

"For me as well," she whispered, holding his gaze without embarrassment as though she tested his reaction. "It was one man, several years ago."

"I don't need names or dates. You in my arms right now is enough."

"I better be the only woman you've laid down in this office. I wouldn't be able to sleep at night knowing this was a habit for you."

"You're the first and the last, the most perfect example of 'endless forms most beautiful.'"

A flicker of surprise crossed her face—whether it was over him declaring his lasting affection or quoting Darwin, he wasn't sure. Sean kissed her once more and straightened, raising Hattie from her wanton pose. He draped her outerwear over her shoulders and took up his own coat and gloves before collecting her box.

"Ms. Keller, I'm out for the morning. Ms. Fernsby's case is my top priority. I'll check in with you this afternoon."

At his automobile, Sean stored Hattie's box on the floorboard of the backseat before helping her into the front. He drove the few blocks to Barton Academy and parked on the side street next to the three story building.

Taking her hand in his, he kissed her fingers. "This will only take a few minutes. Sit tight, dearest."

"I wish to come and speak for myself."

"No offense to you, but Franklin Gentry needs a man to show him the error of his ways."

At the corner of Government Street, he turned and smiled at her elvish face watching him through the windshield. Hattie's returned grin empowered his mission tenfold. Sean strode through the schoolyard and straight to the secretary.

"Solicitor Spunner here to see Mr. Gentry." Sean removed his leather gloves with the air of a man bored. "And no, I do not have an appointment, though you may assure your principal that it is in his best interest to see me promptly."

"Solicitor Spunner, his schedule is quite—"

"I will give him five minutes before I head to the courthouse to file my complaint."

"Ye-yes, sir!" The secretary scurried for the principal's door and knocked. She disappeared inside, then the door flung open a minute later and she raced out before the portly man a decade older than Sean.

"And to what do I owe the pleasure of your visit, Solicitor Spunner?"

"I make a point never to discuss business in doorways, Mr. Gentry."

He reddened and a bead of sweat rolled down his temple. "Of course. Do come in and have a seat."

Sean pretended to sit. As soon as Franklin Gentry's cumbersome backside was lowered into his chair behind the desk, Sean straightened and glared down at the man.

"Hattie Fernsby will be restored to her science classroom in January."

"Ms. Fernsby? How can she afford a lawyer and secure one so quickly?"

"What you need to be worried about is whether or not you want the entire city knowing what the principal of the high school did at the Mystics of Dardenne masquerade in 'ninety-three."

Mr. Gentry's countenance went ashen. Moisture trickled from his forehead.

"I see we are on the same page now, Mr. Gentry. Send Ms. Fernsby a note of apology for your too hasty dismissal by the afternoon post and all will be well."

"But she broke the law!"

"No, Mr. Gentry, that's what you did at the masquerade. Ms. Fernsby did nothing more than respectfully field the comments and questions of curious students. Had you taken the time to listen to her side of the story, you would understand she handled the situation with utmost decorum."

"It's beyond my control. Ms. Fernsby's file has already been sent to the superintendent, along with the authorized letter of her dismissal."

"A one-sided account, which did not include her signature and statement. That is, unless you forged it."

The man went red once more. "It's the last day before the break and—"

"Ms. Fernsby's classroom will not be altered, nor will she collect her personal items this afternoon. Come January third, you *will* welcome back the best science teacher ever employed at the Girls' High School with graciousness."

"But Superintendent Hill will—"

"He will fully agree with me. Promise to do as I instructed and I will have no need to see you again."

"Yes, Solicitor Spunner. And the superintendent's agre—"

"Do not doubt it will be done." Sean pulled on his gloves and turned for the door. "Now pray I do not need to seek another moment of your time."

***

Hattie's clasped hands began to cramp. She stretched her fingers and smoothed her blue dress. Only ten minutes, but it felt like hours before Sean emerged from the school. With a jaunty spring in his step, he rounded the sidewalk.

He patted her hand before starting the engine. "It's going to take another stop, but never fear."

"He refused to—"

"Principal Gentry is ready to welcome you back after the holidays, but I have to follow the paper trail. In his haste to clear things out before Christmas, your file was immediately sent to the superintendent's office. Lucky for you, Mr. Hill and I are members of the same Mardi Gras society."

"The one from your youth?"

"No, my current one, but the Dardenne connection came in handy with the principal."

"That old badger?"

"One and the same. There was quite a report in the society minutes about Franklin Gentry's antics at the masquerade in 1893. It made this backroom deal my easiest yet."

"What did he—"

"A Dardenne brother never spills secrets. No one will hear of his fetishes unless he fails to welcome you back."

"Fetish—Sean! What did you do? It sounds a lot like extortion."

"But it's made possible by his sins, which was all his doing."

Stomach hardened with fear, Hattie laid her hand on Sean's knee. "Couldn't someone hold similar power over you one day?"

"I've never done anything half as bad as *that*. Besides, only Dardenne members serving as president or secretary have access to the locked minutes. I did my time taking notes so I could peruse the past." He parked outside the district office and gathered her hands in his strong ones. "Listen well, Hattie, for I'll tell you this once. My first love was a sweet, pure one. I was seventeen and she fifteen. After a few months of our acquaintance, she died from yellow fever. The following year, I took up with Mystics of Dardenne while studying law. At their parties, I drank too much and acted a fool like many of the others, but I never participated in anything lewd in a common space—if you understand what I mean."

Hattie's face heated, but her heart softened more. "Go on."

"I did, through the years, indulge in the red light district during Mardi Gras. You'll be hard-pressed to find a man raised in this city that hasn't—Davenport is the only one I know of. But all that came to a stop when I began wooing Eliza Melling the spring of 'o-five. She was young but experienced. Not to mention completely uninhibited. Once we were engaged that fall, we held nothing back. When she died the following January, my passion did too. As I told you the other week, she bled me dry. I've focused on my career since then. Using my secret society knowledge and contacts helps with success on the business front, but my personal life has been dead. I've buried myself in books, a habit from my youth. No one has stirred an ounce of my interest until I heard you proclaim Madame Curie's Nobel Prize as the turning point in women's role in science."

His intense stare—amber in the sunlight—caused her to look away.

"When I saw you, Hattie, I wanted nothing more than to bare your curves and lick every inch of you." He took her chin and gently turned her to meet her gaze. "You gave me back my passion. I'll not let you go without doing everything within my power to turn the tides in our favor. If that makes me selfish, so be it. I'm not letting you leave Mobile."

She managed a blushing smile, but couldn't speak.

He kissed her cheek. "Think all that over while I meet with Superintendent Hill."

Think? Hattie could hardly breathe as she watched his steady stride disappear inside the building. Never had a man been as brash, but at the same time tender. He laid his shadowed past bare, though he revealed a future of resplendent colors. Fearing she craved him as much as he did her, Hattie wrestled it over with her liberated lifestyle.

How can I allow him to manipulate others as a means to secure my future while I wait for him in the automobile like an outcast?

One backroom deal and loophole at a time, it appears.

Sean returned a minute later, lips pursed in his thoughtful way. "Apparently he left town this morning to spend Christmas in New Orleans. He will, however, be back in time for our society's ball."

"I'll have no closure until then? What will I do?"

"Shop, of course. You need to be outfitted for the Order of Mayhem's New Year's Eve masquerade."

"But my students!" Frustration over Sean's easy dismissal of her joblessness and his blithe attitude about shopping and parties reminded her of their different stations in life. "Rosella was counting on me."

"And she'll not be disappointed. You will be there with your fossils and enthusiasm the day the students return."

***

The next week and a half was a rush of excursions for Hattie, all revolving around Sean. Two trips to Mademoiselle Bisset's shop for a New Year's Eve gown and fitting, with the bill—at Sean's insistance—sent to him. Dinners together, as well as Christmas Mass at the cathedral. Plus, a chartered boat ride to Dauphin Island with the Davenport family so Hattie could see the Indian Shell Mounds and explore the beach.

Looking back, it was the simple outing of midnight Mass that brought the largest impact. Hattie expected to feel like an outsider within the cloak of the church, but instead saw the beauty of the architecture and felt the peace of the hymns. Sean's warm body beside her and his whispered words after the service as he linked their fingers brought an unexpected rush of joy.

"I feel your peace, Hattie. There's enough good from your childhood for you not to cast it all aside. Leave at least one pinky holding to your faith—enough to allow for a wedding Mass and baptism for any babies we might be blessed with. That's all I'd ask of you." Then he'd kissed her ear beneath her hat and flashed his chip-toothed smile that made him look every bit the young rascal he claimed he once was.

No matter his journey, Sean was an educated gentleman who could quote the likes of Keats, Darwin, Thoreau, and constitutional laws like they were old friends. He was at ease with people of all walks of life and constantly made her feel like the most adored woman in the world—whether he treated her with the respect due a queen or the lusty banter befitting a bar wench. And she loved him for it.

Now, she stood in the middle of her boarding house room in a splendid purple silk gown as she awaited him to escort her to the New Year's Eve masquerade.

A knock sounded, followed by Mrs. Grimes calling through the door. "Mr. Spunner is here!"

Hattie collected the silver beaded reticule that had arrived by delivery that afternoon along with a note proclaiming it a last minute thought over which Mademoiselle Bisset telephoned Sean, saying Hattie needed it to complete her attire for the evening. And the ensemble was stunning—silver shoes, gloves, wrist bag, and mask against the royal purple of the provocative square neckline and short sleeves on the floor-length gown.

"Oh, my dear, you look like a princess!" Mrs. Grimes exclaimed when Hattie opened the door. "Mr. Spunner is most charming. You could do no better, Ms. Fernsby."

Ignoring the baited statement, Hattie went for the receiving room. Sean stood before the fire in a flawless black tuxedo with purple accents and mask that matched her dress.

"Hattie, you look even lovelier than I expected, which says a lot." He took her hand and kissed her cheek before turning to Mr. and Mrs. Grimes. "Thank you both for your hospitality. Happy New Year's."

Surprised to see a hired automobile before the house, Hattie clung to Sean's arm on their way down the walk.

"It's tradition to have a chauffeur for Mardi Gras balls." He helped her into the back of the limousine and settled beside her. "That way the revelers can enjoy every bit of company before and after, as well as not worry about driving home after indulging in too much drink. May I taste a sampling of your offerings, dearest? I've waited weeks to see such a display. I promise not to leave a mark or rumple your dress."

He motioned to her breasts with his gloved hand and she laughed, which caused her cleavage to jiggle. His eyes widened with pleasure beneath the mask and she laughed all the more.

"Oh, go on, you cad."

His smile was soon buried in her décolletage. Lips and tongue explored each swell and the valley they created before he trailed kisses to her mouth.

After he settled back, his hand went for his tuxedo pocket. "I love you, Hattie Violet Fernsby. I want to feast on you every day for the rest of my life. No matter what happens with the superintendent, I want you to consider me for your husband as an option in your future."

He brought forth a purple silk handkerchief and unwrapped it to display a stately diamond ring. Hattie's eyes immediately misted over, a lump forming in her throat.

"We might have met a month ago, Hattie, but it feels like we belong together. I want to continue to get to know all the wonders that make you special as we share a life. Will you at least consider it? Take as long as you wish to answer."

She took several deep breaths, ever aware of his watchful gaze. "I love you too, Sean," she finally managed to say. "I want to say yes, but I feel I must satisfy my critical thinking by forcing myself to mull it over. Will you give me the evening to think on it?"

"Only the evening?" Sean laughed. "I was expecting to wait a year, dearest."

"It will be if I wait until after midnight." She took his cheeks in her gloved hands and kissed him squarely on the lips. "Don't fret. You have more than enough going for you."

Never had Hattie experienced such splendor as when they walked into the ballroom at The Battle House hotel. The chandeliers, silks, jeweled tiaras, and masks created a treasure trove for the eyes. Sean made several introductions, but she could sense him searching for someone.

Superintendent Hill.

He stood twenty feet to the right, along with a lady who appeared to be his wife and another couple. Sean angled directly for him.

As soon as the others turned away, Sean inserted himself. "Superintendent and Mrs. Hill, it is a pleasure."

He kissed the back of the woman's glove and grinned.

"Mr. Spunner, my favorite gentleman." Mrs. Hill beamed like a schoolgirl though pushing fifty.

"You are too kind, Mrs. Hill. May I introduce the young woman whom I am fortunate to escort tonight? Ms. Hattie Fernsby."

"It is good to see you with a companion, Mr. Spunner. I do worry over you. Ms. Fernsby, you said?" She turned to Hattie. "Any relation to the Fernsbys of Moss Point?"

"No, I'm afraid not. I'm newly arrived from Boston."

"Boston! How exciting."

"It is indeed." Sean winked. "And there has been a bit too much excitement these past days. I was hoping your husband could help us. It would only take a minute of your time this fine evening, Superintendent Hill."

"Hmmm?" The man looked up from his champagne.

"Mr. Spunner needs your help," his wife urged.

"What is it, Spunner?"

"Hattie is a teacher at the Girls' High School." Mrs. Hill's hand went to her chest in shock, but Sean continued. "There was a mix up at the school the Friday morning before break. Miscommunication of sorts, as you know happens from time to time. As it turns out, the secretary sent Ms. Fernsby's file with a false letter of dismissal to your office. I am sure you can imagine what a damper it has placed on her Christmas and now New

Year's to worry that her file sits on your desk awaiting your stamp to destroy her hopes of ever teaching again in our fine city."

"And you've discussed this with Mr. Gentry already?"

"The following hour, Superintendent, but his staff was so efficient, the paperwork was already sent. I told Principal Gentry I would see to it myself and be sure the teacher and her file were returned to his school in time for her first class in January."

He grunted. "Very well. Come to my office Thursday morning and I'll give you Ms. Fernsby's file."

"Thank you, Superintendent. I do believe our New Year's is off to a great start."

"Yes," Hattie said, "the perfect time to celebrate our engagement."

Mrs. Hill brightened with the news. "Why, Mr. Spunner, where have you been hiding this delightful creature?"

"In the science department. It's been grand, but we need to find the Davenports. I will see you Thursday, Superintendent. Enjoy your night."

As Sean led her across the room, Hattie felt lighter with each step.

He brought them to a dim corner where he stared down at her. "Did you mean it or did you accept my offer to improve Mrs. Hill's opinion of you?"

Her eyebrows pinched together behind the mask. "Sean Spunner, you're a prig if you think that of me."

"And the same to you, Hattie Fernsby, if you think I was serious." He fished the handkerchief from his pocket and retrieved the ring. "Slip off your glove and let's see if this piece of coal fits."

Both laughing, Sean managed to place the ring on her.

"It's perfect," she whispered.

"Thank you for making me the happiest man alive. Now we need to find Freddy and Melissa so they hear it from us rather than the gossip I'm sure is being spread about the room like wildfire. They did introduce us, after all."

Hattie pulled on her glove and took Sean's arm, hoping to stay within touching distance of him all night.

***

Two mornings after the Order of Mayhem's ball, Sean collected Hattie from the boarding house. She was prettier than ever in a wool walking dress with the engagement ring on full display. After a decorous kiss, he helped her into his automobile so she could accompany him to the superintendent's office. Hattie waited in the automobile when he went inside.

The secretary showed him into Mr. Hill's office where the superintendent looked through Hattie's file.

"Spunner, I hope you know what you're getting into with this woman. Mr. Gentry's note mentions Charles Darwin. You know what an offense that is."

"I do, as does Ms. Fernsby, and it will not happen again. I'll see this file returned to Barton Academy."

"Very well, Spunner. I hope to see you at the Aethelwulf Club soon. Your court stories are the most amusing to hear."

"You can count on it."

On his way down the hall, Sean flipped through the file, slipping the contract labeled CODE OF CONDUCT into the front space.

He swaggered to the automobile.

"You got it?" Hattie asked.

He nodded when he sat behind the wheel.

"Now what do we do?"

"Stop by my house, if you'd like. We can light a fire in one of the hearths, using this as kindling." He presented the contract of behavior standards with a flourish. "Then we may do whatever you wish, Hattie. My housekeeper has the day off."

"Sean, we couldn't burn it, could we?"

"A dismissal over lewd behavior would be difficult without a copy of the signed code of conduct." He kissed her forehead. "Do you want to pussyfoot about when we have so much desire between us? It's all up to you."

Her blue eyes went from his face to the papers and back several times. Then a devious smile spread across her alluring face.

"I do feel a chill, Sean. A fire sounds like a good idea."

"Allow me to see you to your future home, dearest."

Hattie tucked beside him and they blazed a path across town because, as Charles Darwin said, "A man who dares to waste one hour of time has not discovered the value of life."

~~~
~~~

"Mystic Misperception"

A Malevolent Trilogy/Washington Square Secrets/ Possession Chronicles Short

Sadie Marley hurried past the maid into the Beauchamp house and up the stairs to her best friend's room.

"Alice, you'll never guess what happened!" Sadie threw her handbag and blue coat onto the second bed.

Gazing up at Sadie over the romance novel she was reading, Alice Beauchamp raised her eyebrows, closed her book, and sat up from where she'd been lounging on her frilly bed.

"Then tell me."

Sadie perched at the foot of the bed and smoothed her slim skirt about her hips as she crossed her ankles. "I was in Hammel's, near the men's shoe department, when I overheard a few young men discussing the need to buy plain black boots for their costumes."

"What's so extraordinary about that?"

"Costumes! And they were whispering."

Alice continued to stare, unimpressed. "Discussing costumes during Mardi Gras season isn't special."

"They were mystic men—and not just any society." Sadie leaned closer and dropped her voice. "They were Mystics of Dardenne members!"

"What? They never spill a word." Alice lifted her book and opened it back up to where her finger had held her place. Ever since she was nearly ruined by an Italian violinist, Alice had been difficult to impress where men were concerned.

Sadie understood her friend's reluctance, and held her own annoyance under a layer of patience. "They didn't say the name out loud, but I received an invitation from them."

The book lowered once more. "Since when do Mystics of Dardenne members hand out masquerade invitations in department stores?"

"They didn't actually hand it to me." Sadie fingered her blonde chignon. "One of them dropped it on their way out."

"And you didn't return it?"

"They would probably get in trouble if it was found out they weren't discrete. I bet they were greenies. They didn't sound like they knew exactly what to expect."

"Who was it?"

"No one you'd know—some upstarts from St. Matthew's. Unless, of course, you're so desperate for a husband you'd look outside the cathedral parish."

Alice tossed her book onto the side table.

Sadie smiled. "Then you'll attend with me?"

"Not to a masquerade with those barbarians."

"Come on, Alice. All men are wild during Mardi Gras, even my brother-in-law, and he's a respected surgeon. It's time we see what other societies do besides the Order of Mayhem and the Mystic Order of Sirens. Or have you decided on the convent after all?"

"Not on your life, and you know it. I'd rather join a symphony in a northern city that takes women than lead a cloistered life. Besides, you only have one invitation."

"Grace Anne has told me the Dardennes never turn away a pretty figure from their masquerades, with or without an invitation."

"Maybe back when she was single a decade ago. It's 1915 now. I'm sure things are different."

"Don't you want to know if you pass inspection to make it inside their masquerade?"

"I don't care if my figure is desirable to a bunch of upstarts."

"Really, Alice, one would think you'd be pleased with the prospect of unchaperoned time with men. Don't tell me you're still mooning over that Italian. You were just a girl of sixteen back then. It's been more than four years."

"You fawned over Valentino De Fiore as well, so don't tease me."

"Everyone did when he was in town, but unless you're going to chase him around the world and try to make beautiful music together, with or without your violins, I suggest you take better note of the eligible bachelors right here in Mobile. There are plenty, but with talk of the country joining the war, they might not be around much longer."

"I have no desire to marry a man associated with the notorious Mystics of Dardenne society."

"Then come and find out who is a part of it so you can avoid them. I plan to be wed this summer and want to fully enjoy my final Mardi Gras season before marriage."

Alice narrowed her eyes. "And do *you* want to go to learn which men to ignore? It would be safer to find out who hasn't pledged to one of the respectable societies."

"Maybe, but Grace Anne says the best husbands have a naughty side."

"You'll get a reputation if you go to the Mystics of Dardenne ball."

"If I find a beau within the next month, it won't matter."

"You think it's that easy?" Alice sounded offended. "You crook your finger and a man will be at your side."

Sadie shrugged. "Something like that. I've been asked out often enough. Not to mention Grace Anne is always willing to play matchmaker at her supper parties. John has a wide array of friends ready to settle down. I'm sure I'd have an offer from at least one man before the end of Lent if I show the slightest interest."

"You scheming hussy!"

"Don't be jealous, Alice. You could as well, but you have to do more than perform your violin concertos and attend Mass to give a man the chance to talk to you. Shall I inform Grace Anne you're—"

"I'll not be pandered to by your elder sister!"

Deciding not to take offense, Sadie nodded slyly. "You *do* have a plethora of men within easy reach with all your brothers about. Their friends are always ripe for the picking, especially Richard's, but stay away from Clarence's musician friends," she said, speaking of Alice's twin. "The last thing you need is to marry a husband as obsessed with music as yourself."

Alice huffed and crossed her arms. "I'll not look to my brothers any more than to your sister as a means of procuring my heart's true love."

"Sometimes Cupid needs a little help. Begin right now by going with me to Mademoiselle Bisset's shop to look for a gown."

"I don't want to attend that masquerade."

"You don't have to, but will you help your dearest friend find the perfect dress?"

***

Richard Beauchamp, the eldest sibling, returned home at the exact moment his sister and Sadie Marley descended the front stairs. The two women were opposites in looks and temperament, but the difference in their disposition was recent. Alice had grown serious though Sadie remained as joyful as ever.

"Good Saturday afternoon, Alice and Sadie." He lifted his hat and smiled. "Going somewhere?"

"Hello, Richie." Sadie's voice managed to set the twenty-three-year-old's heart on fire, as it had for at least five years. "We are headed to Mademoiselle Bisset's for a bit of shopping."

Richard took her coat from where it hung on her arm and helped the blonde into it. "The wind is terrible. Allow me to drive you, so y'all arrive looking as fresh as you do now."

"That's sweet of you." Sadie gracefully slipped her arms into her coat. "I thought you were still in Montgomery."

"I took the train back yesterday afternoon. I plan to be here every weekend through Mardi Gras. Our state representatives can do without me that much."

"Don't they need your help to stop that prohibition bill they're threatening us with?"

Richard smiled at Sadie as he helped Alice into her coat. "I don't have that much sway yet, Sadie, but someday."

"You're certainly a well-spoken gentleman now, Richie. University and political life have agreed with you. Don't you think so, Alice?"

Alice's brown eyes looked deadly. "Don't get any ideas, Sadie Marley."

Sadie's head went back with a laugh, displaying her elegant neck beneath the unbuttoned coat. "Your sister is darling, isn't she, Richie? Are your friends from the capitol coming down for the festivities? Anyone you think would be especially interested in a pretty violinist?"

Alice stomped out the door.

Turning to Richard, Sadie placed a gloved hand on his for a few seconds. "I'm worried she's turning into a spinster. She needs to be thoroughly kissed this year."

"And you?"

Sadie's full lips quirked up at the corners in that maddening curl that sent Richard's heart racing. "Should I be worried about finding a willing participant for myself?"

He grinned. "Just say the word, Miss Sadie, and I'd be yours to command."

"Alice would never tolerate that." She tucked her arm through his. "But I appreciate the compliment."

Pride inflated to near bursting, Richard walked her to his automobile, and she slid into the backseat where his sister was waiting. They were silent while he backed out of the driveway. As he picked up speed on State Street, Sadie started talking.

"Here's the invitation, Alice. Look it over. You must come with me."

"That's not even two weeks to prepare."

Richard strained to hear more details.

"It's plenty of time." Sadie lowered her voice. "And the venue is only a few blocks from your house. Right there, I can see the roof of the third story. We can arrange that I'm staying with you. It'll be simple."

"Have you forgotten my mother?"

"Then we can ask Richard to escort us. Surely she'd let us out with your older brother as chaperone."

As he pulled to a stop along the curb outside the Parisian dress shop, Sadie leaned forward and set her hand on his shoulder. "Richie, would you be willing to escort your sister and I to—"

"No!" Alice jerked her arm. "That would be as mortifying as the event itself. I'm too old to be escorted anywhere socially important by a relative."

Sadie laughed, her breath warm on Richard's ear as she leaned over his shoulder. "Thanks anyway. We appreciate the ride."

"Shall I wait for you?"

"Mademoiselle has a delivery boy, and I'll take the streetcar home from here." She squeezed his shoulder. "I hope to see you at Mass tomorrow morning."

"I'll be there, Sadie."

Before he pulled into traffic, Richard heard Sadie say something to Alice about the Spanish Inquisition. Fearing they were in possession of an invitation to his society's masquerade, a hot lump of dread twisted through his middle at the thought of his sister stumbling into the debauched scene the Mystics of Dardenne masquerades always presented. Sadie could handle it—at least he thought she might—but never Alice.

***

After settling her luggage in Alice's bedroom, Sadie knocked on a door down the hall on the afternoon of February twelfth.

"Clarence," she called. "Are you there?"

"Of course he is," Alice bitterly whispered. "And I don't approve of you dragging my twin brother into this scheme of yours."

The door opened and Clarence Beauchamp blinked at his visitor.

"Hello, Sadie." He flickered a smile at her. "I heard you were here for the night."

"Yes, supper and then staying over in Alice's room, but listen." She leaned close, causing heat to rise to the twenty-year-old's face. "Alice and I have a late gathering to get to. I was wondering if you'd be able to drop us off to save us the trouble of arriving disheveled."

"I'd be happy to. I'll ask my father to use—"

"No, Clarence." She quickly touched his lips with a fingertip. "I don't want to worry your family. We'll slip out after your parents are settled for the night."

His brown eyes darted from Sadie to his twin behind her. "Do you need an escort?"

"No," Alice was quick to reply as she crossed her arms. "We'll be fine, Clarence."

He nodded and focused back on the blonde. "Our parents don't stay up past ten most nights, but I'll play a few lullabies immediately after supper to help them relax."

"You're a sweet one." She smiled at the plainest of the Beauchamp brothers. He didn't have his younger brother's daring or eldest Richard's square jaw and good looks, but Clarence's piano skills would earn him a woman at some point in his life. "I hate to have to miss your recital, but I'll need to dress for our outing after supper."

Clarence shoved his hands into the pockets of his trousers like an awkward schoolboy. "I practice before supper, if you'd like to join me in the parlor in about half an hour."

"That would be lovely."

"Would you like to do a duet, Alice?"

"I'm not in the mood." She grabbed Sadie's arm and led her back down the hall. Once they were safely in Alice's bedroom, she let loose. "Don't you dare string him along! Clarence is a sensitive soul. The last thing he needs is you flirting with him."

"He's a darling, but not one to flirt with. Y'all look too much alike. But I'll always be kind to him. Have you decided on your gown?"

"I don't want to be recognized in one of my previous dresses."

"That's why I tried to get you to buy a new one at the shop last week."

"I'm not willing to throw money away on something I'll have to toss out after one use. Nothing worn to this scandalous masquerade can ever been seen again."

"So are you going naked? From what I've heard, those men would like that."

Alice shot her a look of incredulousness that made Sadie giggle.

"I got out one of my mother's old dresses. It has to be from at least 1890 because the waistline is from before children. It's red like yours, though not nearly as flattering. I don't want to attract extra attention anyway. I think I'd faint if one of the Dardennes asked me to dance."

"Grace Anne told me the absolute rule of their balls is that you cannot deny one of the members if he asks you to dance. I think she's jealous we're going. She never made it to one, but a few of her friends did and told her all about them. I'll spare you the shocking details." Sadie laughed again, then wished she'd hadn't when Alice paled. "You'll be fine, Alice. Now where's the dress? I want to make sure the mantilla I brought doesn't clash with it."

She took the ensemble out of her closet, laying it on her bed. It was a splendid Victorian two-piece ball gown complete with small bustle and matching red gloves. "I embellished an old mask, mimicking the ruffled edges of the gown around the edges. It gives my face more coverage."

"Very clever, Alice. With your hair under a mantilla and lips painted to match the gown, no one will recognize you. The bustle will even keep your buttocks safe from wandering hands." Alice's face went as crimson as the silk gown, and Sadie hurried to the box holding her masquerade items. "Would you prefer the black or red lace mantilla?"

"Black," Alice said. "It will hide my hair better."

With that settled, Sadie hurried to the parlor to give Clarence her attention while Alice hid the party attire once more.

Clarence played a Beethoven piece, and then Sadie joined him on the bench to pound out a bit of Joplin with him. The youngest Marley sister was the true pianist in the family, but all the sisters had learned to play as soon as they were able to reach the keys. In truth, Sadie didn't think her mediocre music abilities, brains, or manners would help land her a husband. She knew she would be chosen for her looks, and she was fine with that. Blonde hair was fashionable, and though her chest was a tad more than the magazines displayed, she knew some men preferred a little extra on top. And Mademoiselle Bisset specifically chose to highlight that feature with the new gown.

Even without Richard in attendance, supper was lively. Seventeen-year-old Felix was more than eager to show off for the guest, explaining his latest tricks inspired by Houdini's magic. Clarence smiled and offered his thoughts, but Alice was too absorbed in her own anxiety to contribute to the conversations.

Though not as old as Sadie's parents, Mr. and Mrs. Beauchamp appeared to be tuckered out from a busy week of work and club meetings. According to Felix's reports (who happily played spy between the parlor and Alice's room while the ladies dressed), they went like lambs to the slaughter with Clarence's renditions of "Moonlight Sonata" and other dreamy pieces. The Beauchamps closeted themselves in their suite at nine o'clock.

"Come on, Alice," Sadie urged. "We have the opportunity to arrive on time. Your hair doesn't need to be perfect when you're going to have the mantilla over it."

They hurried their final preparations, donned their masks, and pinned on the mantillas. Sadie led the way down the servant's stairs and was met with a low whistle from Felix and the bulging dark eyes of Clarence in the back hallway.

"You're the prettiest girl I ever saw," Felix said.

Clarence elbowed him. "Sadie is a *woman*."

"That she is," Felix replied as he ogled her, "and in all the right places."

"Don't be crude, Felix," Alice said as she came to a stop behind her friend. "Are you ready, Clarence?"

Her twin nodded. "You'll have to tell me where to drop you off."

Felix's intelligent eyes flashed between his sister's tight lips and Sadie's smiling ones beneath their masks. "I can tell you where to bring them." He offered Sadie his arm. "This way, Miss Marley."

"You can't come with us, Felix!" Alice grabbed her brother's other arm. "You have no idea where—"

"Don't I?" He smirked. "I may be the youngest, but I've got ears."

"Shh!" Alice shushed him. "I don't appreciate my brothers being privy to my shame."

"There's no shame," Sadie said. "We're young and adventurous, enjoying what will hopefully be our final carnival season before marriage. Take Clarence's arm and let him escort you to the automobile."

Sadie winked at Felix and allowed him to caress her arm as they followed the twins to the driveway.

"I always said you were the bravest girl," Felix whispered to Sadie. "Ever since you stood up to Richard and the others when they were teasing that dog all those years ago, I knew you would never let anyone hold you back from what you wanted."

Felix helped her into the backseat beside his sister and kissed Sadie's gloved hand.

"Stop fawning over her!" Alice fussed at her little brother.

He leaned over Sadie and kissed Alice's cheek below her ruffled mask. "You look beautiful too, Alice, though I can't imagine you at a Mystics of Dardenne masquerade."

"Oh, go away!"

She shoved him. Felix laughed and jumped into the front seat of the automobile.

"You can't come along! Clarence," Alice said as her twin took the driver's seat, "make him get out."

"I'm not getting out until you and Sadie do. I want to make sure you arrive at Temperance Hall in style."

"No, and besides, we aren't being dropped off in front of the building. Tell them, Sadie."

"That's right, gentlemen. We want to be dropped a block away and arrive on foot so no one will see who brought us. We don't wish to be recognized."

"Men will recognize your luscious lips, Sadie."

"Stop with the flattery, Felix!" Alice snapped.

"How will you get home?" Clarence asked.

"We won't have trouble in that regard." Sadie patted his shoulder over the seat. "Let's get going, though. I don't want to miss their tableau. I hear it's always thrilling."

When Clarence pulled to the curb a block northwest of the hall, Alice clutched the door handle but didn't move.

"Come on, Alice." Sadie nudged her. "I don't want to be late."

"I can't." She shook her head. "I can't do it. I'd die of fright if any of those monsters wished to dance with me."

In the front seat, Felix snorted and Clarence poked him in the ribs.

"I'm not brave like you. Go on without me."

"Alice, don't be a ninny. You're dressed and ready to attend," Sadie said.

"Don't send her in there alone, Alice," Clarence said with indignation.

"I can't. Walk home if you'd like, brothers. I'll wait here for her."

Sadie huffed and exited the door into the street before hurrying around to the sidewalk. She leaned back toward Felix's open automobile window. "Take care of her."

Felix grinned. "Say hello to… never mind. Enjoy the masquerade, Sadie. We'll be here."

***

Richard adjusted the coarse black face netting and then secured the monk's cowl over his head, shadowing himself from all possible recognition when he appeared with the other Mystics of Dardenne members. To help with the air of anticipation in the ballroom, the society men waited five minutes beyond their planned arrival before they solemnly entered in two straight lines of over two dozen each. On the raw wooden tables, the refreshment spread only offered bread and wine.

Their procession of habited monks draped with huge beaded crosses was in direct opposition to the Mystics of Dardenne's reputation and elicited several laughs that turned to nervous titters as they marched the length of the party. Behind the line of the black-clad figures came one in red, arms raised for silence as he swept into the center of the dance floor.

"What heretics are you," he bellowed, "to show your faces within our hallowed walls? Our society demands purity!"

The group's president stalked between the rows of monks as he raved.

"We must sift out the unclean to allow us to focus on our indulgences! You and you," he said as he pointed to one monk and then a second, "bring another brother with you each and ferret out the heretics so our masquerade may commence!"

The two pairs went to opposite sides of the room, circling the guests on their quest. They often paused to grope females, and the men in attendance whistled to egg them on.

"Silence!" The red-robed man went to the dais beside the musicians who stood at attention. He pointed to the wall behind him and a spotlight shone on it. "Bring the heretics to the racks!"

The monks returned, each pair dragging a seemingly uncooperative female. The crowd gasped and angled closer to watch as the chosen offerings were brought toward the torture equipment.

Behind his mesh mask, Richard smirked, knowing that this display was better's than any in recent memory. The women cowered before the man in red, earning every bit of their night's wages for their performance. The leader rent the shimmery gold gown off the first woman, then the blue one off the brunette. As the women were shuffled toward the racks in their corsets and underwear, several shrieks came from the guests.

"They shall be punished until they confess their sins!" The masked president pointed to the crowd. "If you do not dance and make merry, you shall join them!"

He wielded a leather cat-o-nine tails, striking the fleshy thighs of the first woman who was restrained. When the band started a festive ragtime tune, the monks dispersed, seeking their partners for the first dance that only they were allowed to participate in. Several paused long enough to nip from the hollow crosses about their necks that doubled as flasks, drinking the liquor straight through the mesh face shield.

Richard sauntered the edge of the dance floor, seeking a pretty figure though he knew none would be as fine as Sadie's. He caught sight of a voluptuous body in a red gown reminiscent of a Spanish dancer. Gaze traveling her form, he noted the breasts were as fine as Sadie's, and her lips—they were *her* lips!

Painted red like her ruffled dress, Sadie's mouth was open in surprise as one of the monks led her onto the dance floor. When her partner's fondling hands worked from her cleavage to her succulent hips, she looked about the room for a means of escape.

Richard snatched his unknown society brother by the shoulder and shoved him away. He immediately pulled Sadie into a modified Bunny Hug and danced as quickly as possible to discourage interruption.

"Thank you," she said with a trembling smile. "I'm afraid I didn't know what I was getting myself into when I came."

Richard nodded and Sadie looked to the torture scene.

"Everything I've ever heard about your society is true. It's frightful, except for you. There's another monk following us. I think he means to cut in."

"Do you trust me?" Richard asked, forcing a deeper tone to his voice to disguise it.

"Yes," she breathed.

Richard immediately claimed her buttocks with his hands, pressing against her in a suggestive dance as his mesh-covered face went to hers. He had dreamt of kissing her for years, but not through a covering or with an audience. He leaned to her ear, smelling her perfume before he spoke.

"It needs to look like you're mine, that I'm taking advantage of you, so no one else will. Do you understand?"

Sadie nodded, and his chin lowered as his eyes fell to her heaving chest. He licked his lips, glad the net and cowl hid his face from view.

"Good, my sweet. Forgive me." His pelvis continued to move to the beat of the song as he led her in the erotic dance. He bit the inside of his cheek to keep himself from falling completely under the spell of the moment.

"You dance well." Sadie offered a true smile. "I suppose not all the members are monsters."

"A woman like you should never have come here alone."

"There are people waiting for me outside, but my friend was too timid to come in."

"It's better she didn't."

"I didn't say—"

"My turn!" a monk said as he snatched Sadie's wrist.

"I just heard a confession from the heretic. She has agreed to go to the confessional with me for penance." Richard pulled

Sadie behind him. "She is *my* captive. I'll take this to the cardinal if needed."

The other man bowed and stepped back. "Enjoy, brother."

With an arm slung low and tight around Sadie's hip, Richard steered her across the room to the false front of a cathedral. The partitioned room within the miniature church was lined with alcoves made to look like confessionals. They were not divided as a padded bench ran the length of the space and only a thin lace curtain offered a semblance of decorum if used. But the three other couples already filling half the confessionals didn't bother to close the drapes as they necked and groped.

"You'll be safe here for a little while," Richard said as he saw her to the furthest bench and pulled the black lace closed.

Sadie tilted her head, lips tight as she peered through the curtain at the other couples. "Do we need to do something similar to make this appear legitimate?"

"Well…"

"After all you've done for me, I don't want you to get into trouble." She stood, encouraged him to take the bench, and then sat on his lap. She reached for the bottom of his face net, and he raised his hand to stop her. "I won't pull it up all the way. Trust me, as I trusted you."

Her full lips were everything he had imagined as they met his exposed mouth. The netting hung over the arch of his nose as they kissed each other, tentatively at first. As their mutual passion flared, Richard held her closer, feeling the skin on her arms between the long gloves and the ruffled shoulder of the gown. Sadie opened her mouth first, but he rushed to taste her as his hands roamed.

"Oh, Richie," Sadie whispered as his kisses trailed to her décolletage.

He straightened with an intake of breath, the covering falling back over his face.

"I thought it was you, but I knew for sure the instant you rebuked the last monk. Do you think I would have been so forward with a stranger?"

"I'd hope not. You don't think poorly of me after seeing how the society is?"

"It is rather shocking, but after you rescued me like that, I can't fault you." She leaned against his shoulder a moment. "Besides, Mystics of Dardenne membership is temporary—a phase many young men pass through. You'll join the society your father is in when you marry."

"That's right, Sadie." He touched her ear with a fingertip, trailing it down her cheek.

She lifted his netting once more and kissed him until she giggled.

"What is it?"

"Alice is going to have a conniption."

"I'm glad she wasn't brave enough to come. I would have had to rescue her rather than you, but don't tell me she's sitting alone somewhere in the dark."

Sadie's soft lips curled at the edges. "Clarence and Felix are with her."

"Could I escort you there or do you wish to stay?"

"I've seen more than enough of this masquerade, Richie, but I'd like to see more of you."

"Would you attend the Blithe Buckaroos parade with me on Mardi Gras Day?"

"I'd like that, and Alice never attends that one. She claims their humor is too irreverent."

Richard laughed. "It is, but it's nothing compared to this debauchery."

"It allowed me to finally find out how it feels to be in your arms, so I'll always be thankful to Mystics of Dardenne for this time with you."

"Did I pass inspection?"

"I'm going to the parade with you, aren't I?" She smoothed her gown as she stood. "I wish you could leave with me now. I hate to think of who you might grab after I leave."

"My heart goes with you, Sadie." Richard took her hand and went for the door. "I'll not speak once we're outside."

"Your secret is safe with me, Richie."

***

As soon as Sadie and Richard were a half a block from the Beauchamps' automobile, Felix jumped out.

"You didn't last long."

"It was too much for me. Alice was smart not to attend. There was one gentleman out of the lot who was kind enough to see I was not molested." She motioned to the monk beside her. "Thank you, kind sir. Or should I say Father or Brother?"

Richard gave her a silent bow and turned back towards Temperance Hall.

Felix smirked after the retreating form as though he suspected something, but soon refocused on Sadie, seeing her into the backseat.

Alice leaned close to inspect her as Clarence drove toward the house. "You appear rumpled."

"I was touched," Sadie admitted.

"Now you're sullied. I told you not to go!"

Sadie laughed. "It wasn't much. And, like I said, the one who escorted me out was kind."

"What was the masquerade like?" Felix asked.

"She already said it was horrible," Alice snapped.

"Oh, the Dardennes gave a good show, if blasphemous debauchery is considered praiseworthy. You saw the monk. There were dozens like him and a leader in red. They were the Spanish inquisition seeking heretics." Sadie paused when Clarence parked the automobile at the house and then lowered her voice. "They took two women from the crowd, stripped their clothes off, bound them, and then whipped them before the whole ballroom."

Alice shrieked, and Felix laughed.

"But you said he saved you from molestation," Alice said.

"The first monk to try to dance with me did have roaming hands, but—"

"I'll hear no more of it. You shouldn't have gone!" Alice exited the automobile.

With Alice upset, there was nothing to do but follow her inside.

"Sadie," Felix whispered when they were in the hallway. "I'm glad you went."

Understanding that he knew it was his eldest brother who had escorted her out, she smiled. "So am I, but don't tell Alice."

He grinned and hurried up the stairs.

Turning to Clarence, who responsibly locked the back door, Sadie touched his sleeve. "Thank you for the ride."

"I was glad to be of service, though I hope this is the last time you attempt to attend a masquerade like that."

She smiled kindly at his sincerity, so like his twin—and the opposite of Richard and Felix. "It was. Good night, Clarence. I'll see you at breakfast."

Sadie could feel his eyes on her the whole way up the stairs and moved as primly as possible so as not to inflame the young man. He'd get doused as it was when he found out she was stepping out with Richard.

Alice was already preparing for bed. Her gown was draped over one of the chairs and she wore a floral print robe.

"Please shower before bed," Alice told her. "I can't stand the thought of you crawling into the clean sheets after being in that filthy gathering."

Sadie rolled her eyes, collected her toiletries and nightgown, and gratefully escaped to the solitude of the bath before going to the guest bed in Alice's room for the night.

Tucked into her single bed, the remembrance of Richard's firm touch and delectable kisses kept Sadie from falling asleep. When she finally did slumber, the dreams she had kept her warm.

Her disappointment over Richard's empty chair at the breakfast table was difficult to conceal. Fortunately, Mrs. Beauchamp had gone to a fundraiser breakfast for a ladies' aid group. That left Sadie with the two youngest Beauchamp brothers, an un-talkative Alice, and their father, who read the Saturday morning newspaper.

Halfway through the meal, a door opened down the hall and heavy footsteps tread the stairs. No one remarked on it, so Sadie kept eating her omelet. A few minutes later, someone pattered down the stairs and then Richard was in the doorway to the dining room, fresh suit on though his brown eyes were slightly red and his jawline shadowed with the beginnings of a beard.

"Good morning, everyone." His eyes lingered on Sadie the longest, and she hid her smile behind a coffee cup.

Lowering his newspaper, Mr. Beauchamp looked to his oldest. "Just getting in, Richard? You look a bit rough. Did that poker game go all night?"

"Something like that," he said as he took his seat.

"So long as you aren't completely broke, I suppose you'll survive."

"My financial standing is good, Dad."

"Of course it is. I didn't raise any fools, did I?"

"At least not with the first three children." Richard grinned as he helped himself to a cup of coffee and toast from the center of the table.

Felix, in the chair beside him, elbowed him in the ribs. The cook brought in an omelet for the newcomer, placing it before him without a word.

Sadie tried to make her last bit of breakfast stretch by eating slower so she could stay at the table, but Alice must have thought her full.

"Are you finished?" she asked. "You can be excused to finish packing."

"Not quite, but thank you."

"Well, I'm going up. Excuse me, everyone."

Her brothers all rose respectfully, but Mr. Beauchamp's eyes never left the newsprint.

"Let me know when you're ready to go home, Sadie," Clarence said. "I'd be happy to bring you across town."

"Don't bother," Richard said. "I know how you like to practice the piano Saturday mornings. I could bring her so you don't interrupt your routine."

"Thank you, Richie." Sadie dropped her eyes. "I'll be ready in half an hour."

"Allow me to be the porter." Felix knocked his brother's arm. "I'll carry her luggage."

Mr. Beauchamp lowered his paper, a frown beneath his mustache. "She can't have much from a one-night stay, Felix, and you need to study. Your grades have been slipping since the holidays. Classes will only get tougher when you start college in the fall."

"Then I suppose Alice will ride along," the youngest said with a grin meant to show their plans would be spoiled with or without him.

But Alice claimed a headache from the stress of the night before and sent Sadie off with Richard.

Sadie was silent, hands clasped primly in her lap for the first several blocks.

"How was the rest of the masquerade?" Sadie asked when they passed the cathedral.

"Miserable." Richard paused. "I couldn't get you out of my head, so I drank too much. After two dances, I hid in our confessional for an hour."

Sadie smiled. "And after that, or are my feminine sensibilities too sensitive to know?"

Richard tried not to smile and a slight blush colored his cheeks. "Another time, perhaps."

"I dreamt of you," she whispered, half hoping he wouldn't hear, though she needed to confess.

"I'm sure visions of you would have flooded my mind had I slept."

As Richard drove down Government Street, his right hand went to Sadie's knee. A flutter in her middle heightened her craving for his touch. She teased the back of his hand with the tips of her fingers. He gripped her knee, fingers strong around the blue of her skirt.

"Last night was a fantasy come true. I've wanted to touch you for so long, Sadie."

"For how long?" She linked their fingers and brought their hands to the bench between them.

"Since I was sixteen." He glanced at her before returning his attention to the road. "Were you invited to the masquerade?"

Sadie laughed and told of her acquisition of the invitation.

"Those dunces, though I should to thank them for their carelessness."

Richard pulled to a stop in front of the Marleys' home. Sadie looked to the white house on the little rise, wondering if anyone was looking out form the rows of windows on either floor.

"Thank you, again, for rescuing me."

"I'm sure you would have gotten yourself out of his clutches before long. You're resourceful, Sadie. Capturing that invitation proves it."

She smiled when he came around to help her out. "If you bring my luggage to the porch, the maid will collect it."

Swaying her hips a little extra as he followed her up the walkway, Sadie felt his stare and reveled in it. Richard set the two cases on the porch to the side of the front door and leaned in, quickly brushing his lips to her cheek. The stubble on his jawline roughed her skin. His hand slipped into the interior pocket of his suit jacket and retrieved a square envelope.

"Happy early Valentine's Day, Sadie Marley."

Caressing the white paper, she gazed up at him. "Will I see you at Mass tomorrow?"

Richard nodded. "I take the evening train back to Montgomery after supper."

The door opened and a uniformed maid curtsied and went for the luggage. "Welcome home, Miss Sadie."

"Thank you." She refocused on Richard's handsome face. "Tell Alice I hope she feels better. I'll look for your family at the cathedral."

***

"You're really going to the parades with Richard Beauchamp?" Marie asked.

Sadie huffed at her little sister and continued brushing her hair.

"He's not at all like John."

"Good! I don't want a man like Grace Anne's husband." Sadie twisted her hair and secured it.

"But John is splendid." Fourteen-year-old Marie was closer to her brother-in-law than her own sister though there were two decades of life between them. "Is Alice upset about you stepping out with Richard?"

"I expect she will be for a time, but she doesn't know yet." Sadie buttoned on her purple wool cape. "I'll deal with Alice when she finds out."

"Will it be worth the trouble?"

"Richard is worth any amount of trouble." Sadie kissed his most recent letter before pulling on her decorative fur hat. "Don't try to spy on me if you see us."

Marie and their mother would be sitting in the grandstand in front of the Aethelwulf Club with Grace Anne for all the parades that day, something Sadie typically did as well. The excitement of mingling with the crowds on the sidewalks thrilled her, not to mention being with Richard.

After a cordial greeting to her mother and sister, Richard whisked Sadie downtown in his automobile. His out of the way parking space provided an interlude of isolation.

"Sadie," he said as he turned to her, "I hope you enjoy our time together."

"I'm sure I will."

"I have your father's permission to escort you through all the parades, but if you tire of me or aren't enjoying yourself, don't hesitate to tell me. I'm under instruction to bring you to your family outside the Aethelwulf Club."

"I've spent more than enough time on those bleachers. I look forward to being on the streets this time, having an adventure with you."

"But you aren't opposed to the Aethelwulf?"

"Heavens no. My father and brother-in-law are members."

"I'm next on the waiting list for a membership opening." Richard took her gloved hand. "Sadie, I hope this is the first of many outings together. Your father gave me his blessing to court you and I plan on seeing you as often as I'm in town and for as long as you'll accept me. Perhaps next Mardi Gras you'll be sitting in a chair reserved for 'Mrs. Richard Beauchamp' outside the club."

"I might enjoy that."

"Might?" Richard leaned back.

"Ask me in a month or two."

He grinned and angled for her mouth. Sadie eagerly accepted his lips, giving him a taste of what they enjoyed at his masquerade.

"You're an amazing kisser," she whispered.

"I think the same thing of you. I want to shout from the top of the Van Antwerp building that I'm in love with you."

They went at it again until a horn blared on the street behind them as a ragtag brass band stumbled down the road. Laughing, they untangled themselves and Richard helped her from the automobile. He offered his arm, but she boldly linked hands with him.

After the three block walk to the nearest parade route, they angled together to make it through the crowds. They settled in an area where no one knew them, far from Bienville Square. They laughed and joked at the political satire floats of the Blithe Buckaroos, even the one created at the expense of Richard's boss.

Twice, Richard hugged Sadie and kissed her square on the mouth, earning cheers from the good-natured crowd on the day of indulgence. By the time the second parade began, Richard's arms were linked around Sadie's waist from behind, and she leaned against his chest.

The society had more throws than the Buckaroos. Richard caught a string of purple glass beads, laying them gently around Sadie's neck with a kiss to her cheek.

"Let's go to the club now," she practically shouted to be heard over the marching band.

"Are you tired of me?" he hollered as they squeezed through the throng on the sidewalk.

"I want to show you off to our families, Richie." She kissed his lips. "Despite my misgivings about your society, I caught the best prize at the masquerade that night. Alice needs to accept me as a sister if all goes well. The sooner she begins to deal with her feelings about it, the better."

The jaunty tune carried them joyfully as they wove through the multitude. The magic of Mardi Gras could be a blessing or curse on new unions, but Sadie had faith it would be an exultation to her and Richard—that February and always.

~~~
~~~

"Hawthorne's Daughter"

A Southern Gothic retelling of "Rappaccini's Daughter"

by Nathaniel Hawthorne

It was a bright spring day in the city of Mobile, the kind that was full of azalea blossoms, budding dogwoods, and promise. Nineteen-year-old Ralph Salem had just arrived by train from Monroeville to help his great-grandmother after the death of her husband. As a favor to the old woman, her pharmacist had promised to hire Ralph so he could earn his living while he provided assistance to the elderly woman.

"Come here, Ralph," Granny said as he set down his luggage in the front room of her modest home. "You look as handsome as your daddy with that shining blond hair and those eyes the color of the bay on a stormy day." She pinched his square jaw between her knobby fingers and smiled, revealing several missing teeth. "Get on good with Mr. Julian at the pharmacy and you'll be set. He's got no kin and will look to you as a son if you work hard."

"I'll do my best, Granny."

"And that face of yours will catch the eye of any pretty girl in the city. With the protection of the saints, get to the store and tell Mr. Julian you've arrived." She did the sign of the cross over herself and nodded to him to do the same.

Ralph took the streetcar down Government Street to Royal, thinking of the girls he'd known before leaving home. He'd like to add an even prettier lady to his memories—maybe even one to keep. He scanned the sidewalks and passing vehicles for a figure to hold his attention. The horses and buggies were intermixed with a sprinkling of noisy automobiles and twice the amount of pedestrians, but no striking females to hold his attention.

When Ralph entered the pharmacy, a spindly man with wiry sideburns looked up from behind the counter. "May I help you?"

"I'm Ralph Salem. My granny said you were expecting me about a job."

"So I am, Ralph. Welcome to Mobile." The pharmacist sized up the young man—broad shoulders, clear skin, and good teeth—and deemed him an ideal fit for both the physical labor as well as an attractive face to draw in ladies to a soda fountain. "Can you handle a wagon?"

"I have experience with everything up to a four-horse team, Mr. Julian."

"I've got a mule and cart for deliveries. A mule is cheaper to keep and the cart is quick to get around town between the congestion of larger conveyances, so long as you're respectful and don't cause a ruckus."

"No, sir, I wouldn't."

The young man's charming smile gave the pharmacist an idea.

"If you can be here at eight o'clock tomorrow morning, I'll advance you a half-dollar to accomplish your first delivery job on your way home today." After Ralph agreed, the man pulled a small sack from under the counter. "This needs to be delivered to Dr. Hawthorne. He has the mansion across from your granny's house. His back wall along Conti Street doesn't have a gate, so you'll have to go to the front on Government."

"A doctor?" Ralph questioned as he accepted the package. "Does he treat Granny?"

"No, he experiments with botanicals. The man is entangled in science and would sacrifice a person before wrecking one of his trials."

"Then I'm glad he's not seeing to Granny."

The pharmacist nodded, his sharp features softening with a slight smile. "He's a good customer and also a supplier of herbs, but he is not a person to mix in polite society. Go, Ralph, but do not tarry at the Hawthorne house." He spoke the words sure to encourage any youthful mind to test the boundaries, hoping the young man would be a means to the doctor's demise.

With the money in his pocket and the little sack gripped in his fist, Ralph boarded the next west-bound streetcar. A self-satisfied calm gave his countenance an attractive glow, which he shone upon two young beauties on a nearby trolley bench. They giggled and whispered behind gloved hands, stealing glimpses at Ralph. They weren't his type, but he winked anyway.

At his stop, he went up the sidewalk until he reached the correct house number—a gleaming white Spanish colonial. The soaring double columns on the porch and balcony impressed the country lad, and the gabled dormer in the middle front of the roof gave the home an air of immortality similar to a Greek temple.

He stepped onto the deep porch. The symmetrical, arched windows on either side of the front door appeared menacing in their lofty size. Ralph would have to learn to be comfortable around finery if he was going to make a go of it in the city. He knocked on the door, belatedly noticing the buzzer, which he pressed.

A minute went by, but before he could ring again he heard locks being turned. The door squealed inward, revealing a man who practically filled the opening. Ralph looked up into blue eyes between a shock of black eyebrows beneath a crown of wavy gray hair, a dismal moustache adding to his dour countenance.

"What do you need, boy?"

Ralph swallowed his initial misgivings and called upon his reserve of bravado. "I'm from the pharmacy. Are you Dr. Hawthorne?"

"Who else would I be?"

"Of course, Dr. Hawthorne." Ralph gave a respectful nod and smiled as he held out the sack. "I have your delivery from Mr. Julian."

Behind the imposing doctor, a shimmer of air wafted down the stairwell in the right corner of the room. Ralph didn't catch the full view, but it gave the impression of a maiden in violet and was accompanied by the aroma of exotic flowers. A wave of dizziness passed over him, but the intoxicating scent did nothing to his sturdy frame.

The doctor narrowed his eyes, which caused his bushy brows to obscure them. "Do you require anything else?"

"No, thank you. Good day, Dr. Hawthorne."

"Are you the new delivery boy?" the doctor called after him when Ralph went for the steps.

Turning back, he smiled. "Yes, sir. Ralph Salem is my name. I've just moved in with my great-grandmother on the street behind you, should you need anything."

"Very well." Dr. Hawthorne closed the door.

Ralph hurried around the block. Granny's house looked squat and gray compared to Dr. Hawthorne's. Across the road, he noticed the ivy-encrusted brick wall encompassing the yard as though the inhabitants of the mansion didn't want a view of the humbleness a dozen feet from their property.

Granny was on the front porch, rocking in her chair. "Did Mr. Julian take you on?"

"Yes, ma'am, and I made my first delivery to Dr. Hawthorne on my way home."

She crossed herself. "The fame of his garden is almost as notorious as the man himself. Not to mention his daughter."

"Daughter?"

"She'd be about your age. He's kept her home with him since her mother died. Boys peeping over the wall claim she's the prettiest girl in Mobile, though she hasn't walked down a street since she was toddling after her mother. The mother was a pretty thing too. Much too fine for the doctor, though I suppose a title like that might work magic on some women." Granny heaved to her feet, an odd smile on her dehydrated lips. "Supper within the hour, Ralph."

Once Granny was inside, he studied Dr. Hawthorne's property. There was a sprawling magnolia tree outside the wall that could act as a ladder with plenty of branches to perch in.

Ralph crossed the road. Feeling no shame because others had apparently spied too, he nimbly climbed the magnolia until he was several feet above the eight-foot-tall barrier. Cradling himself within the branches, he stared into the lushness of a native Eden, rich with spring colors and scents.

Flowering dogwood trees dotted the yard, but the areas between were filled with budding vines. Jessamine, trumpet, and virgin's bower crept around each other and everything they touched, from bench to trunk to wall. The shady areas boasted ferns of the maidenhair, lady, and rattlesnake varieties that grew to the edges of the flagstone paths curving through the space. Closest to the house—and furthest from Ralph—was an arbor laden with a massive wisteria vine. The lavender blooms engulfed the gothic arch of the structure and cascaded away from it like an exotic rolling tide.

Along the right side of the yard, in what appeared to be a tame herb garden bordered with a low brick retaining wall, stooped the black-clad form of Dr. Hawthorne. His gray head was bent over his task. A few minutes later, he stepped into full view. Soil clung to his gloves, but he brushed it off by rubbing his hands together. The doctor's path went to the center of the yard, where he raised a handkerchief to his mouth. A fountain burbled amid vine-covered statuary with purple flowers as vivid as the moving color Ralph had seen within Dr. Hawthorne's house.

"Una!" the doctor called. "Una, I need your assistance!"

"Coming, Father!" a golden voice replied.

Ralph leaned forward at the sight of the purple-gowned young lady who emerged through the wisteria portal. Her face was delicately tinted from the sun, but flawless. Her dark hair fell in loose waves over her shoulders and down to her slim waist, from which her hips swayed seductively as she followed the path. Ralph knew in an instant that Hawthorne's daughter was who he had been waiting for—the beauty in town to capture.

"She must be seen to, Una," Dr. Hawthorne said with a motion toward the fountain as he leaned away.

"Yes, Father." Obscured from Ralph's view for a second, the young woman was soon sitting on the brick lip of the fountain, reaching a loving arm toward the passion vine whose flowers were the same hue as her dress. "Dear Sister, what are you in need of?"

The doctor circled the fountain as Una sang and stroked the vine. The jeweled brilliance of the blossoms appeared to tilt toward the soprano, while stray tendrils encircled her limbs and snaked through her hair. As the singing continued, Ralph's head swam. He gripped the branches on either side of him to hold steady, not bothering to blink lest he miss a moment of the scene of enchanting beauty below him.

Oh, to be that vine under her tender ministrations! I would give all to be with her like that for five minutes.

Watching in rapture, Ralph unwittingly shook loose a magnolia pod as he shifted for the best view. The *thunk* the dried pod made against a root brought Dr. Hawthorne's attention.

"Come, Una. It is time to prepare for supper." He left his daughter to untangle herself.

Before she could stand, an emerald dragonfly came toward the rippling fountain.

"Hello, my noble dragon," she said as it rattled by the flowers and then her head.

The insect went still, dropping a foot before it took control of its wings once more.

"Do not allow me to cause you concern," she said.

This time, it fell to the flagstone and rose no more. Frowning, Una hurried toward the arbor, her hair and dress swishing behind her. Ralph stared like a simpleton for several minutes after she disappeared before returning to his granny's house.

* * *

At the pharmacy the next morning, Mr. Julian wished to know how the delivery had gone.

"Dr. Hawthorne accepted the package," Ralph assured him. "And he asked if I was the new deliveryman."

"Was he pleased?"

"It's difficult to say." Ralph paused. "Do you know anything of his daughter?"

"Una? Did you see her?"

"Not during the delivery, but Granny told me she is extremely beautiful."

He nodded. "So she is. Men would fall at her feet—for more reasons than one. She is the true leader within the garden, though her father thinks otherwise. One day, she will be in control of his experiments and we shall see what true genius is."

Ralph worked steadily, stocking the shelves and making deliveries, stopping only for his dinner break at noon. At the end of the day, he decided to climb the magnolia tree before going home.

Once in his tree perch, he immediately spied Una Hawthorne. The dark-haired beauty was singing to a bed of prickly poppies he hadn't noticed the day before. Their pale petals tilted in the breeze her pacing produced—either that or they followed some sort of magic as her white dress rustled back and forth before their bed.

To feel the softness of her angelic gown and stroke my hands through her hair is my greatest wish!

Acting on impulse, Ralph maneuvered toward the end of the thickest branch to pluck one of the season's first snow-white blooms from the tree.

"Fair lady!"

Una looked up, pale eyes wide.

"A token of appreciation for your beautiful singing!" He tossed the magnolia to her.

She bowed her head as though shy. "Thank you, kind sir."

"My name is Ralph. Ralph Salem."

"Then my thanks, Mr. Salem." She retrieved the large flower from the flagstone and went for the portal. Before she was through the arbor, the blossom had yellowed in her elegant hands.

* * *

The next day, Ralph repeated his journey up the tree after work. Once again, Una was singing in the garden. This time she was closer—below the magnolia within a crop of spiderwort whose purple petals appeared pale compared to the passion flowers by the fountain. He was sure Una knew he was there, but she never looked up. Ralph, on the other hand, enjoyed the view of her breasts within the low scoop of her blue-trimmed décolletage as she bent and sang to the wildflowers that were the shape of the trinity.

An anole scuttled down the tree and straight to Una as though charmed by her voice. Its bright green faded as the reptile approached, becoming a sickly brown when it was a foot away. There it stopped between the rows of spiderwort and began to convulse as Una finished her song.

"Will you creatures never learn?" She shook her head and quickly went toward the house.

For the rest of the week, Ralph battled nightmares about Una, the dragonfly, the magnolia blossom, and the anole. Decay and death. He couldn't fathom how a figure of such radiant beauty could exist alongside fatality. How life would dare disrespect such an exquisite creation by expiring at her feet. It defied reason!

But his waking hours were filled with fantasies of her magnificent form—her brilliance and splendid voice. Never had he known a woman with such vitality and health. She practically glowed as another bloom in the garden, ripe for the picking.

And Ralph wanted to be the one to pluck her.

* * *

Saturday, the pharmacy was open until noon. Half an hour before closing, Dr. Hawthorne arrived with a selection of herbs and oils for the pharmacist to inspect for possible purchase. Ralph marveled over the stooped appearance of the doctor. He looked as though he had aged a decade, with hunched shoulders, weary countenance, and a sickly pallor. Could it have only been half a dozen days since Dr. Hawthorne had towered over him on his front porch? Was this the true doctor, or was the man more himself at home, within sight of the enchanted garden?

While haggling over prices and ingredients, the pharmacist waved Ralph over. "We will be here a while. Turn the sign to closed and be on your way."

Excited for the prospect of exploring Dr. Hawthorne's garden when he knew the doctor was not home, Ralph hurried to the first streetcar. He noticed no pleasing eyes upon him during the journey, for his mind was filled with Una, the goddess of his desires.

Once on the quiet of Conti Street, he checked in with his granny before scrambling up the magnolia. He shimmied down the branch and hung from the bough before dropping deftly into the spiderwort patch, crushing several of the tri-petal beauties. Remorseful over damaging something he knew Una lovingly cared for, Ralph did his best to right the plants before jumping to the flagstones to avoid more sacrifices.

He strolled the rear half of the yard, hands clasped behind his back and eyes roaming everywhere as he imagined what Una would look like amid the blossoms.

At the fountain in the middle of the yard, he breathed deeply of the perfume in the air. Swaying, he spread his feet as though standing on the rolling deck of a ship and looked longingly at the deep purple of the passion flower. Its tentacle-like embellishments seemed to be reaching for him—wanting a gentle touch as he hoped to give Una one day.

"No!"

Her forceful command made him pause—hand in the air between himself and the nearest flower.

"It is extremely delicate, Mr. Salem." Una approached with a beguiling smile. "You mustn't touch my passion flowers. Sit on the bench and you may observe the fountain and its jewels." She pointed across the path, pale blue eyes flickering to him often.

"Will you sit with me?"

"No, Mr. Salem, I will sit on the edge of the fountain. You would appreciate the view better, would you not?"

"Yes, but would you call me Ralph, Miss Hawthorne?" he spoke across the flagstone gap as she lowered to the brick encasement, fanning her lavender dress around her.

"So you might call me Una?" Her lips parted into a smile once more. Tilting her head so her hair cascaded over her right shoulder, she nodded. "You are welcome to, Ralph."

She began humming and the vines beside her swayed. The deep green of the broad leaves quivered and new tendrils unfurled, wrapping her wrist like a living bracelet.

Mouth agape, Ralph sputtered. "Did—"

"Everything is not as it seems. Wind currents through a walled yard can be erratic, Ralph. Do you not feel something stirring your skin?"

Heat licked him with scorching prickles, but it was his lips that needed movement. To meet those luscious ones on her pretty face was his goal, the space between a gulf of misery as his body pulsed with the need to cleave to her.

"I feel *something*."

Una's rich laugh surged a need far greater than breath within Ralph.

"Will you show me the garden in full?" he asked.

"I would be delighted to."

They stood and he stepped closer, offering his arm.

"I prefer my hands free to tend to needs that might arise as we explore. Come with me."

Una walked several feet away and he trailed in her perfumed wake like a rat following the piper. Under a downpour of descriptions about the flora, Ralph floated in her current. Verbena, orchids, hibiscus, poppies, and flowering vines, but none were as beautiful as Una or her equally alluring passion flowers. Under the magnolia branches, she bent to the spiderwort he had trampled. Her dress that day was the same pale purple as their petals, her hips as pleasingly curved.

"I didn't mean to crush them. Are they beyond repair?"

"Everything in this garden can mend or maim." She hummed and fluffed the green blades. "These will mend."

As she straightened, Ralph moved closer to help. Her fingers brushed his palm before she knew he was there.

He sucked in a breath at the contact—a festering build of caged emotions—and her eyes widened.

"I thank you, but I don't need your assistance, Ralph. I'm up and down all day within these walls. I might be slighter than your powerful frame, but I am strong. Never forget that."

Controlling the urge to pull her toward him and kiss those rosy lips, he nodded and stepped back with a grin that was more leer, though he meant no ill. Everything he envisioned was to bring pleasure. He knew he would enjoy each moment and believed his rapture would be shared by the ethereal beauty before him.

After their stroll, Ralph stooped beneath a wisteria arch and turned back to smile at her. Una pointed to the gate between the side wall and the house. As soon as he was in the front yard, she was gone—the wooden gate closed. He trudged around the block toward his great-grandmother's house.

* * *

That night, impassioned dreams filled Ralph's slumber. Visions of Una's enchanting songs accompanied by dances she performed only for him led to more intimate connections. The taste of his lust for her within his parched mouth seared his throat as he panted through the arousing fantasies.

And again the next night.

The second daybreak brought unease in the form of red marks trailing his hand. On Sunday, they were pale—easily ignored. Could it be a rash from one of the flowers in the Hawthornes' garden? Ralph hadn't touched any. The only contact within the garden Saturday afternoon had been an accidental one stolen between him and Una. With heaviness in his chest, Ralph wrapped his hand with a clean length of cotton. The debauched images from his nighttime visions fled him as he prepared for work with an aching hand.

"You don't look well, Ralph," Granny said over breakfast. "Are you feverish?"

"No, only distracted."

"Then you've met a girl!" Her grin showcased the gaps in her teeth. "Is she pretty?"

"Very much, Granny."

"Bring her around. It's been too long since beauty has come within these walls."

Ralph nodded, but fear over Una's potential danger weighted his heart. He didn't want to expose Granny to possible harm.

All day, corseted figures paraded before the soda fountain counter. The smiles, flirtations, and welcoming conversations were diverting, but afterward all he could think of was Una. Ralph knew he had to have her—no matter what.

After work, he found himself climbing the magnolia tree. As though waiting for him, Una appeared in a white gown through the wisteria portal.

"Come, Ralph," she called. "You are welcome here."

He made his way down the branch hanging over the wall and noticed a piece of flagstone recently placed amid the spiderwort. Laughing, he dropped to the landing spot and then leapt to the main path.

"I thank you, Una. And I'm sure the flowers are grateful as well."

"I find a way to protect everything I love," she replied with her beguiling lips.

They spent an hour roaming the walkways and sitting across from each other that day and each evening thereafter.

Ralph danced through the following month in a haze of impulsive work, living for the hour he spent in Una Hawthorne's presence. He didn't feel nourished until he drank from the living well of her eyes, though they had yet to properly touch and she refused to cross the garden wall.

In the kitchen, Ralph's great-grandmother set his breakfast plate before him and fell into her chair.

"Granny, are you all right?"

"I fear I'm languishing, Ralph. It's a good thing you have a lady friend now—someone who might take care of you when I'm no longer here. I would like to meet her. Could you bring her around?"

"I'll try, Granny." When he finished eating, he offered to see her to her bedroom.

"No, you get to work. I'll be fine." Granny spoke in earnest because she felt the effects of her age and poor health more acutely when he was home. Maybe it was the contrast of a virile young man to her decaying decades.

At work, Ralph asked the pharmacist if he knew of anything that would strengthen his granny.

Mr. Julian raised his dark brows and looked down his long nose at Ralph from his perch behind the medication counter. "She's an old woman, but how long has she been declining?"

Ralph frowned over his neglect, for his every waking hour was spent on thoughts of Una, not the welfare of Granny, though she was the reason he had arrived in Mobile. "I'm not sure, Mr. Julian, but she wasn't in top form before, otherwise I wouldn't have needed to come."

"Then four weeks, I'd guess." The pharmacist's gaze penetrated Ralph's soul. "Did you ever hear the tale of the deadly maiden from India?"

Gooseflesh broke out on Ralph's arms. "No."

"She was cultivated with poisons from an early age and adapted to them, but in doing so, she became a living weapon of seductive beauty and venom. She was sent as a supposed gift—a peace offering to the ruler of a neighboring land—but was the means of their demise. A fatal beauty."

"How horrible."

"Is it? I would think dying in the arms of a beautiful woman would be a mercy—the same for a woman who died within the arms of a handsome man." With a tainted smile, Mr. Julian turned back to his work. "I'll whip up something for your granny. See me at the end of the day."

The hours dragged on for Ralph. If Granny had owned a telephone, he would have rung midday to check on her. As luck would have it, he was given a delivery to make two blocks away after his noon dinner break.

"Stop in on your granny, Ralph," the pharmacist said, "but don't be long."

Ralph drove the mule wagon faster than ever that cloudy afternoon. He hastily delivered the medicine to the invalid customer and then scurried toward Conti Street. Entering the house, he didn't see his great-grandmother in any of the common areas. He found her bedridden in her room at the end of the little hall.

Taking her hand, he leaned over and felt her brow. "Granny, are you well?"

"The flowers. It smells of flowers." She moaned as she paled. "Did you bring me to the garden?"

"No, I stopped in to check on you."

"Heaven forbid, get back to work."

She pulled her hand free, laying it on top the black fabric of her dress. Her papery skin flamed as red as her wrinkled face was pale.

"Granny?" He leaned closer.

"Go, Ralph," she wheezed out the words.

Frightened lest his granny die before his eyes, he fled the house and whipped the mule into a trot to return downtown.

"How is she?" the pharmacist asked upon Ralph's return.

"Terrible. I thought she'd expire as soon as I arrived."

"Did you touch her?"

"Yes, but I think I irritated her skin."

"Redness?"

Ralph nodded. "On her hand, but her face paled at my voice."

"I see."

The pharmacist looked pensive and studied the young man. Under his counter, he released a fly from a small container. It buzzed twice around the workspace before circling Ralph.

"Do you know what that is?"

Ralph followed the motion. "A common fly, Mr. Julian."

As soon as he said the words, the fly dropped upside-down on the counter with a few kicks of its legs before stilling.

The pharmacist pointed to it. "Quick, clean it away before a customer sees it."

Ralph swept it off with his hand, washing it down the sink behind the station with more than a hint of unease.

"Thank you, Ralph. I'll have the elixir for your granny ready by five."

"Would you be able to administer it to her?" His square jaw lowered. "I have somewhere I need to stop first and don't wish her medicine to be delayed."

"Are you sure you aren't worried about my mixture? It's quite safe, I assure you. It's something I take myself."

Ralph shook his head. "It's not that, Mr. Julian. I…I have a standing appointment."

"Ah! So the handsome lad has an admirer."

"I'd like to hope I do, but she has an admirer in me at the very least."

"I'm sure she is very pleased with you, Ralph. Go on now. It's about time for the after-school customers. I know there will be many eyes upon you for the next few hours."

And there were. Schoolgirls on the verge of womanhood flocked to the soda fountain as Ralph served them their refreshments, along with a side of his charming smile. He worked without pause, without thinking, for it would have brought a frown to his mouth and wrinkles between his brows.

At closing, the pharmacist pocketed a silver vial. "I will see to your granny."

"Thank you, Mr. Julian. I'll only be an hour."

"Here. One last delivery. Unless I am incorrect, it won't take you out of your way." He held out a small envelope with Una's name on it.

Eyes wide, Ralph looked at his boss.

"Go, my son. Miss Hawthorne will be pleased with the contents."

The streetcar felt infuriatingly slow, but Ralph didn't want to run and arrive damp with perspiration. Impatiently, he tapped the corner of the envelope against his thigh until he jumped to his feet at his stop and pocketed the letter.

Ralph plucked a snowy magnolia bloom on his way over the wall. When he dropped to his feet a moment later, it was yellowed with age. He released it as though burned, staring as the yellow turned to brown amid the spiderwort.

"Ralph, come to me!" Una called from the fountain. "You're later than usual."

"Granny is ill. Mr. Julian fixed some medicine for her and he sent you a note as well."

Una carefully opened the letter he handed her. Her lips spread into a smile more beautiful than ever.

"I'll be right back," she said as she dropped the note into the fountain where the words ran in blue rivers.

He is ready. The old lady will be safe within the hour.

She was inside only two minutes before returning.

Standing before Ralph, Una reached a hand to his face. The soft pad of her finger grazed his cheek, then trailed around his jaw as she watched for a response. He grinned and put his hands on her waist, drawing her closer.

"I'll be happy to meet your granny this evening, Ralph."

"Are you done being coy with me, Una?"

She nodded. "We can now move on to what you've craved these past weeks."

Their lips met for the first time with a jolt of pleasure. Una welcomed more and Ralph's hands roamed her purple gown as he tasted the desire long denied him. She unbuttoned his shirt and led him to the fountain's edge.

"Forgive me," she whispered as she plucked a passion flower, "but it is for my lover."

Una ran the purple tentacles against Ralph's bare chest, causing him to groan with want as his fingers flexed into her hips. When she was done teasing him, she tucked the flower into her décolletage.

"Come with me, Ralph." She led him under the wisteria arbor and through the back screen door.

Rather than enter the house, she climbed the stairs to a sleeping porch protected by lattice. From there, they went through the door into a long hall. Following the pull of her hand, he soon found himself in a bedroom at the front of the house. The purple chamber of silk and lace overlooked Government Street, but that didn't stop Una from removing her gown. She approached Ralph in nothing more than her chemise.

"Where is your father, Una?" he whispered as she peeled off his shirt.

"A place where he won't bother us while you cultivate my garden."

The words brought a new sense of fervor to his already heightened ardor, and they surged together.

Smiling afterward, Ralph cemented the view of Una within his arms amid the tangled purple sheets. He kept it beside the view he'd enjoyed of her wrapped in the vines of the passion flower at the fountain. Una and the flowering vine were one, and he would have her again within their reach.

"Do you love me, Ralph?" Una whispered.

"More than anything or anyone else in this life. I've wanted you like this since I first saw you in the garden. I'd do anything for you."

"I knew you were my match." She gifted a kiss with her perfect lips and stood. "We need to go downstairs now."

"Is your father expected?" Ralph pulled on his trousers.

"I told you, Father can no longer bother us."

A few minutes later, the couple descended the front stairs hand-in-hand.

The first thing Ralph noticed was the form of Dr. Hawthorne in a wing chair by the corner fireplace. He was about to explain himself when he realized the old doctor wasn't watching them. His deep-set eyes were unblinking, his hands frozen to the armrests with an unclenching power.

Dr. Hawthorne could express no displeasure in the behavior of his daughter or her beau because he was no longer alive.

"Una—" Ralph began, the word choking on horror as it seized his throat.

The front door swung inward and the pharmacist entered with a spritely Granny on his arm.

"Mr. Julian, welcome!" Una bowed before Ralph's employer. "You were exactly right about Ralph."

"All is well?"

"Very well." She laughed and turned to Granny. "And you must be Ralph's dear Granny. Welcome home!"

"Home, my pretty girl?"

"Yes, indeed. You and Ralph are joining me here. You'll be quite well with Mr. Julian's elixir in regular supply."

Ralph took his great-grandmother in a hug and steered her toward the dining room to get her away from Dr. Hawthorne's body. "You look as good as I ever remember, Granny."

Behind him, Una sent the pharmacist to her father.

Once Granny was seated in the other room, Ralph returned. "Mr. Julian, what do we do?"

"Miss Hawthorne has already given me instructions for her father's body."

Ralph looked to Una with trepidation. "And what are Granny and I to do here, Una?"

"Be my companions, of course. The lady may cook and you will do my bidding in all things."

"In all—"

"It will be no hardship on you, I promise." Una gave a devious smile.

"Will I have access to Ralph at all?" the pharmacist asked. "He's become popular with the afternoon crowd. They grow weak in his presence and feel the healing effects of our soda fountain immediately."

Una laughed and ran a possessive hand down Ralph's sleeve. "I suppose I can share him in the afternoons, but only for the soda fountain. No more deliveries, Mr. Julian."

"Agreed. He would have too great an effect on those not immediately partaking of the elixir." The pharmacist nodded. "Now excuse me, I'll see to things."

He left the way he had entered.

"What has been done to me?" Ralph's voice quaked as he looked at Una.

"Father was too old when he began the experiments for his body to handle the poisons, and he's been deteriorating ever since. Mr. Julian has been helping me search for a replacement— one who would be more to me than Father ever could. A man who could grow with me in the garden and provide the outlet for my neglected physical connection. I need a man to love and obey me." Her rosy lips went to the skin below Ralph's ear. "He found you, but I chose you, Ralph. You will fulfill everything for me, both in the bedroom and the garden. Even if I need to share you with Mr. Julian so he can sell his potion-infused fizzy drinks to unsuspecting girls."

Ralph glanced toward the figure of Dr. Hawthorne in the chair.

"He was only forty-five," Una said with a touch of sadness. "But he was suffering and it needed to be stopped. You'll never suffer, Ralph. You and I are invincible—the most powerful pair who ever walked the Earth, though we'll live quietly in our own Eden."

"You've wanted me?"

"Desperately. If I could have fallen into your arms and upon your lips before today, I would have."

"Then let us go to our Eden, Una. There's much more we need to share." A swell of pride and a glow of virility marked his countenance.

With a dismissive glance at the corpse of her father, Una took his hand. They rushed past his dozing granny and plunged through the wisteria portal.

Emerging in the bewitched garden, Una led him to the fountain. She forced him to the bench. Ralph gripped her hips, hands splaying soft curves. Her cold lips met his with a hard press.

When she leaned back, the tendrils of the passion vine wreathed her shining head like a crown.

"I'm so glad you're here." A malevolent smile shone down on him from her angelic face. "You're mine, Ralph."

His previously lusty dreams soured beneath the sickly sweet perfume of his warden.

~~~
~~~

About the Author

While experiencing the typical adventures of growing up, Carrie Dalby called several places in California home, but she's lived on the Alabama Gulf Coast since 1996. Serving two terms as president of Mobile Writers' Guild, five years as the Mobile area Local Liaison for the Society of Children's Book Writers and Illustrators, and helping coordinate the Mobile Literary Festival are some of the writing-related volunteer positions she's held. When Carrie isn't reading, writing, browsing bookstores/libraries, or homeschooling her children, she can often be found knitting or attending concerts.

Carrie writes for both teens and adults. *Fortitude* is listed as a Best Historical Book for Kids by Grateful American Foundation. The Possession Chronicles, The Malevolent Trilogy, and Washington Square Secrets are her Southern Gothic series for adults.

For more information, social media links, and news, visit Carrie Dalby's website:

carriedalby.com

CARRIE DALBY
HISTORICAL, SOUTHERN GOTHIC, AND MORE